A DIRGE
FOR HER

VIRGINIA RATH

A DIRGE FOR HER

VIRGINIA RATH

COACHWHIP PUBLICATIONS
Greenville, Ohio

A Dirge for Her, by Virginia Rath
© 2019 Coachwhip Publications

Published 1947
No claims made on public domain material.
Cover image: Model © OlgaEcat

CoachwhipBooks.com

ISBN 1-61646-487-9
ISBN-13 978-1-61646-487-5

A DIRGE FOR HER

PART ONE

1

According to the publicity releases from her home studio, that sensational young star, Miss Greta Mallon, would begin a prolonged vacation by spending a few days in San Francisco. Miss Mallon was the victim of overwork and nervous strain. She had been advised by her physician to get away from it all. The simple life and bracing air of a Nevada dude ranch were to provide her with a twofold cure.

Or, as the columnist, Jimmy Walter, put it: "The sultry, sloe-eyed enchantress, Greta Mallon, is en route to Reno to sever the bonds that still tie her to ex-Sergeant Thomas Ainslee III."

Being virtually incognito, Miss Mallon was accompanied only by her secretary, Alicia Jameson, and elected to rough it in a simple little two-room, corner suite at the St. Francis. In its living-room, Miss Jameson met the press at about eleven o'clock on Friday morning, August 23rd, 1946.

Miss Mallon had had a tiring trip and was sleeping. Miss Mallon had hoped not to be interviewed during her stay in San Francisco. But in view of this very kind, though quite unexpected interest being shown in her, she would be pleased to meet the ladies and gentlemen of the press, here, between four and eight. And now, if they would excuse her. . . .

Alone, Miss Jameson lifted her trim black shoulders in a movement of repressed irritation. She muttered, "Damned little tramp!" looking at the door into the bedroom, on the other side of which Greta Mallon was presumably recovering from the extreme fatigue of a twelve-hour train trip—

But Miss Mallon was, at that moment, making an entrance elsewhere. Dripping sables, she undulated in the justly famous Mallon manner down the dull green carpet of the gray and green salon in the establishment on Sutter Street known as Gisele's.

A sprinkling of patrons watched her progress toward a door marked PRIVATE and more than one resolved to begin that diet, not tomorrow or next week, but today. The cinematically wise murmured, "Isn't that—could that be. . . ." and were assured by a favorite *vendeuse* that it was Greta Mallon— "You see, she was modeling here when she was discovered by an executive who came here to try to persuade our Mr. Dundas to go to Hollywood. . . . Yes, to have her come in like this must be very gratifying to him. . . ."

Michael Dundas's extreme gratification was somewhat oddly expressed. He leaned back in his chair, stared across his desk at Miss Mallon and remarked, "Well, if it isn't little Gertie Malinowsky." And, unkindly, he pronounced "Gertie" with a broad and unmistakable South-of-Market twang.

Miss Mallon sat down opposite him and arranged herself most decoratively. "Still 'always belittlin',' I see. It would be nice if you'd say, how nice to see you after all these years."

"Consider it said, Gertie. But has it been so many years? When did you come here?"

"January of '41. Julius discovered me six months later, you know."

"And is Julius Lindt still around?"

"He produced one too many flops. He's back in the coat and suit business in New York. But we were washed up long before that. And I gave him value received for everything he did for me."

"I fancy you did," Michael conceded. "Is this the first time you've been back to San Francisco since '41?"

"The first that anyone knows about. For the first three years, I could sneak off and go places. I wasn't recognized, not even," Greta said, grinning, "if I wore dark glasses. My rise wasn't so damned meteoric. I waited nearly four years for my chance because I had so much to learn. Do you know why I never came to see you until now?"

"No, unless you were quite anxious that no one should know that you were in San Francisco whenever you came back here?"

"That was part of it. But I wasn't going to come see you till I could call myself a star. I used to imagine you being very impressed," Greta said candidly. "I should have known better."

It was Michael's turn to grin. "Oh, I am, Gertie. You do definitely make an impression though perhaps not in just the way you'd intended. Why did you want especially to impress me?"

"You called me an ignorant little Hunkie. . . ."

"Did I? I do apologize. I must have been very thoroughly exasperated. I'm not often so crude."

"I'll say!" Gertie Malinowsky agreed. "When you're in good form, there's no hide that tongue of yours wouldn't penetrate."

"But Gertie, I thought that when you came here, you'd already acquired a very tough skin and that, young as you were, you had—to put it nicely—done quite a bit of living."

"That's so. And broad insult, even with some four letter words thrown in, didn't bother me. I could give as good as I got, in that style. But you'd dissect me in a nasty, nice way. Only one other person ever talked to me like that; made me feel like a bug squirming on a pin. . . ."

"Who was that?"

"Never mind. I forgave *you*," Miss Mallon said magnanimously. "It was good training. After you'd heckled me for six months, anything Hollywood could offer along those lines, I could take without batting an eyelash. I still can."

"But I recall only three or four private interviews with you, Gertie. Otherwise, I believe that I confined myself to brief comments in passing. If you took them so to heart, I'm surprised that you stayed with us for six months."

"And I'm surprised you ever hired me, though maybe you thought I looked hungry. . . ."

Michael frowned. "Really, my dear child, I don't remember you as vividly as your charming egotism leads you to believe. But I do remember that I thought you looked as if you'd been ill when you came to ask for a job. Well, you had the perfect model's figure. . . ."

"Though I had to be told to bathe in the showers upstairs instead of out of a bottle of cheap cologne?" Miss Mallon said grimly. "And to wash my hair every week and not to scratch in public when I itched."

Mr. Dundas chuckled. "I'd forgotten, Gertie."

"I haven't. You paid good wages and I learned things here: how to walk and about clothes and so on. The few times she came in here, I'd watch that wife of yours and wonder what she had that I didn't. It all helped—didn't it?"

She let her hands drop to her sides, shoulders squared, a movement arrogantly demanding admiration. "You've seen me on the screen . . ."

"And I've never seen anyone who acted more magnificently—below the chin," Mr. Dundas said mildly. "I presume that few waste time looking at your face, and perhaps it may eventually become as expressive as your shoulders, bosom and posterior already are."

"Why, you dirty. . . ."

Miss Mallon's voice rose a full octave. She stopped, biting her lip, scowling at Mr. Dundas. He shook his head reprovingly.

"Tut! Temper has an unfortunate effect on that ever-throaty, vibrant and low voice that is such an excellent thing in a rising young star. And your new voice had impressed me. It, and your pronunciation, used to be extraordinarily distressing."

"You told me never to open my yap to the customers—that's how bad they were. But I used to listen to you and your wife when people let me get close enough to hear how she talked. I'm good at imitating people so that helped, and then they turned me over to a voice teacher in Hollywood.

"The voice part's almost natural now and I can talk good enough English when I try, but with friends, I just don't bother. I worked like a dog to get a lovely polish," Miss Mallon said. "And paid for it as I went along. But I guess I'm still the daughter of a Polish-born peasant—little Gertie Malinowsky, who. . . ."

"Yes?"

"Who still wants a hell of a lot and is going to get it—all of it!"

Michael raised his eyebrows. "Aren't you unnecessarily vehement? You're doing very well for yourself, I'd say."

"Oh, my career's shaping up all right. Only, I don't really like acting much. If I did, I could wait to be a real star. . . ."

"What can't you wait for, Gertie?"

"Well, I'm not impatient or impulsive. I guess that's the peasant in me. But this is a good time to arrange my life the way I want it to go on. Because now I don't have to jump through hoops if the studio cracks the whip at me, but I'm not famous enough yet, that my whole life has to be an open book to the whole United States. I've got a few loose ends to tie up and somewhat you might call excess baggage to get rid of."

"Such as?"

"Oh, of course you know I got married. . . ."

"Of course, I do not. Why should I?"

Miss Mallon grimaced. "All right, slap my ears back again. I supposed you read movie columns. Doesn't your wife, either?"

"She doesn't read them aloud to me. Though if Valerie were here, she probably would have told me that you were to be in San Francisco. I presume you are en route to Reno?"

"Yes—Sunday night. So your wife's not home?"

"She's visiting her mother in New York. I'm flying back there Tuesday night to come home with her. She took our son and maid with her, and left me and the cat to shift for ourselves."

"Your boy would be about five now? Oh no, I haven't forgotten your wife was expecting when I left here. Well, just for the looks of it, I was going to say to bring her along. . . ."

"Along where?"

"To the hotel. I'm having open house from four to eight. It's not dignified, but if the local dramatic editors want to see me, I'm going to play ball. It's a break, your wife being away. You can come alone. . . ."

"I doubt," said Mr. Dundas austerely, "if I can make it."

"Better try. You won't be conspicuous. I know a lot of good joes here who'll want to see me. Ex-servicemen, most of them. I was a regular at the Hollywood canteen during the war. That's where I met the kid I married. He was on leave from Italy in '44 and—well, why do you look at me like that?"

"You are a nasty bit of work, aren't you, Gertie? Another of those calculating little tramps who. . . ."

Michael paused, rose noiselessly from his chair, and passing Miss Mallon, whispered, "Talk! Say anything you like. . . ."

"What the hell do you mean by talking to me like that!" said Gertie Malinowsky with perfect spontaneity.

She twisted about. in her chair and watched him silently cross the floor to the door that opened into the middle one of three private offices.

She continued, less convincingly, "You don't know why I. . . ." and stopped as Michael yanked the door open and disclosed an unpleasing male object still in the posture best calculated to bring his ear close to the keyhole.

2

"Come out of your crouch, Egbert. That position puts a great strain on the muscles and won't help your lumbago," Mr. Dundas said solicitously.

"I—I wasn't—I just dropped something. . . ."

Egbert was a weedy, pimply individual with skin the color of unbaked piecrust, a repellent Adam's apple, and a not very reasonable facsimile of a chin. He had pale, covertly inquisitive eyes, a marked sedentary paunch, and long, restless fingers. Michael regarded him with unconcealed dislike.

"You have a bad habit of dropping things in front of that keyhole and it always takes you a surprisingly long time to pick them up," he said gently. "Also, you can't keep your clammy hands off the women here. . . ."

"I didn't—I only. . . ."

"I know—a pinch here and a pat there and all good, clean fun. I told you when I took you on, that you'd be one man surrounded by attractive women and would be expected to watch your step. I had another complaint yesterday. As the lady says, she isn't fussy, but you remind her of 'something white and slimy with six legs, all of them hands.' An excellent description, I thought. . . ."

"Oh yeah! 'Lady!' I'll bet she's not fussy where you're concerned. You're the boss; you've got the pick of the. . . ."

Michael's pupils dilated until his intensely blue eyes appeared black. He boxed his bookkeeper's ears with an insulting appearance of negligence and considerable force. Egbert said, "Oof!" and tears welled into his eyes.

"And you're fired," Michael told him. "Draw yourself a check; take two weeks' pay in lieu of notice and get the hell out! But first, give me your keys."

"Look, Mr. Dundas—you know I'm a first-class accountant and I've only taken an interest in the business and. . . ."

"You're a first-class accountant and a revolting little tick. Keys, please!"

In a sudden spurt of defiance, Egbert told Mr. Dundas what he might do with the keys when he had them, and then hastily raised clumsy fists to protect his jaw.

"Oh, let's not do it the hard way," Michael drawled, took a step forward and brought his left foot ungently down on Egbert's right. Egbert howled, stood on his left foot and massaged his right. Michael spun him around, fished a brown key case from his pocket, and appropriated two keys.

"Here's your case, Mr. Knapp." He propelled Egbert into the middle office and seated him forcibly at his desk. "Write that check. . . ."

Mr. Knapp wrote the check in copperplate script while Michael looked into the first of the three offices. His manager and partner, Fanchon Weis, had a desk here but spent little time at it. She was

not there now, nor was their stenographer who
went to lunch at eleven-forty-five, "For which Allah be praised," Michael muttered. He came back
to the middle office with its adding machine, led-
gers and large filing cases, scrutinized the check
Egbert thrust at him and signed it in his precise
backhand.

"And don't," he said, jerking an imperative
thumb toward a gray enameled locker, "forget
your hat and coat on your way out."

Mr. Knapp's venomous mumblings resolved into
words. "You can't treat me like this! I'll—I'll sue
you for assault. You'll regret this. I know a thing
or two. Your wife would like to hear what. . . ."

"If you ever get within talking distance of my
wife, I'll break your goddamned neck," Michael
said agreeably.

He took a step forward. Egbert seized hat, coat,
and a greasy paper bag containing his lunch. The
locker door swung back and caught him on the
funny bone. Miss Mallon gave un unladylike screech
of laughter at his anguished yelp. Egbert scowled
at her, clutched his belongings to him and fled.

"I'm sorry, Gertie," Michael said, returning to
his desk.

"Oh, I got a kick out of it. But where did you
learn those commando tactics? I see your discharge
button but I supposed. . . ."

"Did you think I sweated out the war designing glamorous garments for females?" Michael said acidly. "I was in the Army for more than three years; got my discharge last November, to be exact. I served in Italy, France and Germany. You were saying that the young man you now consider excess baggage was on leave from Italy when you married him. . . ."

"And you called me a little tramp. Why?"

"You won't deny that too many young actresses married servicemen during the war merely because uniforms were the fashion, and it wouldn't help a gal's career to be seen around with a civilian?"

"Well, no. And now they're getting divorces and marrying older guys with money or pull in the studios. I'll admit that. But I liked Tom Ainslee a lot. We had a few swell months together before he went back overseas. He'd say so, too. We might have had a baby. . . ."

"Oh, come now, Gertie. I know that maternity is very fashionable in Hollywood just now, but two years ago you couldn't have afforded to be off the screen for the length of time it takes to produce a child."

"I know. Just the same, I did— Oh, skip it. I got my first big break after Tom and I married. That changed things. Besides, his folks are stuffy—Pasadena socialites—and look down their noses at the vulgar movie people. He'd have asked me to retire, and I knew before he got home that it wouldn't work out. We never lived together again and he don't mind the divorce. There was more than one thing we didn't see eye to eye about—"

"That is, he wouldn't roll over and play dead when you snapped your fingers?"

"It wasn't that. I like a man to be a man and not a mouse," Greta said indignantly. "But there was something pretty important to me and I'd thought maybe— Well, skip that, too. I gave him a break by not keeping him dangling around, and meant to go to Reno a lot sooner, but I just couldn't get away, what with re-takes and everything."

"Yes, and if I'm to get away to New York, Tuesday night, I've a great deal of work to get through before then. So. . . ."

"So this is where I came in? Well, I want to come in tomorrow to order clothes and you can have them ready for me when I come back from Reno."

"Tomorrow is Saturday. We close at one. . . ."

"You still get away with that? But that'll fill in tomorrow morning." Suddenly, Greta brought her hands together in an unstudied gesture expressive of restrained impatience. "I wish it was tomorrow evening! Oh, yes, I have a—an important engagement then. Can I use your phone to call my secretary?"

"Certainly," Michael said, and while she dialed, began to read his morning mail.

"Jamesy? How are things going, darling. . . . Oh, that's all right. If they say they know me, chances are we've met. Come one, come all. . . . What? . . . No, I absolutely will not make any engagement for tomorrow evening! That's final. . . . Why, you'll damned well cover up for me!" Greta said with a sudden flash of temper. "It's what I'm paying you for and the only reason I agreed to let you come up here with me. . . . Oh, let it go. . . . I'm coming back to the hotel now. Be a pet and order lunch sent up. . . ."

She put down the telephone. "Jamesy's in a tizzy because too many men have been calling up, wanting to see me. She's afraid this will turn into a brawl. Won't you try to drop in this afternoon?"

"I'll keep it in mind," Michael said evasively. "I'll see you tomorrow when you come in. You'll be a good advertisement for Gisele's."

"Thanks. Look, do you think that little twerp will make you sorry you fired him like you did?"

"Egbert? Good God, no. What harm could he do me?"

"I hope you're right. Little rats like that can be dangerous. Well, it's been nice, Mr. Dundas. I'll see you tomorrow, if not later on today. . . ."

Michael returned to his mail and had time to read two letters and make cryptic notations on them before his sanctuary was invaded again. This time it was Miss Poole, an excellent stenographer but a twitterer.

"Oh, Mr. Dundas, Fanchon went to lunch and I can't find the smelling salts—but perhaps brandy. . . ."

"Smelling salts? Don't tell me that Egbert collapsed on his way out?"

"Egbert? Oh no, one of the customers fainted and since Fanchon is out, I thought you might. . . ."

Michael groaned. "*Por Dios,* is this going to be one of these days? Very well, where is she?"

3

"She" lay on one of the gray-green love seats, a slight woman with long, narrow hands and feet; an ash-blonde with over-delicate features and skin that had the unvital flawlessness of a pearl. "Probably a fine example of overbreeding," Michael thought. "A pedigreed racer with no stamina. . . ."

He turned to the saleswoman in attendance, "There's nothing I can do that you haven't done, Mrs. Tyson."

"Of course not. I told Poole not to bother you. This poor girl hasn't been well and all of a sudden she just keeled over. . . ."

"Should I know her?"

"I guess not. She's Mrs. Alan Furness. . . . Here, dear, take a sip of water. . . ."

"I'm so sorry. It was so silly of me." Mrs. Alan Furness tried to sit up, closed her eyes and lay back again. "Give me just a minute. I skipped breakfast, which was stupid of me and the ghastly raw-egg-and-milk I'm supposed to take in mid-morning. . . ."

"'Ghastly' does not adequately describe that nauseating concoction," Michael observed. "I'm Michael Dundas. . . ."

"I'm very glad finally to meet you, Mr. Dundas, even if our meeting is the result of my foolishness."

Marie Antoinette mindful of her manners even on the steps to the guillotine, Mr. Dundas reflected rather uncharitably. "Would you like me to call a taxi, Mrs. Furness? Or have you your own car?"

"Mrs. Furness, senior—Mrs. Zachary Furness—is in one of the fitting rooms now," Mrs. Tyson said. And, being an old and privileged employee, added, for his ears only, "And a regular Tartar, that one is. . . . Don't try to get up, Mrs. Alan. . . ."

"Oh, but I must." Viola Furness pulled herself erect, her pale mouth resolutely curved into a smile. "I'm quite all right and my mother-in-law is so. . . . would be so concerned about me that I'd rather. . . ."

She raised a hand to her eyes and let it drop in a despairing gesture as a crisp voice demanded, "Have you fainted again, Viola? Really, my dear, there are times when I despair of you. I left you here to rest and you've done nothing more tiring this morning than to sit at your ease in various shops and give Catherine and myself your opinion of our proposed purchases. . . ."

Michael had never seen Mrs. Zachary Furness before, but he recognized her instantly. What her name happened to be was unimportant. Under any name she belonged in his large collection of those who are so thickly overgrown with the complete arrogance of the elect, that imagination perished years ago for lack of air.

The Mrs. Furnesses could not be deliberately unkind, imagination being essential to deliberate unkindness. Only a favored few had the power to wound them, a circumstance which they believed was due to their own strength of character, not to an inborn imperviousness to approval or disapproval. And if others were foolishly sensitive, they must "just learn not to take offense so easily."

"I know, Mother Furness," her daughter-in-law was saying placatingly. "You've taken very good care of me and I don't know why I—Mother, this is Mr. Dundas. My mother-in-law, Mrs. Furness. . . ."

At fifty-odd, Mrs. Furness was tall, straight
and spare, with cold blue eyes under a widow's
peak of white hair, and a mouth tightly buttoned
up against laughter. She turned and regarded
Michael as she would have any other object in
the establishment that was offered for her inspec-
tion.

"Hmm. Isn't that name of yours Scotch? You're
dark as a Mexican or any of these foreigners. I did
expect you'd be given to bowing, clicking your
heels, that sort of thing. You don't look like a
dressmaker—too masculine . . . ."

"Mother Furness! Please—Mr. Dundas has been
very kind and. . . ."

"Hmm? Oh, Viola considers me rather outspo-
ken. I trust I haven't offended you?" Mrs. Furness
said indifferently.

Michael counted ten. And decided that three
years in the Army where it was often wise to lose
your temper if you wished to be at all highly
regarded, had had an unfortunate effect on his
ability to control his.

"Oh, not at all," he said. "Though I must con-
gratulate you for having gotten something for
nothing. . . ."

"Eh? I'm afraid I don't understand you. Now,
Viola, if you—"

"You see, the privilege of insulting me comes under the heading of special attention," Michael continued blandly. "And one pays extra for that. Then, some of my patrons who demand my personal attention, really pay me to insult them. Either way, it's strictly a matter of business. But you aren't on the preferred list, Mrs. Furness, so whatever you purchased today, you have a bargain; special items not on the table d'hote menu thrown in at no additional cost."

Viola Furness did not look as if she laughed easily nor often, but now she gave a sudden delighted giggle.

Mrs. Furness regarded Michael blankly for a minute; then, "Well, upon my word," she said in genuine astonishment and let out a short bark of laughter. "You do have a tongue in your head and you don't care at all if I take my trade elsewhere, it that it? Well, well, let's forget it, shall we?"

Viola murmured something that sounded to Michael like, "As if one always could, so easily. . . ." and drew Mrs. Furness's attention to her again.

"Well, Viola, I suppose that this is the end of our excursion for today. You must go home and rest. I couldn't face Alan if I didn't see you home myself. Now, if Catherine would come with the car. . . ."

"She's coming now, Mother Furness."

Michael turned to look at the young woman who was striding down the salon as if the carpet under her large brogues were the rolled green of the fairway of some golf course. She was as tall and as strongly built as her mother and twenty pounds heavier. She had beautiful teeth, a smile that showed two-thirds of them; skin that spoke of a healthy, semi-outdoor life and a rather too generous use of soap and water.

Made her debut, but no takers the first season, Michael guessed. Since then, golf, tennis, horses and—or—dogs, good works, Red Cross and so on. If she were married and had children, she'd be well on her way to being as impregnable as Mamma. I'll wager it's the fact that she's still Miss Furness that keeps her so well under Mamma's thumb. . . .

Viola looked at him with a faintly ironical smile, as if she had read his thought and stood up abruptly. "Miss Furness, Mr. Dundas."

"What? Oh, how-d'you-do," Catherine said. "I've never come here for my things, but perhaps I'll give you a try one day. Mamma and Viola think so well of your things that I really should give you a chance, shouldn't I?"

Michael opened his mouth with every intention of withering Miss Furness where she stood, but Mrs. Zachary Furness spoke first. "Nonsense! There's no point in paying high prices for the type

of thing you wear. But if you ever need a trousseau, which is unlikely, I'll gladly order it from
Mr. Dundas."

The words flicked a harsh, unbecoming scarlet
into Catherine's cheeks. She shifted from one foot
to the other and smiled, the incredulous smile of
an adolescent who has been ridiculed again by
a trusted grown-up but who still believes it will
surely never happen another time.

"Oh, Mamma. . . ."

"Please, let's go!" said Viola Furness and moved
toward the door into the entrance hall without
waiting to allow Mrs. Furness to take precedence.

Catherine and Mrs. Furness followed, reaching
the door in time to receive a smile and bow from
Fanchon Weis. Michael motioned to her to follow
him and stalked back to his office. She was grinning when she came in.

"What's the matter, boss? Did that Furness out-
fit get under your skin?"

"I should have stayed in the Army. War was
never like this."

"You're spoiled because a lot of our customers
let you get away with murder."

"Should I know who the Furnesses are, Fanny?"

"No. Viola got her trousseau here but that was
after you were in the Army. Her folks are old San
Francisco but short on cash. Old Mrs. F. started

coming here after that. The Furnesses came here from the East about ten years ago. They never did any splurging but old Zachary had plenty of money."

"Had? Is he dead?"

"He died last year—about the time you got back from overseas. I heard someone say that. . . . Look, where's Egbert?"

"I fired him a little after twelve noon."

"Oh, God! I knew you would in time, but I hoped you'd hold off a couple of weeks. And you haven't done a lick of work today." Fanchon frowned at the untidy litter on his desk. "If you don't get things in shape before Tuesday evening, you'll go to New York over my dead body. You get to work!"

4

It was six-thirty when Michael left Gisele's. He got in his car, only to sit there indecisively for several minutes. "I deserve a drink, two or three drinks," he muttered and produced a coin. "Heads I go home; tails I stop in a bar. . . ."

He flipped the coin. It eluded him, rolled across the car floor and came to rest, leaning against the car door—on edge. He raised his eyebrows. "Oh, well, solitary drinking is a pernicious thing. I'll stop by and see how Gertie's doing. . . ."

Miss Mallon, he saw at once, was doing quite nicely, thank you, though she was keeping her voice in its place and had control of her grammar. She greeted Michael with considerable manner and was most graciously inclined to acknowledge any small contribution he had made toward "what little success I have so far achieved. I was so very young and crude when I went to Gisele's; Mr. Dundas taught me so much. . . ."

"Less of it, Gertie. You've put me quite at my ease, thank you," Michael said in a cautious undertone, and made his escape when a fatuous middle-aged colonel stroked her arm and suggested that they all have a little more champagne.

He secured a highball and two squares of toast topped with lobster, saw a familiar, round, red face in a corner and made for it. "What are you doing here, Jube? Have you suffered the fate worse than death and been put to reviewing movies?"

"Unh-unh. I never pay for liquor when I can get it for free," said Mr. Jubal Chambers of the *News-Bulletin* truthfully. "I heard about the brawl and came along. The so-called drahma critics just left. They were here at four-thirty and Greta kept them waiting till after five. Maybe she was just getting into those things. . . ."

He regarded Miss Mallon's black metallic hostess pajamas approvingly. "But if she was right next door until she made her entrance, she'd been hoisting a few in the bedroom. She put on a good act, though. Smart of her to admit Pop was a Pole with more kids than he could feed, so she came out here to live with an aunt. . . ."

"An aunt? Oh yes, that aunt. Well, well," Michael said thoughtfully.

Mr. Chambers, who had hoisted a few himself, disregarded this and prattled cheerfully on, "Local girl makes good against heavy odds. Corny but effective. She had a good word for you and all the other guys who gave her a boost up the ladder. She's sort of taking off her shoes, now the most important people are gone, and the secretary doesn't like it."

He waved his glass toward Miss Jameson who was sitting very straight, ankles precisely crossed, talking to the only other women in the room— two young things, all eyelashes, shining blonde manes and flowery hats, who were gazing enviously at Miss Mallon.

"Knew Greta when they were all bit-players. They gave up fame for marriage and three squares per day," Jubal explained. "Smart of her to ask them up. Don't know who all the men are. The public relations department at her studio would bust a gut if they saw this. 'Taint the way a rising young star should comport herself. Looks to me

like Greta's pretty sure of herself for one reason
or another. Since you're on your feet, how's about
another drink?"

Michael nodded and started toward the elderly
waiter who was presiding over a portable bar with
the long-suffering disdain of one who, in better
days, had snubbed certain people of importance.
He was given two flattish highballs, turned without looking behind him and stopped short to avoid
collision with a handsome, middle-aged male, who
put out a steadying hand and said genially, "Sorry,
m'boy. Wasn't looking where I was going. No damage done, I hope? Aren't you Michael Dundas? I'm
Nathan Ridley. . . ."

"The name doesn't register but I do feel I've
seen you before."

Nathan Ridley laughed, the sort of deep, ever-
ready laugh that on first hearing is labeled "infec-
tious," but soon becomes irritating to the listener.

"You don't know me. It's just that I look like so
many other men of my age."

Michael was not obliging enough to contradict
him, though he thought that few men in their
fifties were lucky enough to be so sleek and glossy
as Mr. Ridley. He suspected that Mr. Ridley agreed
with him. At least, the movement with which
he smoothed his thick, curly white hair back from

its widow's peak, invited admiration of both hair and a shapely hand.

"Good to have this chance to see Greta again. . . ."

"Is it?" Michael said uncooperatively. "I haven't seen her since she left here to go to Hollywood."

"Oh, I didn't know her when she lived here," Ridley said hastily. "I worked for Pacific Ship during the war. That was in Los Angeles and I got to know people there—studio and radio writers among others. Greta was very cooperative about appearing at bond rallies. As the boys say, she's regular. Nice of her to remember an old duffer like me."

For want of anything better to do, Michael had finished his drink during this monologue. He looked toward Jubal Chambers. Jubal made gestures meant to indicate that he was perishing from thirst. Michael exchanged his empty glass for a full one.

"Yes, well, if you don't mind, Mr. Ridley. . . ."

"As I was about to remark," a languid voice broke in before Michael could get away, "we'll be late for the tomato juice aperitif and Hester will not be pleased. Or impressed, if we tell her in what exalted circles we've been moving. For one thing, she will know that we've been drinking something more potent than tomato juice."

"Afraid you're quite right, m'boy. And it does no good at all to chew cloves. My nephew, Louis Hilton, Mr. Dundas."

"Not that I am really his nephew," Hilton said, "but Nate's the ideal uncle—all the benefits of relationship with none of its inconveniences, in this case. I've heard of you, Dundas. . . ."

This was so often merely introductory to, "You're the guy that designs women's clothes. . . ." that Michael's "Yes," was deliberately unresponsive. Louis Hilton grinned. His angular chin, over-long nose and high knobby forehead at least guaranteed his narrow, sallow face a certain distinction that his uncle-elect's lacked.

"Not what you think," he drawled. "I knew a guy who knew you in Italy and was pretty well sold on Captain Dundas, as you were then. Art Bradley, it was. . . ."

"Were you in Italy?"

"No. I was too old for combat and for some reason or other, I could teach other guys to fly. I sweated the war out in Bakersfield and Chico—and I do mean sweated, in the summer months."

"Louis came to Los Angeles when he could and roughed it with me," Nathan Ridley said. "I introduced him to Greta. She did yeoman service at the Hollywood canteen during the war. . . ."

"And hooked the poor sucker who married her there," Louis said cynically. "I'm surprised that she threw him overboard so quickly. Tom Ainslee III was a nice little step up for her."

"Come now, Louis, one mustn't be uncharitable. Hundreds of other women, not in the public eye, married too hastily during the war. Very sad, but. . . ."

"I'm not criticizing Greta," Louis said coolly. "She's a shrewd operator and I like to see her work. Meanwhile. . . ."

"Yes, of course. Mustn't keep Hester waiting," said Mr. Ridley. "Glad to have met you, Dundas. . . ."

"Apparently, but I wonder why," Michael muttered, going back to Jubal Chambers. "Do you know those two who were talking to, and, at me, Jube?"

"Not the young fellow. The perennial playboy is Nathan Ridley. You've seen him around."

"Have I? Who would 'Hester' be, do you think?"

"Haven't any idea. What do you care?"

"Oh, I wonder why Ridley thought he needed to explain at some length how he and his so-called nephew happen to know Greta."

"Maybe they both have wives. And somehow or other, stories get around. Your wife hasn't come home yet, has she?" Jubal finished his own drink and absent-mindedly picked up the glass Michael had put down on a table. "By the way, what do you hear from Nick Prevost?"

"He's still convalescing in New Mexico. After all, he did just escape a ruptured appendix after having been badly overworked for four years. He should be back next month."

"You'd better not stumble on any bodies while he's away. The other detective inspectors, especially Hoyt, think there's not much choice between you and poison," Jubal said tactlessly and put down an empty glass. "Are my eyes crossed?"

"Slightly."

"Then it's time Mrs. Chambers's little boy Jubal was on his way. Be seeing you. . . ."

"But I wanted to ask you. . . ."

Michael stopped, shrugged and allowed Jubal to go on his erratic way, realizing that whatever he might know about Nathan Ridley, Jubal was in no state to be terse or too accurate. And, as Greta's laughter had grown somewhat shrill and much too frequent, he thought that he would not risk additional demonstrations of gratitude and esteem, but make a quiet exit.

She caught up with him before he reached the door. "You can't run out on me like this, darling," she said playfully, slid her arm through his and

accompanied him into the hall. Michael regarded
her with a reluctant grin.

"Having fun, Gertie? You are *en grande tenue*
this evening, aren't you?"

"Whatever that means. But I'm having fun. Oh
boy, have I had fun today," said Gertie Malinowsky. "And the evening's young yet. I'm. . . . You
always used a lot of British phrases, didn't you,
even before the war made them popular? And isn't
it English to say you're getting a bit of your own
back? And I am and I will!"

"With no wish to be a spoil-sport, I advise you
to lay off the champagne for a while. Another
half-hour and you'll be drunk as a fiddler's owl."

"Not another drink now, so help me. I'll take
a cold shower, have some coffee *and* some more
fun. Thanks for breaking down and coming to my
party. Thanks a lot. . . ."

Her kiss landed, due to his involuntary back-
ward movement, below one ear. Miss Mallon giggled. "Not scared, are you?" she said sweetly.

Mr. Dundas said resignedly, "Hollywood stock
situation, number ten," grasped her shoulders and
kissed her, not at all casually. Miss Mallon looked
well pleased and he admitted to himself that the
pleasure was mutual.

"What," she inquired, "would that wife of yours
say?"

"That some such proceeding was necessary for the preservation of my masculine ego. And quite right, too," Michael said, reaching for his handkerchief.

"Don't get lipstick on that good linen," Greta said thriftily. "Besides, you don't want that turning up in the family wash. I don't wear the same shade as your wife. Here, I'll give you a Kleenex . . .

She opened her black cordé bag and handed him a small, folded square of paper. "Don't miss that smear by your left ear—Oh, nuts, that isn't Kleenex. Well, it's ruined now so it don't matter. Yes, you've got it all off."

Michael thrust the crumpled paper into his pocket without looking at it. "Hadn't you better go back and be kind to your other guests? And, though I doubt that you care to be good, at least try to be reasonably careful . . .

5

The telephone's determined ringing jerked Michael from his first, deep sleep. He groaned, feeling for the switch of the bedside lamp. He loved his wife dearly but deplored her habit of making her long distance calls around midnight because "it's four o'clock here and I can't get back to sleep. . . ."

But it was only twenty minutes past ten, and the voice that came to him over the wire was not that of a long-distance operator.

"Michael—Mr. Dundas—I know you're going to be sore at me for calling you. . . ."

"What do you want, Gertie?"

"Do you know this big apartment house on the corner of Jones and Green? I mean the one right at Jones, not the bigger one over by Green Street steps. . . ."

"Certainly I know the Verde Vista. I live less than two blocks from it."

"I thought you did but I wasn't sure. Mr. Dundas, could you come over right away?"

"Is that where you are now? Alone?"

"I'm still alone but—Oh, I don't blame you for being suspicious. It does sound like it could be a frame-up but honest, it's not. I'm sober, Mr. Dundas, and I don't scare easy and I'm not really scared now—but maybe it'd be better if I had someone else here; someone I could trust never to talk. I've been thinking it could be dangerous . . . If you don't come and—anything happened, you'd be sorry."

"Quite a judge of character, aren't you?" Michael snapped. "Yes, I'll come. I suppose you couldn't be persuaded to explain, first?"

"It'd take too long. You'll find out soon enough if you hurry. Will you?"

"I won't venture into the streets without my trousers but I should be with you in twenty minutes. Are you incognito?"

"What? Oh. Well, just come up to apartment 801. You don't have to ask for me. No one'll stop you. Or you could use the service elevator like I did. I'll be watching and let you in. And. . . ."

"Yes?" Michael said impatiently, as the pause lengthened. "Have you changed your mind—I hope?"

"Just making it up. Just in case, there's a name I want you to remember: Bella Voss. Got it? She. . . . But look, it's ten-thirty already. You can't get dressed if I keep talking. Apartment 801. . . ."

Michael had been an air-raid warden for several months in 1942 and was familiar with the Verde Vista's capacious garage that had been designated an air-raid shelter then. He knew that the service elevator could be reached by a door that paralleled the driveway into the garage and was only a few steps from the street, but Michael chose to enter the building by its front door. "Because," he thought, "if anyone saw me sneaking in the back way, they'd take for granted I was keeping an assignation here . . .

There was no longer an impressive bottle-green doorman to wave one toward the elevators. A middle-aged woman, half-asleep in one of them, took him up to the eighth floor without asking whom he wished to see.

The radio was on in 801, not loudly, but just high enough so that he could hear a band rendition of *To Each His Own*. Michael tried the door, not surprised to find it on the latch, and then rang the bell perfunctorily.

"She's probably touching up her face in the bathroom," he decided and stepped into a long hall, at the end of which he could see a triangle of living-room. "Soft music! Now, if she has the lights turned down low. . . ."

But there was, after all, too much light in the big room—from the fixtures along the walls, from the squarish glass and plastic lamps on three low tables. Gertie Malinowsky lay dead in the light. Her head rested in a soft pool of it, against the polished, blond wood of a table leg. There was an angry bruise across one temple and the pulpy wounds in the back of her head had stained the pale carpet. . . .

Michael made a quick tour of the apartment. Dinette, bathroom, kitchen and two small bedrooms, all in perfect order. "No murderers hiding under the bed," Michael muttered and returned to the living-room.

It, too, had an unused look, like an expensive garment well-cared for, but hung away in a closet for future wear. Greta's occupancy had hardly

disturbed its contours. There was a pack of cigarettes, a bottle of whisky, three unused glasses
on a coffee table. A square of heavy, brown paper
and a tangle of string lay on the chartreuse couch,
along with a blue, sport felt and a coat of no distinction whatever.

Michael turned and looked down at Greta again,
seeing that she wore little make-up, had combed
her black hair straight back from her forehead,
put on flat-heeled shoes and a severe wool dress.
There was no purse in sight, none beneath hat,
coat, or wrapping paper. Michael regarded the
latter, frowning for an instant longer, before he
moved toward the telephone in the hall.

He started to dial, thinking, "Nick Prevost will
say I've taken my time about. . . ." and stopped.
"Oh, Lord!" he murmured, not irreverently. "Nick
is in New Mexico and if they send that bastard,
Hoyt. . . ."

He shrugged fatalistically and dialed Police
Headquarters.

PART TWO

1

"So when Miss Mallon called you up at ten-twenty and asked you to come right over, you didn't make her tell you what it was all about," said Inspector Matthew Hoyt. "You just got up, dressed and came right over. Though you didn't hurry too much, dressing—didn't get here till ten-fifty. The elevator operator brought you up. You found Miss Mallon dead and didn't call us until eleven-five. Is that right?"

"Your facts are correct," Michael said. "You state them in a rather intriguing fashion, too, Inspector. You omitted to say that it was ten-thirty when she rang off. And I haven't told you that she. . . ."

"One thing at a time," Hoyt said repressively. "First facts first, you know. Get the groundwork and fill in details later. Got all that, Quinlan?"

Quinlan nodded. He was an earnest-looking young man who breathed through his mouth and suffered from an excess of saliva. Conversation with him was a moist affair unless you kept your distance, and his shorthand was damp, too, since he was a constant pencil ticker. He was also Hoyt's son-in-law, and Michael eyed him with what dislike he could spare from the inspector. It was a new experience for Mr. Dundas to have his first informal statement formally taken down by a police stenographer. Good for my soul, no doubt, he reflected, and very deflating.

He said, "May I finish my story and get on home?"

"We're in no hurry. I don't work the same as Nick Prevost. You'll have to get used to my methods," Hoyt said and might as well have added, "I've got you where I want you and I'll take no nonsense from you."

Hoyt had four daughters, seven grandchildren, and a wife who said frequently, "My, how right you are, Matt." Sarcasm angered him, flippancy baffled him, and he felt that verbal levity must be the offshoot of genuine licentiousness. Hoyt was moral, upright and incorruptible. He knew it and intended that anyone who didn't know it should damned soon find out.

So he said reprovingly, "You won't get special favors just because I know you. You've told us how you come to find the body. Now you'll have to wait a while. Bring the elevator operator in, Costello."

And you, Michael decided, will wait to hear the name "Bela Voss" until I'm bloody well ready to mention it. Then he grinned and settled back in his chair as it occurred to him that, by putting him in his place, Hoyt had given him an unexpected opportunity to hear the testimony of other witnesses.

The elevator operator was voluble as soon as she saw that the body had been removed. She'd been on duty since seven and the elevator had been overworked for a while, it being Friday night. There were parties on the tenth and twelfth floors that she knew of, and lots of the tenants went out. But lots of people came in and she didn't remember one person from another until things quieted down about nine o'clock.

"After that I recall four strangers coming in. A couple went up to six and a woman to eleven, I think it was. A young fellow went up to ten, said he was late to the party there. They all mentioned who they were going to see. People usually seem to think they ought to, the first time they come to a place. This man . . ." she nodded toward Michael, "didn't bother."

"You didn't make me feel that it was necessary to do so," Michael remarked.

"No. I put you down as one of these explanations-be-damned people. And I didn't take this Greta Mallon up to eight. The service elevator's automatic and even the tenants use it sometimes rather than wait for me."

"The telephones are all private?" Hoyt said. "No apartment house switchboard? No? Now, whose apartment did you say this is, and why aren't they around?"

"The Yellands rent it and they're characters. In their fifties. Lots of money and no sense. They have a little fifteen-room dump down the peninsula. . . ."

"Oh, *those* Yellands?" Michael said.

"So you know them, then?" Hoyt asked.

"I've never met Yelland. His wife has been in the shop several times and I think she owes me money now."

"Oh, they're quite the society bugs," the elevator operator said. "Get their names in the papers and all that. I will say they're goodhearted. Not that they'd give up this apartment that they don't really need to someone who does need a place to live. But during the war, they began lending it to friends when they weren't here themselves. . . ."

"And they don't stay in the city much?" Hoyt said.

"Never over a week end and they've been up at Lake Tahoe for three weeks now. And don't ask me

who all they let use this place in the four years
I've been here. The Yellands know so many people
that they don't always seem to know quite who
they do know."

"We'll get a list when we've talked to the manager and day force here," Hoyt said omnipotently.
"We're good at digging out things like that."

"I wish you joy of your job." The woman was
not impressed. "Because the Yellands handed out
keys like crazy. They were always mislaying their
own, so they kept a dozen extras around. Screwballs!
I know this place's been occupied week ends even
when I never saw anyone go into it or leave it."

Hoyt closed his right eye and looked disapprovingly down the left side of his nose. "Like
that, was it? Well, during the war, too many people confused liberty with licentiousness."

"You think so? Mrs. Yelland's kind of innocent for a dame that's been around. She'd hand
out a key and the use of the place and never even
wonder if there was any funny business going on.
Mr. Yelland just wouldn't care if there was or not.
And I warn you," the elevator operator added,
"that I think some people who were given keys to
this place didn't ever return them and sometimes
passed them on to others who wanted a place to
sleep for a night or two. That wouldn't worry the
Yellands, if they knew it."

"You don't like the Yellands," Hoyt stated.

"I like them all right. But they think they're entitled to anything because they can pay for it. They're not as bad as some, but I could live for six months on what they spend on their pedigreed pups in a year."

"Comes the revolution and we'll make street cleaners of all people with pedigreed dogs who consistently refuse to kick the little dears over to the curb when walking them," Michael said.

"Now, now! I don't go for this Communist talk," Hoyt said heavily. And could not understand why the woman grinned companionably at Mr. Dundas.

"That's the idea, brother," she said.

"May I ask the lady a question, Inspector?" Michael said deferentially

"Oh . . . Yes, let's hear your bright idea."

"Of course you don't know the names of all of the Yellands' friends and couldn't recognize by description all those who have used this apartment," Michael said. "Still. . . . the man I have in mind is middle-aged, very good-looking and with hands and hair of which he is proud, the hair being gray and curly and growing to a widow's peak. His name is Nathan Ridley. . . ."

"Yes. He's come here to see the Yellands. He's the sort that tells his name like you should know it, and where he's going and why, like it mattered to you. He came here the first year or so I worked here, then when he came back last year, he seemed to think I'd remember him right off or had missed him. Told me he'd worked two years in L.A. during the war. That the one you mean?"

Michael nodded. Hoyt said, "And who is Nathan Ridley?"

"I don't know. He was at the St. Francis this evening when Greta entertained and he bothered to tell me, in detail, how he happened to know Greta. There was a young man, Louis Hilton, with him. Tall, sallow, narrow face, big nose, sharp chin, high forehead. . . ."

The elevator operator asked, "Would he have been in uniform?"

"During the war, yes."

"Well, there were so many in uniform and it changed their looks. . . . Why don't you just ask the Yellands the names they remember that might be important?"

"We'll decide that," Hoyt said. "You can go now, Miss—Mrs.—thank you. . . . So there were other men besides this Ridley and Hilton up in Miss Mallon's suite this afternoon? Including yourself? You did say your wife's in New York?"

"Yes. And she would want me to give you her best regards if she knew that I'd had the unexpected pleasure of seeing you again."

Hoyt sniffed. He did not consider Valerie Dundas the ideal type of young wife and mother. "Well," he said, "since you've mentioned this. . . ."

"The brawl in Miss Mallon's suite?" Michael suggested.

Just then Costello, who was on duty at the front door, returned to the living-room. "The secretary's here, dame by the name of Jameson," he told Hoyt. "She insisted on coming over when they told her what'd happened. Says she wants to talk to you before the reporters get wise."

"Why, that's very co-operative of her. . . ."

"Yes, Inspector, and I wish to co-operate, but may I not speak my little piece and go home?" Michael said cagily.

He was rewarded with a stern, "You sit where you are. Bring Miss Jameson in, Costello."

2

"Who might have wanted to kill Greta?" asked Miss Jameson in her light, agreeably fastidious voice. "Many people disliked her and she may have made some men and women unhappy. A person like her does."

"This guy, Ainslee, that she was going to divorce. . . . He could have followed her up here," Hoyt suggested.

Miss Jameson shrugged. "You'll check on that, won't you? But I think Tom was quite resigned to the divorce. When he was home again, out of the Army, he got his perspective back. At least, so I judged, and he talked to me quite frankly."

"Well, I suppose there are other men. . . ."

"Only one on the active list, Inspector. Greta did conduct herself circumspectly while Tom was overseas. But though it hasn't leaked into the gossip columns yet, I believe that she was going to marry Victor Borck, who is a power in Hollywood. I admire him," Miss Jameson added quickly. "He is one producer who has taste and intelligence and courage. He is fifty, very wealthy and very lonely. I don't know what he saw in Greta but I think they planned to marry. I'm rather glad that I don't have to break this news to him."

"Borck is a V.I.P. and I suppose that's why Greta dared to do more or less as she pleased on this little jaunt?" Michael said.

"I think so. She knew she had his backing. The studio wanted her to postpone her divorce. They certainly wished to make the usual arrangements regarding her activities while she was in San Francisco. She defied them. She allowed me to come along because I would be useful. She needed someone to cover up for her."

"Cover up, hunh?" Hoyt said.

Miss Jameson frowned. "I'd better tell you that I've been with Greta for only a year. I know nothing about her but what she chose to tell me and that's what everyone else knows. Born in Chicago of Polish parents; youngest of ten children, came out here to live with an aunt. I should think that might be where Mr. Dundas comes in."

"Greta came into my shop in January of '41 and asked for a job," Michael said. "She was alarmingly dressed, needed washing but had obvious possibilities. I took her on as a model. She looked as if she had been ill but said she'd been working as a waitress out in the Mission. She said she was eighteen and looked it. At least, the school authorities were not on her trail. I don't know how long she'd been in San Francisco then. She was vague about that, only said that she was living with an aunt."

"We can check on that and with her aunt," Hoyt said. "What was the aunt's name—Malinowsky?"

"No. I don't remember the name, but it was Italian and so was she. Gertie put her down as the person to be notified in case of emergency when she made out her employment papers. One evening Gertie took one of our model dresses with her when she left the shop. I was told what she'd done and drove out to her home. The address must still be in our files and I could find the place easily enough. It was in the Potrero district, and the place was about the crummiest rooming house I've ever seen.

"Gertie had already departed in her borrowed frock," Michael continued. "Her so-called aunt was not helpful. Her English was rudimentary and though I speak her particular Italian dialect, she wouldn't talk, except to insist that she was Gertie's aunt by marriage, though she couldn't explain why her name was something like Guisto instead of Malinowsky if that were the truth."

"Then you don't think they were really related at all?" Hoyt asked.

"No, I thought the woman was probably a procuress in a small way. Her roomers seemed to be mainly very tough customers who worked in the Potrero. I have no idea how Gertie happened to drift to that place. I do suspect that she may have run away from home when she was quite young."

Miss Jameson nodded. "Publicly, she said that her parents were dead and her brothers and sisters so scattered that she'd lost touch with them. Privately, she never mentioned her family except that she said to me, only once, that they would never bother her and that they didn't even know that she was Greta Mallon."

"Her name may not even have been Malinowsky, which makes the job of tracing her back a tough one," Hoyt said. "Well, Mr. Dundas, you didn't fire her, in spite of what she did?"

"I should have. But she made no excuses. And her personal wardrobe consisted of two very old dresses and one shabby coat," Michael said thoughtlessly. "And she was a born model. I made her pay for the dress she borrowed. . . ."

He did not add that he'd allowed her the usual employee's discount and increased her wages soon afterward. "And she didn't do it again. Soon after that, she got herself a housekeeping room in a respectable establishment. That address should be in our files, too."

"And you visited her in that place, too?"

Michael regarded Hoyt speculatively. "Not that I recall. And there is a flavor to your questions that I don't like, Inspector. My manager, Fanchon Weis, will give you access to any records we may still have on Gertie. I've no idea to what extent Gertie may have confided in Julius Lindt, who discovered her. He's back in New York now."

"Make a note of Lindt, Quinlan. And I guess it's your turn to talk again, Miss Jameson."

"I'd better be selective, I think. Others can tell you more than I can about Greta's first three years in Hollywood. She lived very economically; that was necessary when her salary wasn't large. But even when she could have afforded to live less simply, she didn't. It's the fashion for actors to be sensible about money but most of them have business managers. Greta didn't, and she never allowed me to handle her check book. She gave me cash for household expenses. Which may not be important. . . ."

"But you think she could've been blackmailing somebody?" Hoyt said.

"I think it's more likely that someone was blackmailing her. The studio thought, after she made such an impression in her last three pictures, that her establishment—only a maid by the day—was too simple. And I was supposed to be half-duenna. Greta was usually docile," Miss Jameson said. "She listened to people who told her what would or wouldn't further her career. But at least three times during her first years in Hollywood, she simply vanished for a week without telling anyone where she was going or, when she returned, where she had been."

"I believe," Michael said, "that she'd been either in this city or somewhere near it. She told me that this was the first time she'd been here 'that anyone knows about'; that for three years it was easy enough 'to sneak off and go places' without being recognized."

"Yes. But now it was nearly impossible for her to do that. Well, I expected, as her secretary, to open her personal mail. But she wouldn't allow me to do that. Not that there was a great deal of it, directed to her home. . . ."

"I suppose a lady like you wouldn't ever look at any envelopes?" Hoyt said, ponderously jovial.

"I have my fair share of curiosity," Miss Jameson said dryly. "Every month a letter came to her, addressed in a rather illiterate handwriting. Now and then it would be fairly bulky, as if there was some enclosure. Then, just lately—during the past two months—she received four or five letters postmarked San Francisco, the address typewritten. The other letters I spoke of had various postmarks: San Leandro, Hayward, and Oakland. You see, I was never in Greta's confidence. There's another odd thing I have to mention. She had something in her possession that she prized greatly, that I never saw. . . ."

"How was that?" Hoyt asked.

"Whatever it was, she kept it in a lacquered bronze box, a rather heavy thing that must have been made to order because it had a small, but quite intricate lock. Greta always kept the key, if not on a chain about her neck, in her purse. She took the box with her even when she spent only one night away from home," Miss Jameson said.

"It was a rather odd shape—about five inches across, one way, only about four the other, and about four inches deep. Whatever was in it was heavy, too, I'd say, and there was space enough in the box that it—well, it didn't rattle, but it shifted just a little. And the box isn't in our hotel suite now," Miss Jameson ended.

3

"Quinlan, that wrapping paper!" Hoyt said impressively and, when it was produced, "Now, Miss Jameson, you see the creases in this? Could it. . . ."

"Oh yes, it could have been used to wrap that box. Greta certainly took it with her. To carry it unwrapped would have made her conspicuous and she obviously didn't want that. You didn't find the box here, with her. . . ."

"Mr. Dundas didn't report finding it and he's shaking his head now," said Hoyt with horrible geniality. "Why do you say Miss Mallon didn't want to be conspicuous tonight, Miss Jameson?"

"Shall we go back to our departure from Hollywood? As soon as we were on the train, Greta told me that she would not be free tonight. 'Probably not after eight,' she said. And that she would not be spending tomorrow—Saturday—night in the hotel.

"Protest did no good. Greta said, 'I'm clearing out of the hotel in the late afternoon Saturday and you'll just have to cover up for me.' We got into the city, reached the hotel. She told me to stall off the newspaper people until between four and eight, and to tell anyone else who wanted to see her, to come up then, too."

Miss Jameson lifted her slim shoulders in another of her admirable shrugs. "It wasn't at all the thing for her to do. Then she went to see Mr. Dundas, returning to the hotel for lunch. A little after two o'clock, the telephone rang—again. But this time, she happened to answer it herself."

"Make a note of that, Quinlan," Hoyt said. "We'll check with the operator. Go on."

"Listening to whoever was talking, Greta began to smile in an odd, almost triumphant way. She said something like, 'Of course I remember. I'm not apt to forget.' And then, 'Oh, that would be a pleasure.' Then she looked at me and I was forced to walk out of hearing distance. In a minute or two she hung up. She told me that she was going out—and went."

"How long was she gone?"

"Until nearly five, Inspector, which was embarrassing as people began to come in at four. She came in by her bedroom door, of course. People stayed on until eight o'clock, when she simply announced that she must be excused because she had to rest."

"Have you any idea who all was up there this evening, Miss?" Hoyt asked.

"I can give you a list of those to whom Greta bothered to introduce me. There would still be a great many whose names I don't know. If she wished to contact someone without making elaborate preparations for a meeting, her open house gave her an excellent opportunity to do so."

The Inspector blinked and then said hastily, "As I was just thinking. Well, after eight o'clock. . . ."

"She had coffee sent up, took a shower and laid out a plain dress, hat and coat. Then she lay down for a while. We didn't talk. She didn't care to, and I was exasperated," Miss Jameson admitted. "I wanted a breath of air. I asked Greta if I might walk to the nearest drugstore. This was a little before nine-thirty. She told me to do as I wished for the rest of the evening.

"So I walked across Union Square to the Owl drugstore opposite the City of Paris, walked back along Geary, window-shopping. It was about ten minutes of ten when I got back to our suite. Greta was gone—and I'm afraid that's all I can tell you, Inspector."

"We'll check with the elevator boys. She probably grabbed a taxi. And what," Hoyt said, "did her and you talk about when she was at your store, Dundas?"

"We talked over old times. She spoke of her marriage and impending divorce, insisting that young Ainslee was resigned to his sad fate. And she did say that she had an important engagement on Saturday night and seemed rather impatient for Saturday to arrive."

"Yes," said Miss Jameson, "I got the impression that she was waiting for Saturday—impatiently."

"Well, you went to this party she gave," Hoyt said. "What'd she talk to you about then?"

"The only interesting thing she said was that she'd had fun today and that the evening was young yet," Michael said. "But the evening isn't young now, Inspector. Before I go, I should. . . ."

"Weren't you still in San Francisco or around here for a while even after you got into the Army?" Hoyt said abruptly.

"I wasn't sent overseas until April of '43."

"Then you were around here for nearly two years after Miss Mallon went to Hollywood. Are you sure she never dropped in to have a little talk with you when she made one of those hush-hush trips back here?"

"I've told you I hadn't seen her since she went off to Hollywood with Julius Lindt."

"But it would've been the natural thing for her to let you know how she was getting along, even if she didn't want anyone else to know she was up here for a day or two. Or maybe she wrote you now and then? She certainly must've thought of you as a good friend, to have called on you tonight like she did. . . ."

Mr. Dundas rose. Afterward he liked to remember that when Hoyt interrupted him, he had been about to pass on Greta's request that he remember the name "Bella Voss." But now, in a quiet way, he lost his temper.

"I'm a patient man," he said untruthfully. "But I'm fed up with your insinuations. You have a mind like a stopped-up sink and Quinlan may make a note of that. Good night."

Hoyt bellowed after him but he proceeded unhurriedly through the hall to the front door and Costello. Costello was an old crony of Nicholas Prevost's and knew Michael well. He permitted himself a guarded smile, but the shake of the head that went with it was a distinct warning. Mr. Dundas acknowledged it with a vulgar and expressive gesture, then went on his way.

If the police cars, meat-wagon, and rumor of violence had drawn a crowd earlier, it had melted away long ago. The fog had come in and a spiteful wind was badgering a drowsy city. Michael had not worn a top coat. He paused outside the Verde Vista's ornate front doors to button his sport coat and shrug deeper into it.

As he stood there, he looked across Green Street at a small, unpretentious apartment house on one corner of Jones and a white stucco duplex on the other. The duplex had a tiled outer vestibule with a short flight of twisting stairs leading to the front door of the lower flat. A man was standing motionless, well back against the side of the steps, hat slanted down over his eyes.

Somehow he did not look at all like a householder just come out of his home, or as if he was on the point of returning to it. Michael reflected that it was impossible to loiter convincingly in a neighborhood like this at one-thirty in the morning. And with the police in force in the Verde Vista, one wouldn't dare take cover at its entrance.

Still, he doubted that he would have noticed the fellow if he hadn't stopped to take a deep breath and had not reached a state of nervous irritation that went hand-in-hand with an oversensitive alertness to his surroundings. The guy's interested in the Verde Vista, he decided. I can't see why that interest should extend to me, but it might. We'll find out—And, instead of taking the short way home, along Jones to Vallejo, he turned and started along Green Street toward the steps that led down to Taylor.

He walked rapidly, without looking back, until he reached a walk that led into a house halfway down the hill. He left the steps to stand quietly in the walk. After several minutes, he heard heavy feet starting down the steps, but in less than another minute the sound ceased abruptly.

"He realizes, now, that he can't hear me," Michael thought. "*Está bien, hombre;* if you want to play games, we'll take a nice walk together. . . ."

Quickly he put the remaining sixty-odd steps behind him, turned into Taylor and led the way up the steep slope between Green and Vallejo. He stopped on the crest of a hill where a dirt path led into a small park, sat down on one of the rocks left to mark this entrance and lighted a cigarette.

The man behind him stopped, too, halfway up the hill. And probably, Michael thought maliciously, damn glad to rest. The fellow was not tall but was powerfully built. Michael could not see his face clearly. For he was also lighting a cigarette, using a great many matches, shielding cigarette and face with a cupped hand and making unconvincing gestures of annoyance.

Michael considered his next move. His shortest way home now was by the steps just across the street that, skirting the old Verdier mansion, continued on up to the brown hump of earth that had once been a Russian burying ground. A nice climb, that, but he was still amused and not winded. And in this neighborhood, the difficulty was not to find hills and long flights of steps, but to avoid them.

"Perhaps," he muttered, "the gentleman would find Fallon Terrace interesting. . . ."

He rose, went on down Taylor until he reached a tree that had a green-lettered sign *Fallon Terrace* nailed to it. A wide, brick wall that soon gave way to pinkish cement steps took one down the hill. To the right were three solid, drab-colored houses; to the left, a damp, dripping growth of fern, ivy, hydrangea and assorted shrubs. During the day, Fallon Terrace was picturesque. At night it was unpleasantly dank and inadequately lighted.

The steps were succeeded by steppingstones that curved across a stretch of moist earth to more steps—these, rather rickety wooden ones. They came to an end when a board walk turned at right angles back toward Vallejo and the middle level of the little park.

Michael turned into the board walk, stopped and listened. He thought he heard a profane noise behind him. The steppingstones were dangerously slick and arranged in a rather haphazard fashion. He smiled smugly, continued along the walk past two excessively quaint, ramshackle cottages, to a wooden gate marked *Private*.

He got it open after a short struggle with a crotchety latch that needed oiling, stepped out of the terrace, closed the gate and leaned back against it. Presently feet made themselves heard along the boards on the other side of the gate, then stopped abruptly. Michael waited, wondering just how patient the man who was stalking him could be.

Apparently, for the second time, the next move was up to him. They were now halfway down the hill between Taylor and Mason. He could double back up the hill toward home or go on down to Mason and after that, the possibilities were endless. What he would have decided on, he never knew.

For, as he stood there, from a little down the hill came an easily identified voice, saying irritably, "For God's sake, Cathie, if you're not through talking, come back inside. But otherwise—and preferably—go home!"

4

There was a thick growth of shrubs and ivy to one side of the gate. It hid Michael from anyone below but, parting the ivy a little, he could see the front of a white stucco cottage with long windows opening onto a narrow redwood balcony, redwood steps leading up to a square landing before the front door. Catherine Furness was facing Louis Hilton and the door, slapping her pigskin gloves nervously against her tweed skirt.

She said, with something of the same anxious desire to please that had been apparent when she spoke to her mother, "Oh, of course you're provoked with me, Lou. I shouldn't have come here so late—alone. . . ."

"I'm not worried about the conventions, babe. We are first cousins, aren't we? And what you had to say was very interesting but it could have kept or you could have managed to talk to me after dinner."

"But you and Alan left so early tonight. Mamma was hurt. . . ."

Mr. Hilton snorted. "It would take a meat cleaver to hurt Hester. She was displeased. Trouble is, Cathie, you can't just tell a thing once. You hash and rehash and indulge in useless speculation."

"But Lou, it's so worrying and I don't understand. . . ."

"And don't call me Lou! It always reminds me of the lady who's known as."

"I'm sorry. But you're the only one I can talk to. Mamma ridicules everything I say and Uncle Nate is completely under her thumb. . . ."

"Hester's thumb is large enough to cover a lot of people besides you and Nate, babe," Louis said. "Look, there's no one home in the next cottage and sensible people don't stroll through the park at this hour. There's a gang that goes in for robbery and plain and fancy rape that sometimes operates around here. Still, why discuss family affairs in the wide open spaces? I'll take you down to your car. . . ."

"Nonsense!" Catherine was brisk and self-reliant again. "It's parked at the bottom of the hill. Wait here, if you like, and I'll toot the horn when I get in. . . ."

Michael waited until he heard the mournful hoot of a car horn and then walked quickly across a square of pavement and a little way down the steps that led to Mason, paralleling the front of Louis's cottage.

"Good morning," he said politely.

Louis stopped with his hand on the doorknob and stared at him. "What. . . . Oh, it's you? What are you doing here at this hour? Airing the dog, maybe?"

"There's a bloodhound behind me but he won't come when I call. I'm only taking my insomnia for an airing. I live nearby: Russian Hill Place. I didn't know that you lived down here."

"Why would you? This house is the only property that my sainted Pa ever managed to hold onto. But what do you care where I live?"

"I don't," Michael said mildly. "But I'm intrigued to learn that you're related to the Furnesses.

I had the pleasure of meeting three female Furnesses today, including the one that just departed, her mother and sister-in-law."

"Oh. Yes, Hester—Mrs. Zachary—does make a definite impression. My mother was Zachary's sister. . . ."

"And Nathan Ridley is Mrs. Zachary's brother?"

"Yes, but how did you know?"

"The hair and the widow's peak."

"Oh yes, that runs in the family. Look, Dundas. . . ."

"I stood behind a convenient clump of ivy and listened to you and Catherine," Michael said coolly. "Tell me, was Viola Furness in moderately good health at dinner this evening?"

Louis's long jaw dropped. "She wasn't even at dinner and Hester said she'd been dr— How did you know Viola wasn't well?"

"She fainted in my shop this afternoon for no apparent reason. Greta Mallon had just swept regally through the salon where Viola was sitting. It was stupid of me not to connect those two happenings before."

"But I had no idea that Viola knew Greta and. . . . How's about you coming inside?"

"No. But I'd advise you to tune in early on the radio newscasts if you don't take a morning paper,"

Michael said, backed up the steps, turned and opened the gate into Fallon Terrace.

He found himself confronting a dejected male sprawled against the unsteady railing that bordered the wooden walk on its right side.

"Did you wish to speak to me? Fun's fun, but I'm not young enough to be overflowing with energy and I need my sleep."

The "bloodhound" removed his slanted hat, revealing short-cropped, kinky, brown hair and a reddish scar that was like a third eyebrow.

"Christ Almighty, I'm not proud," he said in a quick, sharp voice with a marked nasal twang. "And I'm no mountain goat. I'm dry as the great Sahara, so if you've got a home, give a guy a break. I'll go quietly, anywhere I can take the weight off my feet for a while."

5

"Say when," Michael invited.

"If that's Scotch, just let it run until it's good and cold."

The man lifted his glass when Michael gave it to him, inhaled deeply and put it down empty. He settled himself more comfortably in the largest chair in the Dundas living-room.

"The name is Woodrow Wilson Weller. . . ."

"Born during the first war to end war?"

"Before that. Pop was a black Republican and so sure Hughes would win in '16 that he bet a guy twenty bucks against anything he'd like to name, that Wilson would be defeated. I arrived two days after the election and the guy said he'd like to have me named Woodrow Wilson. Pop wouldn't welsh on a bet but being quite a reader, he began calling me Sam. Everyone does.

"A break for you, Mr. Weller. What's your interest in this business?"

"I'm a private operative by inheritance. I was born in New York State though I've been around. . . ."

"European theater or South Pacific?"

"European. Where were you, bud?"

Michael raised his eyebrows. "Since I wear my ruptured duck only during business hours, for business reasons, and I'm past thirty-five and look it, thank you for the compliment."

"You probably looked it ten years ago and still will, ten years from now," Mr. Weller said astutely. "As to the other, a guy can tell. Can't you? For instance, what would you say I was in the war?"

"A sergeant, for one thing, and a gunner for another. You have those lines around your eyes. So you inherited a detective agency? A pity you didn't inherit someone to coach you in the finer points of tailing a man. Or did you, but just haven't had enough practice?"

"I only inherited a sourpuss office girl. I fired her. Uncle Ike's agency was in L.A. and I thought I might like it there. His office turned out to be a crummy hole on Main Street but there were living quarters in back. Yeah, I'll take another but pass the soda once over lightly this time.

"Thanks. Well, I wasn't bothered with clients till this last Monday when I was sitting on my prat with my feet on the desk and a bottle at my elbow, making like a movie detecatiff, and this guy walked in. . . ."

Mr. Weller drank, produced a stumpy pipe and lighted it. "He was about my age but he'd tried to disguise himself. I'm no detective but I'm noticing. You know, you get like that. If his mustache wasn't a phony, I'll put in with you. It was a good job, but it didn't look like it was growing. He was light-complected, tanned, with light blue eyes. Kept his hat pulled down which don't do any good unless you have a scar like mine that folks will notice. I had a hunch he was from Frisco. A few guys in L.A. wear conservative business suits in summer but they don't carry topcoats over their arms."

"Not very bright, was he?" Michael said.

"I got the idea he was used to being at his ease, socially. But not, maybe, very adaptable. He didn't know quite how to act in that situation but he had to keep on trying to be the little gent; it wasn't in him to be rugged about it. I think he just picked out the crummiest looking agency on Main. If Uncle Ike's old sign, 'Twenty Years in One Location' lured him on, that proves he wasn't quite dry behind the ears. But he set his teeth and came on in. . . ."

Mr. Weller displayed an unexpected gift, not for actual mimicry, since he could not alter the character of his own voice, but for conveying the essential quality of the person whose words he repeated. His prospective client had said, courteously but hesitantly, while resenting his own hesitancy, "I was looking for Mr. Weller. . . ."

"Speaking," Sam said negligently.

"Oh. I'd expected someone older. . . . But—but have you any objections to—uh—collecting divorce evidence?"

"I can't afford to have," Sam said truthfully. He added, "I'm no Peek-a-boo Pennington but I do wield a mean camera," which was also true, since for fifteen years photography had been his hobby.

The other man gave the impression that he winced slightly. "Well, you've heard of—or perhaps you've seen photographs of the moving picture star, Greta Mallon?"

Mr. Weller whistled. "Hubba, hubba! A luscious tomato and one of my favorite pin-up girls."

His client blinked and then smiled, not quite soon enough. "No doubt," he said dryly. "It's— common knowledge that Miss Mallon is leaving for Reno Thursday night to divorce her present husband. . . ."

"Is it?" Sam said. "Maybe I should read the newspapers more carefully. Go on."

"I want you to follow her to San Francisco. Her movements here don't matter but guard against her slipping away from here before Thursday. Plan to go up on the same train that she travels on."

"Yeah. Then what?"

"What she does in San Francisco itself probably isn't important—though it might be. So watch her. If she leaves the city before she goes on to Reno, I must know where she goes. You—you might even carry a camera just to—to back up the evidence of your own eyes, if necessary. . . ."

"And I am," Sam Weller told Michael, slapping a protruding, green tweed pocket. "Of course there was a smell of rotten fish about the whole thing. That wasn't the guy Greta Mallon was divorcing. I've seen his picture. And this guy just smiled in his polite way and said, oh, let's just call him Mr. R."

"Mr. R.? I take it he gave you a retainer?" Michael said. "But how were you to report to him?"

"He gave me two hundred smackers and said he'd get in touch with me. He said Mallon would be at the St. Francis and that he'd reserve me a room at the Brighton, a small hotel around on Geary."

"And he managed to get you a room there?"

"I know, he probably had a pull with the management to be able to do that. If the deadpan desk clerk knows who reserved the room, he isn't telling. I checked in, then settled myself as a permanent guest in the St. Francis lobby. Before lunch today, Greta comes out, muffled to the eyes in furs and went. . . ."

"To a place on Sutter called Gisele's. My shop. . . ."

"I know, now. I cooled my heels outside there till Greta came out and went back to the hotel. Then I had another spell of waiting with my eyes glued to the elevators."

"Until shortly after two o'clock?" Michael suggested.

"No," Sam said gloomily. "When you gotta go, you gotta go. I didn't know she'd been out till she came back a little before five, minus her furs and wearing a smaller hat. Among a million other people, I saw you come in later on and noticed and remembered you. . . ."

"But you did not see Mr. R. during that time?"

"No. Look, Mac, do you think you know who he is?"

"I don't think I'll make a guess just yet. Well, I know that Greta was in her suite from five until some time between nine-thirty and nine-fifty. . . ."

"Nine-forty-five," Mr. Weller said. "I damn near didn't spot her then. You know how she was dressed? But I was alerted because I'd missed her once and I had a hunch that if there was any funny business, it might come late at night. I trailed her out to the street. Noticed she had a brown paper package under one arm. She went down Powell, turned into Geary, walked to—Mason, I guess the street is. There were two cabs there.

"She got in one of them and I had one break. My hearing's sharp and I heard her say 'Green and Jones' to the driver. But then a little twerp edged in and grabbed the second cab before I could."

"They do it," Michael said absently. "What then?"

"All at once there weren't any cabs. Took me twenty minutes to flag one down. It was past ten by then. And I didn't sniff the driver's breath first. More bad luck. He tangled with another car three blocks on. We got away before the cops came but the other driver had a heat on, too. I had to pry those two lushes apart and when we got going again, I made my driver throttle down to a crawl and it was ten-forty-five before I got to Green and Jones."

"And when you arrived there, you thought that the Verde Vista seemed the most likely building to have been Greta's destination," Michael asked.

"Yeah. So I hung around. And in five minutes or so, you came along and I was interested because I recognized you."

"Did you have the garage in view during that time?"

"Just a little of the front of it as I looked down the hill. But no one could've dodged in and out of it without me seeing them, from ten-forty-five till about eleven-fifteen when the cops came. I didn't know if there was a service elevator in there, but I thought there could be. And later on, someone in the crowd says there is.

"I didn't even know that Greta had gone into the building but I didn't like the setup," Sam went on. "And a cop finally tells one hysterical dame who don't live in the place herself but has friends that do, that the deceased was 'a lady who was visiting.' He can't deny there's a body because we see them bring it out."

"Did you see Miss Jameson arrive and recognize her?"

"Sure. They had a drawing-room, but we came up from L.A. in the same car. When she turned up, I was pretty sure I was out of a job as far as tailing Greta went. But I'd been paid in advance and I was curious."

"Why didn't you show your credentials to the cop on the door, ask to see the officer in charge and tell him your story? As if," Michael said, grinning, "I didn't know."

"You mean I owed it to Mr. R. not to tell the cops about him before I'd reported to him? Yeah, there was that. And I don't like flatfeet much. I've tangled with a few in my time."

"So you stayed around even after the crowd had melted away? But were you waiting for me? You didn't know me. . . ."

"This game is new to me, doc, but I don't take too much for granted. Greta went to your shop first off. Then I read in the afternoon papers how she's in town and that she'd been modeling at your place when she was discovered."

"Oh, Lord," Michael said. "Though I suppose it was inevitable that someone would print that. But. . . ."

"Then when you went through the St. Francis lobby this evening, a guy behind you called out your name and caught up with you."

"I'd forgotten, since it was no one of any importance, but you're right."

"And," Sam said, "I'd already found out a lot about you. I asked the cabby that took me from your shop back to the St. Francis, following Greta this noon, what kind of dump Gisele's was. He gave me an earful."

He grinned. "You're a well-known character in these parts, Mac. The cabby says you're supposed to be one of these amateur detectives; that the cops let you tag along and help in some murder cases. I liked that. And I had a hunch, seeing you around, that me and you might be able to do business."

"Then why didn't you approach me in a businesslike fashion?"

"You went away from the Verde Vista like a singed cat out of a burning barn," Mr. Weller protested. "And I got curious again. It's a failing of mine. I wanted to see what you were up to, so I tagged after you. But I was going to yell at you when we got off that damn overgrown hillside you led me through. I'd begun to tumble you were just stringing me on. I knew you were on the other side of that gate and I could hear voices down the hill, though not what they were saying. I thought you were listening, so I kept still. What was that all about?"

Michael shook his head. "I wish I knew. Then I suppose you heard me talking but still didn't interrupt. That winds up that. But I'll be greatly surprised if Mr. R. ever contacts you."

"You and me both, pal. I'll give him till noon tomorrow and then I'm not his hired help any longer. Then I guess I should go to the cops."

"Yes. I've no doubt that I'll be having another session with them tomorrow. But I should tell you that even a slight acquaintance with me will not recommend you to Inspector Hoyt."

"He's in charge of this case? And you don't like him, either?"

"The feeling is intensely mutual. Hoyt won't listen to anything I have to offer. . . ."

"What've you got to offer, Mac?" Sam asked.

"I think that before she went to Hollywood, Greta was involved in some way with a family here in the city. Which would include your Mr. R. But I've no evidence to prove that. Of course Hoyt is thorough and has a passion for routine. He may eventually hit the right trail and follow it to the end."

"I'd say to let the guy sweat it out by himself."

"I'm more than anxious to divorce myself from this affair as quickly as possible but I don't know if—I didn't care for the manner in which Hoyt. . . . And I did blow my top and walk out on him. . . ."

Michael stopped and snapped his fingers impatiently, not being addicted to unfinished sentences and having always been irritated by those who were.

"I'm not a timid soul," he said in his usual incisive fashion, "but I have forebodings. Would you consider not going back to Los Angeles for a day or two, Mr. Weller?"

"I'd consider putting it off forever. I don't like the place. Too much weather that no one talks about anything else but. Think you might have a job for me?"

"I might need your help. I'll call you around one tomorrow afternoon. And it's after three now, so I'll get the car out and take you back to your hotel."

6

The alarm went off at nine-thirty. Though he had set it for that time, Michael scowled at it resentfully before he remembered what it was that he'd wanted to be certain to do before ten o'clock, and reached for the telephone.

"Is that you, Miss Poole? . . .. No, don't call Fanchon. Tell her that I'll be in this afternoon. I can't make it earlier. And tell her to co-operate with the police in every possible way and. . . . Oh,

don't dither, Miss Poole! Give Miss Weis my message and tell her that I'm short on sleep and she'd
better not call me back before eleven-thirty. . . ."

He slammed the telephone down on the table,
slid back under the covers and went to sleep. At
eleven-thirty he rose, reluctantly, and was butter-
ing toast in the kitchen when someone knocked
on the back door.

Michael opened it to admit Mehitabel, the cat,
who looked even more than usually pleased with
himself and his night about alleys; and Detective
T. P. Costello, who did not look as if anything
pleased him.

"I come in the back way in case Hoyt's got a
man on you," he said without preamble. "It's this
way—me and you and Nick Prevost's always been
friends. I never liked Hoyt; he's always hated
Nick's guts because he's smarter and younger and
slated for promotion again soon. I'll take my pen-
sion next year and I can pound a beat again out
in the sticks if Hoyt finds out and wants to get
tough. . . ."

Michael put the coffee pot down without having poured any coffee from it. *"Por Dios, amigo—*
is it that bad?"

"Hoyt's working on the angle you killed the
Mallon dame, Mr. Dundas, it's that bad."

"Why, goddam his soul!" Michael said bleakly. "Does he think I'd deliberately march into the Verde Vista, letting myself be seen, kill Greta and then calmly call the police?"

"Hoyt says you're just the boy who'd have the guts to go in the front way, figure that'd be a point in your favor and that you could get away with it, brazening it out, because you're who you are."

"Well, now I've heard everything—"

"Oh no, you ain't," Costello said grimly. "This morning, early, a ratty little guy turns up saying it's his duty to inform the police that you'n Miss Mallon knew each other better than you'll admit. His name. . . ."

"His name is Egbert Knapp. But still I don't see quite what he could. . . ."

Michael stopped and for some minutes said nothing at all. Finally he whistled, a prolonged and uncheerful sound.

"*Mama mia!* Now that I recall my conversation with Gertie in detail, I see that a great deal might be made of it, if Egbert repeated only carefully selected items and conveniently didn't hear the perfectly innocuous stretches in between."

"He admits he listened at the keyhole. Says his attention was first caught by Mallon's saying, 'Why, you dirty. . . .' without finishing. After that,

Egbert says he listened all he could. The thing is, Hoyt knows now that Mallon had a baby sometime or other, and it certainly wasn't after she went to Hollywood. . . ."

"She had. . . . Oh Lord, I should have thought of that!"

"Don't you talk like that, Mr. Dundas. It sounds like. . . ."

"I'm not the father of her child," Michael said indifferently. "But the fact that she had one may explain so many things. Basically, Gertie was pretty primitive. . . ."

"Yeah, and so is this pretty primitive," Costello remarked dryly.

"Hmm? Well, what's the full strength?"

"The case Hoyt's building up? Well . . ." Costello ticked his points off on his broad, short fingers. "No one's admitted they knew Greta longer'n you did. Hoyt says you had to admit that, and that you knew where she lived and was there once, anyway. He thinks you knew her before she worked for you; that she made you give her a job. Because Egbert heard her say she was surprised you ever let her work in your shop and that you told her never to open her yap to anyone."

"I underestimated Egbert. He arranged his material to suit his purpose. And he had his ear to the keyhole a longer time than I'd supposed, because those remarks were made before Gertie started to call me a dirty so-and-so. Go on."

"Egbert says Greta said she used to watch that 'wife of yours' and wonder what she had that Greta didn't. And that she mentioned your son and said she hadn't forgotten Valerie was expecting when she left here for Hollywood. . . ."

"Indicating jealousy of my wife and legitimate child?" Michael suggested.

"Yeah. And she says it's a break, Valerie being out of town. And that she—Greta—wanted a hell of a lot and was going to get it. Then you called her a greedy little tramp and she asked what the hell you meant by talking to her like that. And then. . . ."

"And then I caught Egbert at the keyhole and fired him rather forcibly. Never tread on a worm, Costello. It might be a scorpion in disguise."

"Oh, Hoyt knows Egbert would be a poor witness. He's boiling with spite. But he's given Hoyt an angle. The Hollywood end don't seem promising. Greta sneaked up here several times; probably twice, while you was still here. She got typewritten letters from here lately. You admitted you're a little acquainted with Mrs. Yelland. Hoyt argues you know others who know the Yellands. People who'd hand over a key so's you could meet Greta there. I'm saying what Hoyt would say. . . ."

"Yes. He thinks I had an affair with Gertie, that she bore my child and, I presume, that I looked after her and it, in a fashion, but without mentioning my little lapse to my wife. And that I allowed Gertie to blackmail me for six years until she threatened to tell all. Then I became fed up and killed her."

Costello grinned briefly. "And Hoyt has a the'ry you got so used to killin' overseas that it released the inhibitions you used to have against it."

"God help him, he would. Yes, well, it's a neat, tidy little picture and, worse luck, Hoyt thinks that I'm a natural for one of the two central figures."

"That's it; he knows you too well without knowin' you at all," Costello said shrewdly. "You got a lot of friends, boy, and they'll go to bat for you. But there's some guys hate your guts. The kind of things you say, stupid and conceited people don't forgive you for."

"People like Hoyt have never shown any regard for my tender sensibilities," Michael retorted. "He not only believes that to be a dressmaker is unmanly; he thinks it's slightly immoral."

"Yeah," Costello said with another reluctant grin. "He can't believe a guy could be surrounded by good-looking dames for years without getting out of line now and then. Hoyt's—well, unsophisticated. He imagines that shop of yours is a cross between a high-class whorehouse and a harem."

"No!" Michael was, momentarily, diverted. "Reeking with incense, I suppose, and thronged with scantily-clad models? And myself giving a good imitation of a barnyard cock? Phui! How quickly will Hoyt move, do you think?"

"Not very quick. Slow and sure, that's him. And he knows you'd hire Jake Ehrlich for your lawyer and sue for false arrest and damages to your character if he moves too quick. Not that he can ever make it stick. . . ."

"But I can't afford to be publicly suspected of murder! Even my innocent connection with Gertie won't do me any good. The backbone of my business is the conservative matron who pays her bills, not too promptly, but regularly, and trusts me with her debutante daughters, and daughter's trousseau. That type of woman would gather up her skirts and flee Gisele's forever if I were seriously suspected of having murdered one of my former models, or even detained for questioning."

"Oh. Yeah, I see what you mean."

"And there is Valerie to consider. She'd stand by me. More remarkable, she'd even believe that I knew Gertie only as a model. But, a nice thing for Valerie, to have people whispering that she'd 'certainly kept up appearances' or. . . ."

"I know, I know," Costello said hastily. He was fond of Valerie Dundas. "I was going to say, play it safe. Wait Hoyt out. But I see you think you can't afford to. Well, I'm off duty now and I've a hunch I'm off this case, too."

"Hoyt's using only his pet stooges?"

Costello nodded. "Including that dumb son-in-law of his, Quinlan. I got a lot outa Quinlan this morning before Hoyt warned him to clam up. I never was ambitious or worked for promotion which is why I got friends. Maybe I won't be on the inside, but anything you'd like me to try to find out for you. . . ."

"I'd like to know what names are on the list Hoyt will get from the Yellands, of persons who might have keys to their apartment. And what results he gets when he fills in the details of Gertie's life before 1941. And if he finds out where she was between two and five yesterday afternoon. . . ."

"He found the cabby that took her from the hotel around two, but she was cagey; she had him drop her at the El Capitan theater in the Mission. That's kinda out where you said she lived once, but it'll take time to trace her from there."

"Yes. If I were willing to risk running into Hoyt or his underlings, I'd go out to that rooming house and tackle the old witch that ran it—if she's still there. My Sicilian is more fluent now than it was in 1941. It's quite possible that she delivered Gertie's child; that abortions and midwifery were her sidelines. Do you think Hoyt's put a man on me yet?"

"No. Right now he's more interested in what you did in the past than what you'll do today," Costello said. "And we're still short of experienced men. Too many guys didn't come back from the war. If you'll just try to keep your tongue and your temper under control when you talk to Hoyt again, Mr. Dundas. . . ."

"Oh come, Thomas Patrick," Michael said with the smile he reserved for his friends. "Surely we can dispense with formality?"

"I guess so. Well, try, will you, son? I always knew you had a naturally quick temper and I used to admire the way you'd hold yourself in. . . ."

"That was merely a matter of expediency."

"I know. And I can guess how you kind of lost the habit during the war. And I know what your war record was, though you'll never capitalize on that. But it'd be a good thing if you'd go along normally for even half a day, whatever you have in mind. . . ."

"I suppose I'd better sweat it out in my office this afternoon. But tell me, does the name Zachary Furness mean anything to you?"

Costello frowned. "A rich old guy of that name died last fall from natural causes. I don't remember anything out of the way. . . ."

"Very likely there wasn't. I'll get in touch with Jubal Chambers later. I do have some good friends and I'm afraid that this is the time when I'll have to make use of them. Beginning with Saul Hirsch, though that's off the record."

"The doctor that runs that so-called sanitarium? Well, at least he's a good doctor and probably does more good than harm. He's smart; we've never caught him with his pants down. But why him?"

"I think he can tell me something I'd like to know, after what you've told me, and remembering one bit of information that Miss Jameson gave Hoyt. And you'd better get home and pretend you haven't been here."

When Costello had gone, Michael went into the bedroom to dress. He put away the sport coat and slacks he had worn to the Verde Vista the night before; got out the dark blue suit he had worn during the day and early evening.

He removed a nearly empty pack of cigarettes and Valerie's last letter from one coat pocket; thrust his hand into the other, frowned questioningly and drew out a folded square of paper, stained on one side with lipstick. But now he saw what he hadn't noticed when Greta had given it to him; that it was a cheap cocktail napkin—on one fold, *Joe's and Pete's,* and an address in the Mission, in pale blue letters.

Michael whistled. "I must be slipping, not to have looked to see what it was that Gertie gave me instead of Kleenex. Not that I'd have passed this on to Hoyt. He'd have wanted to know whose lipstick I'd removed. I suppose Gertie collected these things automatically. It's a damned useful find, but. . . ."

But, he realized, he couldn't be certain that no one had seen him with Greta in the hall outside her suite yesterday evening. Had anyone come out of the elevator at the end of the hall? And would he have noticed a stray maid or bellboy?

He had to admit that, during the most crucial moment, his mind had been pretty well on his work. If Hoyt learned of that little episode. . . . Mr. Dundas quite frankly flinched at the picture presented by this possibility and cut himself while shaving.

PART THREE

1

Fanchon Weis was at her desk and Michael, passing by on his way to his own office, invited her to "bring in anything we have on Gertie, please." When she joined him with a few papers in her hand, he was talking over the telephone.

"That's it; Bella Voss. . . . I didn't think you could, offhand, Saul. This girl wouldn't have had much money in '40 or '41. But there were some things she probably would have demanded and been able to pay for, later. . . . Yes, somewhere near here though not, I think, actually in the city. . . . So far as I know now, I'll be here until six o'clock. *Gracias, amigo.*"

Pulling the telephone directory toward him, he said to Fanchon, "Sit down." And, as he looked through the classified ads, "The police have been here?"

"Yes. They were polite. So was I. But we don't have much on Gertie. Two addresses and the name of the woman she said was her aunt, Mrs. Guardino."

"Will you copy those addresses for me?" Michael dialed the number of the Brighton hotel. "And what is dear Egbert's home address, just in case? . . . Mr. W. W. Weller, please. . . . Weller? This is Michael Dundas."

"I've been waiting to hear from you on account of I consider myself out of a job," Sam said cheerfully. "Mr. R. hasn't gotten in touch with me. Still think you might have something for me to do?"

"Yes, but I must warn you that I am even more than just slightly unpopular with Inspector Hoyt this morning."

"That so? I wondered if he might not try to fasten this on you if he couldn't find anyone else to work on. What you want me to do, Mac?"

"I think I know where Greta was yesterday between two and five. There's a bar in the Mission called *Joe's and Pete's*." Michael gave him the address. "That should be about a dozen blocks from the El Capitan theater, which you can't miss. See what you can find out."

"Sure thing. Do I say I'm a private op or use my ingenuity?"

"Whichever you like. Hoyt doesn't know you exist and he can't forbid me to hire a private detective. But to protect yourself, you shouldn't put off telling him about Mr. R."

"You want me to? Would it help you?"

"Not a great deal, just now."

"Then let's save it," Sam said airily. "What else?"

"Here's another address. . . . That's beyond Potrero Avenue but cabs aren't difficult to find at this time of day. The place is a very unsavory rooming house. You won't get anywhere trying to talk to the woman who runs it, Mrs. Guardino, if she's still there. And it's not too likely that there's anyone there now who lived there in '41. . . ."

"Did Greta Mallon live there then?"

"Then, and probably for some time in 1940. You can only fish about to see if you can find out anything that will be helpful."

"Such as the man or men in her life that far back? Okay, doc, I'll give it a try. Shall I call you back?"

"I expect to be here until six or after." Michael gave him the telephone number. "Got that? Good hunting. . . . Well, where were we, Fanny?"

"Saying how little we know about Gertie. All the models that worked with her are gone, what with getting married or putting on weight. The saleswomen snooted her and she never talked much, anyway. Even if I gave her hell, it never cracked that Polish deadpan of hers."

"I know. I suppose I had a reluctant liking for her because she could take a beating without whimpering."

Fanchon nodded. "You know I do try to look after the girls. You told me what kind of dump she lived in and I knew she didn't eat enough. I got her the housekeeping room she moved to, but she never unbent. Except just once. . . ."

"Yes?" Michael said, lighting cigarettes for her and himself.

"My kid sister had a baby and I was showing some things I'd bought, upstairs before opening time. Gertie drifted closer and closer like she couldn't help herself. I'd bought the very best and I remember now how she fingered the things and the way she said, 'I didn't know they made such beautiful things for babies.'

"And later she asked me if kids shouldn't have orange juice and cod liver extract and things like that. She never bought herself any clothes and was afraid that housekeeping room might rent for too much. But other girls manage very well on the kind of wages you've always paid."

"Did you pass this on to the police, Fanny?"

"I told them as much of it as I thought they needed to know."

"Did you also assure them that I have never exercised the *droit de seigneur* over any of my female employees?"

"I didn't think it was smart to act like I knew what the cops were driving at. But hell! You can prove you've never given any woman who worked for you so much as the time of day. . . ."

"And what a bloody ass I'd look, producing character witnesses to swear that I keep fair— through faith and prayer—a virgin heart in work and will. Sir Galahad Dundas. Only another man who'd been surrounded by women, as I have been for twelve years or so, would see that one couldn't make a go of this business unless he deliberately ignored all opportunities for dalliance. I say 'deliberately' because I don't claim that I haven't thought, often enough, that it would be fun."

Yes, you dope, it could have been, Fanchon thought. And, smart as you are, you never ask yourself why I've never married. . . . Instead, she said, with apparent irrelevance, "Well, it's been a long time."

"Since we set up business on nothing-plus and you were saleswoman, model, and even bookkeeper because my multiplication and subtraction are erratic?"

"But you always knew by instinct whether we were in the black or the red. Remember the time you managed to pay the rent on the first shop with your winnings in a blackjack game? And you did all the cutting yourself, and I'd pray whenever you slashed into anything that cost more than two bucks a yard. . . ."

"Yes, it has been a long time," Michael said and something in the tone of his voice made Fanchon look at him sharply.

She said quickly, "Look, boss—you don't think this is really serious? That dope, Hoyt, can't do us any real harm?"

"He can wreck the business if he really believes that I may have killed Gertie. And, knowing Hoyt, I'm afraid he does believe that. With luck, I may be able to keep him from doing anything too drastic for a day or two, but . . . I thought you should be warned, Fanny, as you've been a full partner since I went into the Army. I hope," Michael said with a rather stiff-lipped smile, "that you've put aside something against old age and possible unemployment?"

"But it's not like you to take such a dim view of things. You're too apt to just ride roughshod over anything and everything that might cause you a little temporary annoyance and . . ."

Fanchon stopped. At last, she said carefully, "If you think Hoyt's out to prove that you were—uh—mixed up with Gertie when she worked here. . . . Well, Valerie would never in this world think . . ."

"Let's leave Valerie out of this—if you don't mind!" Michael said savagely.

"I'm sorry. I was just trying to. . . . Well, you're not going to close Monday?"

"If you feel that something more than business-as-usual is called for, we can tack a picture of Gertie on the door and surround it with flowers."

"No wonder so many people think you're a stinker—"

"Do you wish me to pay Gertie the tribute of a suitable quotation? How about, 'A dirge for her, the doubly dead in that she died so young'?"

"Not bad. But anyone who still enjoys living, dies too young," Fanchon said. "The police haven't talked to you again today? Is that good?"

"No. If Hoyt really believed my story, he'd make me go over it again, merely to be annoying. What did you start to tell me about the Furnesses yesterday?"

"Well, old Zachary died last fall and someone said he didn't leave his money the way they thought he would. But if I heard anything more, I didn't listen. You know how you get in this joint, where you hear so much."

"Are there any grandchildren?"

Fanchon shook her head. "There was one, but it didn't live long, which is probably what's wrong with Viola Furness."

"Should I know Nathan Ridley?"

"That old rip? You might have seen him in here a long time ago. Maybe when Gertie was still here. He came in twice with a pretty little tart who called him 'daddy.' Paid for what she bought but I guess daddy's sugar didn't last long because he didn't come in again. You know he's Mrs. Furness's brother?"

"Yes, and I would have supposed that she'd keep a stern eye on brother."

"She probably tries to. But I heard someone say she has a soft spot for brother; that he can always live off her, after a fashion. Look, do you think. . . ."

"I think I'd better do some work while I can. . . ."

The telephone rang. Michael picked it up, said, "Yes? . . . . Speaking. . . ." For some time he listened, his mouth tightening perceptibly before he said, "No, of course it doesn't help matters in the least, but it's water over the dam now, I'm afraid . . .

2

The cocktail lounge was on an alley and had certainly started life as a neighborhood saloon. The bartender, however, did not date back to pre-prohibition or even prohibition days. He was in his early thirties and the shirt under his soiled white jacket was, Sam noted at once, government issue.

He pushed his hat to the back of his head, straddled a rickety bar stool and asked, "What d'you say, Pete?"

"I'm not Pete; I'm Joe."

Sam snapped his fingers. "I keep forgetting. The usual— Hell, you don't remember me, do you?"

"We see a lot of guys in here, Jack."

Sam managed to appear slightly downcast. "Yeah, and I usually come in nights when there's a crowd. I haven't been in Frisco long and I don't know anyone yet. Rye with a water chaser. I been seeing the country since I got out. . . ."

"Where was you, bud?"

"Where wasn't I? Africa, Sicily, Italy. . . ."

A look came into the bartender's eyes. "Gawd, that Italian vino! But better than some stuff we drunk around Sissonne. . . ."

Three drinks and two campaigns later, Sam allowed himself to laugh explosively. "Speaking of dames, there was a hot number that came in yesterday afternoon as I was leaving. I'd like to fraternize with her. Though she did have class and I wondered what a doll like that was doing in here."

"Oh, her?" The bartender served two beers with a speed calculated to discourage conversation from other customers and planted an elbow on Sam's end of the bar. "That was funny enough that I thought about it quite a bit. We gotta mean the same dame. She looked kinda familiar to me. . . ."

Sam nodded. "Like some of these pin-up girls. Suppose she's ever had her picture in the papers?"

He waited with some anxiety for the bartender's answer but the man shook his head. "Could be, but I don't get time to read the papers, working these hours. She spoke to me very friendly; said this didn't use to be called *Joe's and Pete's,* did it? I says, no, Pete bought the joint three years ago, but the place itself's been here years under one name or another. Then she says, can she wait for a friend?"

"What'd the lucky stiff look like?"

"It wasn't a guy." Joe absently poured two on the house. "It was another dame and she had class, too. More than the black-eyed number if you like 'em pale and skinny and blonde. I don't. And Black-eyes didn't seem to mind coming in here but Blondie looks around like she was slumming. Then Black-eyes gets up and goes to meet her like it was one of these fancy teas and she was hostess—only did that doll know how to walk!"

The bartender whistled reminiscently, frowned at a customer who demanded a shasta-high but consented to serve him.

"And she says to the blonde, kinda purring-like, 'You don't know me? I'd have known you anywhere. Well, some change for the better and some don't change. So nice to meet you again. . . .' The blonde looks like she's gonna faint. They go off in that back booth. . . .'"

He waved a hand toward a murky corner. "Not that there were many people in here. Those two sit there and talk for—oh, half an hour or more."

"That's a funny thing, isn't it? Why," Sam said flatteringly, "do you suppose they met here? It's easy for women to find places to get together without anyone thinking anything about it.

"That's what I wondered." Joe abstractedly downed another shot of bar whisky. "I couldn't hear what they said. Black-eyes laughed a lot, though, like she was having fun. And she had me keep the drinks comin'. Once she says to Blondie, 'Drink up, dear. Good for what ails you.'"

"Hadn't Blondie been drinking?" Sam said.

"Not at first, but she finally had four. That, or something, made her kinda stagger when she started out. The black-haired one takes her by the arm, laughing again and says, 'I'll see you to your limousine.' And out they go. It's things like that makes a guy think he oughta write a book. No ending to that story but I could tell you. . . ."

The bartender did. Sam did not want to abandon his role too quickly, especially as the drinks continued to be on the house. It was after three when he got back to Mission Street and found a drugstore with a telephone.

"Mr. Dundas? Well, Mac, you gave me a good steer. This is what the barkeep says. . . ."

Sam told his story in detail and felt that it deserved a more enthusiastic reception than, "Oh? So that was it?"

"It surprised me. I supposed she'd sneaked off to meet a guy. Look, don't it help?"

"Yes, of course it will," Michael said hastily. "Don't mind if I don't jump up and down and clap hands. I'm rather disgruntled."

"Something happen since I talked to you?"

"Hoyt is in possession of some information I'd hoped wouldn't float his way. But I've learned one thing more quickly than I expected to. I'd like you to take a little ride with me tonight. But we'd better settle on some out-of-the-way meeting place. There's a small park at Steiner and Geary that you can find easily. I'll pick you up on the Steiner Street side as near eight o'clock as possible. You can tell me what else you find out then, unless you think it can't wait."

"Okay. . . ." But as he left the phone booth Sam was thinking, "I'd like to know what kind of ride you're taking me on. Oh well, I was bitching because life was too dull. Maybe not, after all. . . ."

He walked on until he was able to flag down a cab and gave the driver the second address on his list. Eventually he found himself in a grimy neighborhood of slatternly, bedraggled houses. Sam sniffed disparagingly. "'Unsavory' is right," he muttered and told the driver to let him out before a small, dejected, corner grocery. "This is close enough, Mac; I'll walk from here."

The house he was looking for should have been not more than a block from the grocery. Sam walked along, kicking absently at the paper and trash that blew about his feet, dodging an over-abundance of children racing about the streets, until he came to a space where there had been a house but where now only blackened foundations, overgrown with weeds and grass, remained.

Mr. Weller whistled mournfully. He checked the numbers of the houses on either side of the lot; went across the street and studied house numbers there. He shook his head, then started back toward the grocery.

"That store looks like it's been here for a long time," he thought. "I guess I won't need to interrupt Dundas to give him another report, whatever he's doing now. . . ."

At about that minute, Michael was reaching for the telephone. He dialed a number that he had looked up some time previously, having been rather surprised to find that the Alan Furnesses did not live with Mrs. Zachary on Vallejo, but had an establishment of their own on Jackson.

Viola Furness answered the telephone. Michael identified himself; went on quickly before she could express well-bred amazement at his having called. "Mrs. Furness, I know and, if necessary, can prove that you met Greta Mallon yesterday afternoon in a bar out in the Mission . . ."

He heard her gasp and waited for a full minute before she said faintly, "G-go on, please."

"The police already want to know where Greta was between two and five yesterday afternoon and eventually they'll find out. Neither of you would pass unnoticed in a place like that. It was foolish of you to meet there."

"I know. We'd have been more apt to escape notice in some downtown cocktail bar. But she— Miss Mallon—would have it that way."

"And you were sufficiently anxious to talk to her that you let her have it her own way?"

"Yes. Mr. Dundas, are you telling me this to warn me that the police may question me, or are you warning me that you must tell the police what you know?"

Michael did not answer immediately. He sat staring at a disturbingly lifelike photograph of his wife on his desk.

"The age of chivalry," he said at last, "is past, Mrs. Furness. I'm not in a pleasant position myself and I may have to throw you to the wolves. Just now, that wouldn't help me too much. It isn't good policy to give out driblets of information. But you might persuade me not to tell the police what I know, if you care to explain. Not over the telephone. . . ."

"I can't meet you this afternoon. You've encountered my mother-in-law, so perhaps you'll believe that she has a rigid schedule, rigidly adhered to. A family dinner at her home every Friday night, for one thing. And she expects tea here every Saturday afternoon. And as I'm in disgrace with her just now. . . ."

"You aren't used to drinking, but you did drink with Greta yesterday afternoon?"

"I . . . You know that, too? Mother Furness dropped by yesterday evening—natural solicitude

on her part since I'd fainted in your shop earlier in
the day," Viola said bitterly. "She found me fairly
plastered and advised me not to attend the usual
Friday night family dinner. She'll arrive before
long, expecting apologies and explanations and . . .
I just heard the front doorbell. I'm talking in my
own room. . . ."

"I've only your word for that but I'll give you
until tomorrow. If you don't get in touch with me,
I'll have to come to you."

"Oh, I will get in touch with you tomorrow! I
will; I promise. . . ."

3

Viola put down the telephone, answered the
maid's, "Somebody to see you," with a quick, "I'll
be there in an instant," and then sat staring at
herself in the oval mirror over her dressing table.

I'd thought it would be the police if it happened.
Is it better that it's Mr. Dundas who knows? He
won't act hastily. I might persuade him not to tell
what he knows. . . . She recalled the harsh angles
of his profile; the expressive, controlled, arrogant
mouth, the glint in the eyes that were startlingly
blue in his swarthy face. No, he won't be chival-
rous unless it will do him no harm to make a grand
gesture, she decided. I'll have to talk to him. But
what am I to say? What will he believe. . . .

She got up and started downstairs. The house
that they'd thought themselves so lucky to find
was a story-and-a-half affair, two bedrooms and a
bath on the upper floor. A bedroom for Alan and
one for her, despite Mother Furness's plainly expressed disapproval. . . .

Viola put a hand to her mouth, set her teeth in
a knuckle and didn't laugh, after all. She went on
down to the square, formal living-room to find,
not her mother-in-law, but Nathan Ridley.

"My dear, I hope I haven't cut your afternoon
rest short? Can you spare a cup of tea for an old
uncle? I'd hoped to find you feeling better. We
were sorry not to see you last night."

Viola smiled faintly. "Don't be tactful, Uncle
Nathan. I'm sure Mother Furness discussed my
disgusting conduct with all of you last night."

"I can't deny that she did, until Alan told her
very rudely that he didn't care to hear any more.
Didn't think the boy had it in him," Nathan said
approvingly. "And I don't think it harmed you to
get off this beastly healthful regimen you've been
on; take your mind off yourself for a while. But
it's worrying for Alan, y'know."

"I do know. And he was very sweet. . . ."

She'd cried for a long time against Alan's shoulder when he came home. But of course, she hadn't
dared to tell him the truth. She'd sobbed out a

fantastic, incoherent story about being "fed up," being unable to rest, feeling she couldn't stay alone in the house, Friday being the maid's day out.

And so, she'd told Alan, she went for one of the brisk walks that Cathie was always recommending, found herself on Fillmore on the point of collapsing and had gone into a bar there. She'd felt she must order a drink; had wondered if several drinks wouldn't help. . . .

"Yes, sweetheart, I understand," Alan had said patiently. "And I don't blame you. You'd been shopping with Mother, too, and she'd been more trying than usual, hadn't she? She. . . . Don't you think, darling, that we'd better just tell her and get it over?"

"No—no! I can't listen to her—I know what she'd say and she'd say it over and over and. . . ."

"All right, Viola; we'll wait. But next time you wonder if several drinks won't help, wait for me, won't you? And we'll get tight together," Alan said.

And he had smiled and tried to convince her that he thought there was something rather humorous about the episode. He hadn't wanted to leave her but she'd persuaded him to go to his mother's for dinner, as usual, on the plea that there was no food prepared at home and that he had better begin peace negotiations with Mrs. Furness that night.

One paid one's parting respects to Mrs. Furness at ten-thirty on Friday nights; no earlier, no later. But Alan had insisted that he would telephone after dinner to make certain that she didn't need him. He had called before nine-thirty. She'd promised not to stay awake until he got home. She'd been in bed when he came in—later, it seemed to her than he would ordinarily have been, coming straight from his mother's home.

But she hadn't turned on the light to see what time it was. She'd wanted him to believe that she was asleep and didn't answer when he spoke to her, very softly. Some time later, she'd gotten out of bed, still in the dark. . . .

"You aren't listening, my dear," Nathan was saying. "I asked if you don't know the Yellands? But perhaps I should ask, have you read the morning papers?"

"I've read about Greta Mallon. And we do know the Yellands. I knew them when I lived in Burlingame, as a child. Alan's never liked them though we've visited them here a few times. But Uncle Nathan, why. . . ."

"The newspapers didn't mention the Yellands' habit of letting people have the use of their apartment, nor of handing out keys to it without making certain all the keys were returned to them. But you know about that; everyone does who knows them . . ."

"Did you borrow their apartment? Because you know the Yellands, too, and though you've always lived with Mother Furness, you. . . ."

"My reputation is greatly exaggerated, Viola. In my youth I may have been a devil with the ladies but I'm too old now to be a wolf. I'd no reason to want to borrow the Yellands' apartment. But there are others. . . ."

"Louis?" Viola said quickly.

"Yes. His cottage was rented during the war and he disliked staying with Hester when he came to San Francisco on leave. He did use the Yelland apartment one week end several years ago at a time when I was up here myself. He gave the key to me before he went back up to Chico and asked me to return it.

"And you didn't?"

"It slipped my mind. I threw it into a box of odds and ends on my bureau. Louis saw me do it and," Nathan said slowly, "I've always made him free of my belongings and my room at Hester's. And it's worried me—because the key isn't there now."

"Oh, I know," he went on hastily as Viola looked at him with a faint, slightly skeptical smile "I had the key and I was acquainted with Greta, too. If the police are as thorough as I've heard they are, I suppose that will come out. Though Louis and I are only two of many. And anyone might have

taken that key. . . . Alan isn't home yet? I supposed that he would be, on a Saturday afternoon."

"He often works Saturday afternoons. It's not
easy, getting back into harness after having been
in the Army for so long. He wants to make good
on this job; it carries some responsibility and Alan
doesn't take that lightly."

"The dear fellow's always been overconscien-
tious," Nathan agreed absently. "I've been wondering to what extent the police may think this
fellow, Dundas, is involved in Greta's death. The
newspapers are very discreet. They would be. . . ."

"Why?"

"There is a law of libel, my dear, and I understand that if he's pushed too far, Mr. Dundas is
an unscrupulous fighter. But, of course, that is no
concern of ours. . . . Ah, that is probably Hester,"
he added as the doorbell rang.

They waited. The doorbell rang again, admon-
ishingly, before doors banged at the back of the
house and clumping footsteps were heard in the
hall. Viola said nervously, "Our maid resents having to get tea on Saturday afternoons, and when
she must answer the bell besides. . . . I do hope
Mother Furness won't—isn't. . . ."

Catherine strode into the room, tossed her hat
onto a chair in a characteristic gesture and looked
them over, hands in her tweed pockets.

"Well, old girl, you're looking better," she said, and winked in a way that was meant to be humorous and encouraging. "Don't worry. Louis says Mamma can't be really shocked; that shocks just stir up her liver and keep it from being sluggish and so she thrives on them."

Nathan chuckled. "Blessed if I don't believe the boy is right."

"But only Louis would dare say so." Catherine glanced quickly over her shoulder. "Oh, Viola, before I forget it again. . . ."

She took a cheap, white envelope from her pocket. "This came for Alan yesterday morning. I suppose it's from someone who thinks you're still living with Mamma. Give it to him, will you?"

Viola held the envelope fastidiously by its edges, looking at the tipsy, clumsily printed address. She thought, I'll have to give this to Alan. Catherine has seen it and probably her mother and now Nathan. . . .

"I didn't know Alan was acquainted with any semi-illiterates," Catherine observed. "Probably some private who served under him in the Army. Uncle Nate, since Mamma has read the morning papers, she approves even less than she did last night of your acquaintance with Greta Mallon."

"Don't babble, Catherine," her mother said, she swept into the room, established a beachhead on the chesterfield and entrenched herself.

"If your mind wasn't an arid waste you wouldn't give two thoughts to this Malinowsky person. You think a moving picture actress must necessarily be glamorous—a nauseating word. Whereas," Hester Furness said baldly, "almost all actresses are simply high-class tarts. Kept women. I can see why that fact intrigues Catherine, who hasn't found a man who's willing to keep her even in holy wedlock. . . ."

For once Catherine did not blush and stammer, "Oh, Mamma." She turned her back, marched over to a window and busied herself rearranging marigolds in a blue bowl.

Mrs. Furness continued calmly, "I am sorry that Nathan knew the woman, though of course the police will never bother us. Nathan's his own worst enemy; everyone likes him and he can't bring himself to snub anyone. . . ." The smile that she bestowed on her brother was at once reproving and affectionately tolerant. "As for Louis, he prefers low company. Did you give Viola that letter for Alan, Catherine?"

"Yes, Mamma."

"He should have had it last night. But Catherine said that she would see that he got it. Then, as usual, her wits were straying about like lost sheep and she forgot. From some ex-soldier, no doubt, presuming on a wartime association with Alan, asking him to use his influence to get him work that he's too shiftless to obtain for himself. . . ."

"We know your theories regarding the working classes, Mother Furness," Viola said deliberately. "Have you. . . ." The unmistakable sound of breaking chinaware suddenly floated in from the kitchen. "Yes, you've been instructing our maid in her duties. When her feelings are hurt, she always drops cups and saucers. . . ."

"Feelings? Don't be ridiculous, Viola. You speak of domestics as if they were persons. If they wish to succeed in their work they must be instructed by those who are qualified to do so. Most of you younger people are not. You'll put up with anything in the way of service. . . ."

"We have no choice, Mother Furness," Viola said sharply. "Alan and I are glad to have any sort of full-time maid. Your servants are elderly survivals. We've lost one maid because you took it on yourself to criticize her dress and manner of answering the telephone and doorbell, and. . . ."

"Good Heavens, girl, let's not be hysterical, shall we?" Hester Furness said disgustedly. "This woman won't do. She's slatternly and she's too young. You must try to find an older woman who likes children. . . ."

"Yes. Oh, yes, of course," Viola said, and began to laugh and kept on laughing, beating the slick, cheap envelope with its sprawling address against the arm of her chair until the front door banged shut and Alan Furness hurried into the room. . . .

4

The fog had come in before the sun went down and, since he was early at the rendezvous, Mr. Weller was very weary of the little park at Steiner Street by eight-thirty when a black roadster slithered along the curb and Michael Dundas leaned out and beckoned to him.

"I'm sorry," he said, "but I wanted to be quite certain that no one would be following us."

"Do you think someone was?" Sam asked.

"Yes, but not one who knows this city as well as I do, or can drive better than I," Michael said modestly. "It was amusing, shaking off my tail, but it took some time. I'm playing safe, going where I want to go by a more or less roundabout route."

"Are you? I don't know this town. . . ." However, Sam did have a good sense of direction and he knew that they were heading toward the Mission. "Look, fella, that rooming house's burned down."

"Oh? When? And does anyone know where Mrs. Guardino is now?"

"The dump burned down in '43. I asked questions at the corner grocery. The owner's been there for ten years. I told him I was looking for a guy whose family wanted to find him, who'd lived there the last they'd heard from him. . . ."

"You're coming along fast, *amigo*."

"Yeah. The guy at the store told me one of the roomers went to bed with a skinful of booze and a cigar. But the dame that ran the joint had already gone back to Italy before the place burned down. So you'll never get any information out of her."

"Yes, she was the type who would return to the fatherland with her savings," Michael said.

"That's what the store owner said. He wasn't chatty, though. The police had already talked to him. He wanted me to describe the guy I was supposed to be trying to trace. I described Mr. R.—without a mustache. But the storekeeper just shook his head."

"Did you ask him if he remembered Greta?"

"Not right out. He broke down and said the cops had been questioning him about a girl who used to live at the rooming house. He'd seen her around. I said right away that my clients thought their son had been mixed up with some girl when he'd lived in that joint and I wondered if it could be the same girl."

"Very good. Did he rise to that bait?"

"He sniffed and said that if my clients' son had been mixed up with that girl, he might have something to account for. He said, 'the girl was in the family way at one time.' And that he didn't know if the girl had the baby, or when, or where, but that the old hag could have arranged all that for her."

"I take it that Mrs. Guardino didn't have a good reputation in the neighborhood?" Michael said.

"It stunk. But then the grocer clammed up and I beat it; went back to the hotel and caught up some on my sleep. How's things with you and where are we headed for, Mac?"

Michael did not answer the last question and he waited until they were on the Bayshore Highway before he said, "You haven't been briefed yet. It's time you were. I did tell you last night, while we walked home from Fallon Terrace, how I happened to be the one who found Greta dead. You know how I came to know her, that she called on me yesterday at the shop, but not what we said to each other. Or that I had, when Gertie arrived, an accountant named Egbert Knapp. I'll start from there. . . ."

It took some time to tell Sam not only all that had happened the day and night before, but also everything that Michael had learned from being present while Hoyt interviewed Miss Jameson and the elevator operator at the Verde Vista. To that he added the information that Costello had given him, and outlined Hoyt's case against him as he supposed it existed in Hoyt's mind. Sam whistled.

"Brother, you ain't been living right!"

"No," Michael said grimly, "and Costello called me just before you did this afternoon. Some bellboy witnessed that apparently amorous passage between Gertie and me yesterday evening in the hall outside her suite."

"Jeepers! Did you kiss her just once?"

"Once was enough; take my word for that. A man's entitled to make a damned fool of himself now and then, but my timing has been spectacularly bad. Also, the bellboy heard Gertie ask me what my wife would think. But not my answer. And he heard her remark that I'd better not let my handkerchief turn up in the wash with Gertie's lipstick on it."

"Dames are poison. But there must've been plenty of guys in Greta's life and Hoyt will find that out, in time, if he's as thorough as you say. . . ."

"And I repeat what I said to Costello, I cannot afford the sort of publicity that may develop if I give Hoyt time to bumble along in his own inimitable, slow and sure way. By the time Hoyt has investigated me thoroughly, I'll resemble a bone that a large dog has gnawed on for a week. And, like the bone, might just as well be buried."

"I see what you mean, pal. You can't risk going through channels. How much will he tell the newspaper boys and how soon?"

"Very little and not soon. He's cautious and besides, he doesn't like reporters. Nor is he one of their favorite flatfeet. I don't think there will be anything startling in tomorrow's newspapers."

"Well, by Monday we'll be in a position to make Hoyt look foolish," Mr. Weller said cheerfully.

They had reached San Mateo and left it behind, turning off into a road where traffic was much lighter than it had been on the Bayshore Highway. Sam peered out discontentedly at fields and an occasional shadowy house.

"You've told me all about this Furness gang" Weller went on, "and you tell me it was Viola Furness that Greta met out in the Mission yesterday. So . . ."

"Viola will keep," Michael said, "though I would have insisted on talking to her tonight if there hadn't been something else I wanted to do—after dark."

"Which is?"

"Greta gave me a name to remember—Bella Voss. I had no idea who Bella Voss could be until Costello told me that the post-mortem had showed that Greta had had a child. Then several things fell into place if you presume that the child is living. . . ."

"Funny she had the kid in the first place or that she didn't let it be adopted as soon as it was born," Sam remarked.

"It's often the girls like Gertie who refuse to give up a child. I'm afraid I did her an injustice when I pooh-poohed her statement that she'd hoped she and young Ainslee would have a child. I imagine she'd have liked to have a baby whose existence she didn't have to hide."

"But she couldn't turn up in Hollywood with a bastard brat hanging to her skirts. I see that," Sam said. "And someone would have to look after the kid. . . ."

"Yes. And she made several trips up here without telling anyone why, or where she had been. She warned Miss Jameson that she would not be in the city tonight. Greta said to me with unusual feeling that she wished it were already Saturday. And Miss Jameson said that she regularly received letters addressed in a rather illiterate hand; that they were sometimes bulky and postmarked from San Leandro, Hayward or Oakland."

"Oakland, I know. Not the first two."

"Keep on driving through East Oakland and you come to San Leandro, then to Hayward," Michael said. "We're heading for Hayward. This is one way to get there and I wanted to avoid the Bay Bridge and the toll gates. I argued that if someone was caring for Greta's child, that someone could be named Bella Voss. Bella could be anyone—some housewife, perhaps, anxious to add to her income.

In which case, she wouldn't be easy to find. However, when Gertie came to Gisele's as a model, she had no money and, apparently, no friends."

"Nobody seems to be admitting they knew her in those days," Sam said. "But she did at least know the old hag in the rooming house. Is that it?"

"Yes. And there are women who make a business of caring for children whose existence can't be openly acknowledged. Sometimes it's quite legitimate; sometimes it's not. Well, I know a doctor that I believed could find out if Bella Voss was a professional at this baby-farming business. He did find out. I don't know just how and I didn't ask him."

"And who is this Voss woman, pal?"

"At one time she was a small cog in the abortion mill. I'd guess that Mrs. Guardino knew her, professionally. But some years ago, Bella took up 'child care.' Oddly enough, she's fond of children and takes excellent care of them. The police have nothing against her on that score. She cared for many children of working mothers during the daytime. That was a good front for her during the war when so many women worked in essential industries. She had several different establishments in San Francisco, but two years or so ago, she moved to a small farm, several miles out of Hayward."

"Three guesses who put up the money for that," Sam said.

Michael nodded. "She must have forced Greta to pay through the nose as her earning capacity increased, and especially after she had her first real success and became a public figure. That's why Greta wouldn't have a business manager or allow Miss Jameson to handle her checkbook. Which, just in passing, may have driven Greta to put the bee on a third person, if she'd never done so before."

"Bleed Peter to pay Paul. Well, Hoyt doesn't know about Bella Voss. . . ."

"And if I told him now, he'd say, well, isn't it odd that you know all about her? In fact, I'm glad now that I didn't mention her name to him last night . . ."

"Because this morning he'd twist that around to suit himself?" Sam said. "Well, if this dame's always looked after Greta's kid, she may be able to tell you everything you want to know, if she isn't planning to sell her information to someone else."

"I'll pay cash, and women like that have a weakness for cash-in-hand. It was Egbert's job to take money to the bank. When he departed, no one else thought to do it, so there was a satisfactory amount of folding money in the safe this afternoon. But I have more than one reason for wanting to get to Bella Voss as soon as possible. There's the child to consider."

"Yeah. If that's Greta's hookup with Bella, Greta had the kid on her mind when she told you to remember Bella's name. And I don't live right, either. If that little twerp hadn't beat me to the cab just behind Greta's, I'd have gotten to the apartment house at just about the right time, instead of too late to see whoever met her there go into the joint."

"Yes," Michael said inattentively. "If we knew what else was in that box that Greta always kept with her and took to the Verde Vista. . . ."

"What else? You mean you think you know one thing that was in it?"

"Yes, considering the size and weight of the box as Miss Jameson described it. Women like Gertie have streaks of sentimentality here and there. And. . . . We'll be in Hayward in a short time. The only address is a certain rural delivery route. There are flashlights in that dashboard compartment. You'd better get them out. . . ."

5

Michael backed his car into a rutted, uncared-for road off the highway and they walked back the hundred yards to the tin mailbox on a post that had B. VOSS lettered on it. Mr. Weller was inclined to complain about this and Mr. Dundas snapped, "Why advertise our approach when we don't have to?"

"Infiltration, hunh? Oh, my aching back! But maybe she's in bed. It's after ten, you know."

There was a little orchard to one side of the un-paved driveway and an unplanted oblong field on the other. The driveway curved slightly, and then they could make. out a small, low house ahead of them, and the large oak tree that brooded over it.

"I don't see any lights," Sam said. "Though maybe she sleeps at the back and. . . . Wait, did you see that?"

"Yes. A light came on at the back of the house and was turned off almost at once. We'd better split. You take the front. Go in, if you can, and no one stops you. . . ."

"Illegal entry? Okay. You'll cover the back?"

"Yes." They had reached a graveled walk that bisected a neglected lawn and ended at four steps leading up to a narrow front porch. Michael slipped away into the darkness around the side of the building.

No one, Sam thought, was very apt to hear that guy coming. The further reflection that he was no herd of thundering elephants himself, bolstered up his confidence. He mounted the steps, crossed the porch and twisted the knob of the front door tentatively. It turned easily in his hand; he shoved the door open with his foot and waited. When the complete quiet beyond the open door persisted, he risked turning on his flashlight.

He stepped from the porch directly into a square living-room. The furniture was sturdy, scarred, old-fashioned stuff—an obese davenport, several rocking chairs, a round table with nothing on it. There were no curtains at the windows but a pile of them, neatly folded, lay on the davenport.

The door at the back of the room opened into a short hall. Sam shaded his light with one hand and ventured cautiously into the first room on his right. He was surprised that it was so large, until he remembered that the house, seen dimly in profile through the dark, had jutted out some distance on one side. This room was unfurnished. There were feathers of dust on the uncarpeted floor; a broken toy engine lay in one corner.

Sam whistled soundlessly and continued his self-conducted tour. There was a dismal, dark blue bathroom across the hall and a bedroom adjoining it. The covers on the wide, old walnut bed had been turned down and the pillows lay flat and unrumpled.

A closet door was not quite closed. Sam went over and looked into it. There were a few black wire hangers with no clothes on them, and a large,

brown suitcase on the closet floor. Sam stooped to
open it, yanking impatiently at the slightly rusted
buckles that held the straps tight about it.

The sound of a shot from somewhere back of
the house jerked him erect. He kicked the suitcase
aside, darted back into the hall and recklessly on
through the door at the end of it. Instinctively
he looked for, and miraculously, without delay,
found a light switch.

The glare from a large, unshaded bulb flooded
an empty kitchen and, when Sam kicked the back
door open, threw an oblong of light over a stretch
of bare, hard-packed earth. Here Mr. Dundas was
engaged in hand-to-hand combat with a taller
man, whose back was to Sam. Sam dashed forward
like a pugnacious terrier, stopped, shook his head
and became an admiring audience of one.

He conceded that the other guy knew a few
tricks but Michael knew too many more. Besides,
the fellow wanted to box straight up, nice clean,
smacking blows all above the belt. Those tactics
earned him only an unquestionably foul punch
that made him grunt. He gasped, "You dirty. . . . ."
and flung himself at Michael, clawing for his
throat.

"*Y puta tu madre!*" said Mr. Dundas, tripped
him neatly and, as he staggered forward, hit him
over the head with a gun—a deliberate, savage blow.

"Jeez, was that necessary, Mac?" Sam said disapprovingly.

"This is not my gun," Michael said coldly. "It's this gentleman's and he fired it at me. Perhaps he didn't intend to hit me. Certainly he came nowhere near doing it. Nevertheless. . . ."

"You probably scared the pants off him. He didn't know who you are, any more than you know who he is . . ."

Michael grasped the man's shoulder and rolled him over on his back. "Take a close look at him."

"I. . . . Why, hell! This is Mr. R. without his mustache!"

"Yes. The mysterious sound offstage. And, one will get you fifty, Alan Furness, loving husband of Viola, dutiful son to Hester. Would you like to take him into the kitchen?"

"It's a pleasure," Sam said and heaved his ex-client up and over his shoulders in one smooth, practiced movement.

The kitchen was obviously the real living-room of the house. It was large enough to accommodate not only stove, sink, cupboards and a big, square pine table but also an easy chair, an unpainted bookcase and a wide couch. Sam laid their captive on the latter, pushed up an eyelid and said judiciously, "Well, you didn't hit him too hard but he'll be out for a while yet. How'd he get here? In a car? I didn't see one."

"It's parked past the end of the driveway where we couldn't see it. But he didn't hear us. There's a large shed back there some distance from the house. He went toward that and I followed him. Evidently he sensed that someone was blocking his exit and his one idea seemed to be to get away. He ran almost full tilt over me," Michael said resentfully, pulling two long splinters from the palm of his left hand. "Among other odds and ends, the shed contained kindling."

Sam grinned. "You must've landed on your feet all the same and caught up with him."

"I caught up with him and he lost his head and pulled a gun on me. So. . . ." Michael shrugged and dabbed with his handkerchief at two moist scratches low on his throat. He fastened the top button of his sport shirt "He wears his nails long. I take it there's no one home?"

"It's the damnedest thing. One room's got nothing in it but a broken toy engine. It would have made a good playroom or bedroom for kids. There's furniture in the other rooms but no little do-dads in the front room like women have around and the curtains are down, folded up. . . ."

"That is, Bella Voss has pretty well dismantled this establishment and disappeared?"

"She's not here, but. . . ." Sam looked about the kitchen. "Well, there's nothing here worth taking away. She had a radio. . . ." He pointed to the ends of aerial wires projecting over a window sill. "But that's gone and there's nothing in the book-case but old stuff."

"No." Michael glanced at the heap of dirty mag-azines and newspapers on the bottom shelf of the bookcase. "What's troubling you?"

"There's a packed suitcase in the bedroom. I was starting to open it when I heard that shot. And the bed's made up and all nicely turned down. Of course I didn't look under it, not being a nervous or hopeful old maid—Jeez! I know that's a corny joke and you don't suppose. . . ."

"We can find out easily enough," Michael said.

"It's a big bed and a high one," Sam said uneas-ily, following him toward the bedroom. "And the bedspread hangs down quite a ways, you see. . . ."

"Yes." Michael flung the covers up over the bed and dropped to his knees. After an instant he said, "You'd better see this, too. Turn on your flash. . . ."

The woman lay on one side, her face toward them. She had on a warm, blue flannel robe over a high-necked nightgown, bedroom slippers on her feet. She had been in her fifties, a small, plump-ish person with thick, white hair. It was in a long braid that hung over one shoulder and across her breast, looking uncannily as if it, at least, was still alive. The braid was white but the back and top of the white head were a dried rusted red.

Michael stood up, automatically brushing lint and dust from his hands. "She's been dead a good many hours, don't you think?"

"It's certainly not very recent though I'm no expert about rigor . . ."

"Even experts do not always agree on that subject. I don't think we'll take time to look for the murder weapon. Obviously it was the well-known heavy, blunt instrument but it's not in this room and may not even be still in the house. Eventually, the police will look after that angle. Well. . . ." Michael restored the bedcovers to their former condition, erased with his feet any marks their hands and knees had left on the old carpet. "We'd better get back to Mr. R. Will you bring that bag in so that we can look at it?"

When Sam entered the kitchen, carrying. the heavy, brown bag, the man on the couch was sitting up, leaning back against the wall, one hand over his eyes. Michael regarded him with a marked lack of sympathy.

"I should introduce myself, I suppose. I'm Michael Dundas. You, I presume, are Alan Furness. And this gentleman you have already met. . . ."

Mr. Furness looked at Mr. Weller and visibly braced himself against the wall. Sam said quickly, "I gave you till noon to get in touch with me. You didn't, so now I'm not working for you. When I've figured up my expenses, I'll give you what's left over from your retainer."

"If you could bribe Mr. Weller, which I doubt, I'd outbid you," Michael said pleasantly. "He can testify that you hired him to follow Greta Mallon. . . ."

"But he obviously didn't follow Gertie here. . . ."

"Gertie, Mr. Furness?" Michael said. "So you think of her as Gertie, too. Our presence here needs to be explained, I know, but I'd prefer to hear your explanation first."

"And I fail to see why you should dictate to me!" Alan Furness said.

For an instant he slightly resembled his mother but the resemblance was fleeting and superficial. Hester Furness's arrogance was impenetrable; her son only achieved an effect of dignity, grievously affronted. Michael smiled unkindly.

"Take your choice. If you don't care to explain, we'll notify the proper authorities at once that someone has killed Bella Voss. . . ."

"K-killed? You don't mean. . . . Oh God! The house is empty . . . I thought it was. . . . There's no child here. I thought she'd gone and . . . Oh Christ! What could have happened? What. . . ."

Michael took a flat flask from a hip pocket. "Have a drink," he said, "and tell us all about it."

6

None of it would have happened, Alan Furness said, if he hadn't majored in sociology in college and taken it seriously.

He'd never worked with his hands or known any real workers and he'd wanted to. . . .

"You wanted to get closer to the great heart of the masses by living as they did, for a limited time only—spending your week ends in comfort at home, of course," Michael said nastily.

Alan flushed. He had thinner, fairer skin than his sister and well-cut, rather delicate features that would have been a greater asset to her. He resembled his mother physically only in the way his fair hair grew to a pronounced peak on his forehead.

"Father laughed at me, too. But I got a job in a foundry in January of 1940 and chose a rooming house convenient to my work. Do you by any chance know that rooming house?"

"Yes. And that it burned down. Of course you met Gertie there. How long had she been there, then?"

"Only a month. She told me she'd run away from home when she was fourteen. She worked as a waitress in a lunch room near the rooming house. We lived in the same place and I'd never. . . . I'd been shy of women and. . . . Well, even with that frightful voice, Gertie was. . . ."

"I know. Gertie was. And Gertie was conveniently at hand, and nature took its course," Michael said.

Alan flinched. "Y-yes," he admitted, "for a short time. Then in March, at home, I met Viola, my wife. I fell in love with her like—like that!" He snapped his fingers. "Then I wished—wished desperately that I'd never seen Gertie. Well, do you know my mother?"

"I have met her. She made an impression somewhat like that of a large, devastating foot on a doormat. I've met all of your immediate family so you needn't bother to explain them to me."

"Oh. Well, I knew that Mother mustn't learn of my—my relations with Gertie. She had plans for me. I did know I must break with Gertie at once. I didn't go back to my job or return to the rooming house. But I felt that I owed Gertie something and . . ."

"And she might have embarrassed you by turning up at the old family homestead in a driving snowstorm with a shawl over her head," Michael drawled. "And I've always felt, myself, that an about-to-be-discarded mistress is entitled to at least one grand scene."

Alan bit his lip. He said evenly, "There was no scene. I was very callow but Uncle Nathan and Louis were not. I consulted them. Uncle Nate tut-tutted and Louis laughed. But both of them went to see her. Not together. Neither of them mentioned Viola to her. I managed to get five hundred dollars together and I wanted to be sure that she—she. . . ."

"That she wasn't pregnant," Michael said wearily. "*Por Dios, Senor!* We know the facts of life. This coyness is a waste of time."

"Very well! When Uncle Nate saw her, she was angry and threatened to get even with me. But when Louis talked to her, later, she told him to tell me to forget it; that it was fun while it lasted."

"And when was this?"

"It was in April of 1940, not a month since I'd seen her last. So she couldn't have been certain, then, that she was going to have a child. Later that month, I went East to my mother's people. Viola was to visit eastern relatives of her own in May, so I went very willingly."

"And you didn't know that Gertie was going to have a child? Did anyone—but Gertie?"

"Not that I know of. I'm sure she didn't go to my father. He was a mild-spoken, essentially kind man. He would have provided for her generously and have had a word or two to say to me. Uncle

Nate and Louis swore I had nothing to worry about and. . . ."

"Yes, well, you and your present wife did finally marry?"

"There was a definite period of—courtship," Alan said with his ready flush. "And a long engagement. Viola's mother was ill and died before we were married. In June of '42, that was. I hadn't been called up and was waiting around for a commission. I got it and was shifted about from one camp to another. Viola insisted on being with me. I shouldn't have allowed it; she'd never been strong. We lost our first baby during that time. Then I landed in Africa, was wounded slightly, sent home and never sent back overseas."

Sam looked at Michael who raised an eyebrow but said nothing. He thinks like I do, Sam decided —Furness was one of these well-meaning spit-and-polish officers who could take good care of their men in camp, but didn't have what it took to make them die for their country alongside of him in a fight.

And Alan added, half apologetically, "I spent the rest of the war behind a desk and was still a first lieutenant on V-J day. I got my discharge in October just before my father died. Meanwhile, we'd had a son, Viola and I, born last August. And Father made a new will at that time that surprised everyone and which wasn't too fair.

"Viola and I wanted children very, very much," Alan said with the characteristic trick of understatement which carried the suggestion that though he could express himself more adequately, it would be slightly ill-bred to do so. "And my father was extremely anxious to have a grandson. Mother was at least on a branch line of so-called Philadelphia mainline society and felt she'd married beneath her. She was always talking about the Ridleys as if the Furness name was hardly worth perpetuating. Perhaps that was why Father was so anxious that it should be perpetuated."

"There is a community property law in California," Michael remarked.

"Father was much older than Mother. He acquired most of his property before he married. The bulk of his estate was separate property—his, to dispose of as he wished. And he had already provided generously for Mother by outright settlement when his health began to fail. Not, I will admit, that that satisfied her."

"And how did your father dispose of this large amount of separate property?"

"He left Cathie only the income on a hundred thousand dollars. I don't blame her for being resentful. But she isn't married and her children wouldn't be Furnesses in any case. And Father may not have—have thought her capable of handling a great deal of money. She has not always been—she isn't always as practical as you might suppose."

"She won't starve to death on the income off a hundred grand," Sam Weller said unsympathetically.

"No. But she may have—have had—plans," Alan said and went on quickly, "Uncle Nathan got fifty thousand outright and so did Louis. Father had loved his sister—Louis' mother—and had a tolerant sort of liking for Uncle Nathan. But I was the residuary legatee."

"That must have been a great strain on family feeling," Michael said. "But I suppose that your father's real intention was that you were to be merely a steward for your son."

"Yes. I'd rather he had created a trust fund, but he trusted Viola and me to hand on the bulk of the property to our son. Our baby wasn't strong and we knew, after its birth, that Viola would never have another child. Father expected me to keep my affairs in order. He said that wills are easily made; there's no reason why they shouldn't always be up-to-date. And he said that if our son should die, he supposed Cathie should receive a more nearly equal share of the estate. He left that to my judgment and conscience. Well, he died in October. And then, in spite of all our care, our baby died this February."

7

"I see," Michael said, almost gently and poured what was left in his flask into three drinks.

Alan gulped his down and went on, "After that, I made a will. I acquired that property by bequest so it's my separate property, too, and I can dispose of it as I wish. It isn't fair that Viola should inherit all of Father's holdings so I've willed her only half of it. And Uncle Nathan another fifty thousand and the residue to Cathie."

"Nothing to Louis Hilton?" Michael asked.

"Father was more than generous with him," Alan said stiffly. "My existing will was simply my effort to keep my affairs in order in case I died suddenly. The estate won't be settled until this coming October. I'd promised that, at that time, I'd see to it that Nate got his fifty thousand outright and Cathie at least a hundred thousand. Nate's not young and Cathie's nearly thirty and I didn't want them to be wishing I'd die."

"How much money is involved in this deal, doc?" Sam said.

Alan frowned. "Oh, something over half a million. And I was considering, eventually, turning over to Cathie all that she'd receive if I died. If. . . ."

"If she proved herself fit to handle money?" Michael said blandly. "I presume you're the executor of the estate? Then you are, at this moment, a well-to-do man. And your will and your promises were made when you thought that you'd probably die childless."

"He could get him another wife and try again," Sam said baldly. And slid his chair back a foot or two as, for an instant, Alan's face was twisted with blinding anger and he half rose from the couch. "Take it easy, pal," Sam said. "That's just a practical suggestion."

"I wanted a son—very much but Viola is. . . . I don't want any other wife but Viola," Alan said haltingly. "Of course. . . ." He grimaced distastefully, "Mother's reaction would be the practical one. That is why she wasn't told, until this afternoon, that Viola will not have another child."

"You mean she'd want you to divorce your wife for that? Your mother must be an old hellcat," said Mr. Weller with refreshing candor.

Alan did not dispute this verdict. He said, "I took a position with a steel products company last fall. Their main office is in Los Angeles. This June I had to go down there. Nathan went with me, 'for company.' One night he insisted on taking me to various nightclubs to 'cheer me up.' In one, we encountered Gertie. I should say, Greta. Very much Greta."

Alan smiled wryly. "She was a little tight. Nate said, 'Oh, be civilized, m'boy,' so she sat at our table and made the usual civilized remarks. She was with some unimportant man and a couple who didn't join us. Nate went off to the bar because the drinks weren't coming fast enough to suit him. Greta said she knew I was married and had we any children? I said simply, 'No,' but she saw she'd hit me on the raw and laughed and said, 'So your fine lady wife didn't do as well by you as your peasant light-of-love?'"

Sam whistled. "Why," he asked the room at large, "do dames always deliver knockout blows in public places?"

"She was tight. I suppose I said, 'You're joking.' She said, 'Oh no, I had a baby that November and, take it from me, it was no joke.' Of course I asked, 'Is the child living?' I think she was already sorry that she'd spoken. She said, 'What's it to you? Oh, you're its father and I could prove that. But it's my baby and I can take care of my own. . . .' Well, was that such an odd thing for her to have said, Mr. Dundas?" Alan asked as Michael frowned.

"No. It reminded me of something Gertie said to me that I suppose could be construed in more than one way. Go on."

"That's all she would say. She went back to her friends. I had more thinking to do than I could do at once. In fact, Nate had to pour me into bed at the hotel that night. But I tried to see Greta the next day—Nate knew where she lived. . . ."

"Oh, did he?" Michael said.

"Some mutual friend had pointed out her cottage to him. But Greta wasn't home and I had to be on the train home that evening. As soon as I could, I went south again—three weeks later, in July. I saw Greta for a little while. Miss Jameson wasn't in, but Greta expected her at any moment and didn't want her to see me. She said she must be discreet—with a divorce in the offing—and she didn't want me underfoot, having to be explained.

"She said, justly, that she'd asked nothing from me six years ago and she wanted me to leave her alone, now," Alan said. "As for my interest in 'her child,' that had come six years too late. But she seemed to think I might not believe what she'd told me. And she said, 'All right, if it will shut you up, so you'll go away, I'll show you something.' She showed me this. . . ."

Alan took a small, rather soiled snapshot from his pocket and passed it over to Michael. It showed a pale-haired boy whose hair already grew in a widow's peak and whose features promised to be Alan's, once they were firmly set. A penciled notation on the back read: "Five years, three months."

"That is, she showed me another copy of this picture, the latest one she had. I left her, then,

and came back to the city. I had a difficult decision to make. I could not just shrug and go on my
way. Though Greta said she was well able to provide for my son, he was half-Furness and we owed
him something.

"He was going on six and what sort of life would
he have if she went on concealing his existence?"
Alan said angrily. "Yet she must do that for the
sake of her career. She told me that she hadn't
risked visiting him for more than a year; that the
woman who looked after him sent her snapshots
every three months. And that he'd been well taken
care of, though I wouldn't approve of the person
who'd had him in charge."

"She was quite right, wasn't she?" Michael said.
"But didn't this come to be more than just a matter of conscience with you?"

"I couldn't—forget that picture. It might have
been one of my own baby pictures. I found I
wanted my son and couldn't bear thinking of him
hidden away. Oh, I cringed when I thought what
I was letting myself in for! But I decided to persuade Greta to let me have our son. No one need
have known that she was his mother. The scandal
wouldn't have touched her. . . ."

"But it would decidedly have touched your
wife."

"Do you think I didn't realize that! But Viola and I have been very—unhappy. She'd already suggested that we adopt a child. She'd mother any baby but I didn't want just—anyone's child. And while it still isn't as if this were Viola's child, still it is my son. And I knew that Viola would be courageous and understanding. . . ."

"But first you had to deal with Gertie?"

"Yes. I expected her to drive a hard bargain. So my first thought was to try to find out where the boy was. She wouldn't tell me; laughed and said he was well hidden. I could not expect her to believe at once that I wanted the boy very—very much."

"Did you try to see her again in Hollywood?" Michael asked.

"No. Last month I made my decision and began writing to her. I urged her to let me see the boy, to allow me to have a voice in planning his education. The answer, in that frightful scrawl of hers, was always, 'No!'"

"You addressed your own letters on a typewriter?"

"Yes. Then I began urging her to try to meet me, to talk. To my surprise, she finally wrote that she was coming up here, and that if I could arrange for us to meet secretly, she'd see me 'just to get me out of her hair.' I know the Yellands and their peculiarities and that they're at Tahoe now.

I had to take the chance that someone else might be using their apartment that night.

"Apparently the arrangements appealed to Greta's love of intrigue," Alan said distastefully. "And I knew that Louis had left a key to the Yellands' apartment with Uncle Nate; that he still had it. Greta wrote that we'd have to meet on Friday night. We always dine with Mother on Fridays. It's difficult to break any sort of engagement with Mother so I told Greta that I couldn't meet her until after eleven; that she'd better get to the meeting place first and I sent her the key."

"Then you had a bright idea and came down to L.A. and hired me to watch her?" Sam suggested.

"Yes. I flew down and back. It occurred to me that she'd see the boy before she went on to Reno, and that it might be worthwhile to have her followed, but I didn't care to engage a local detective."

"Well, I did my best, Mac, but I was held up getting to the apartment house. I got there too late to see anything that would help. But how come she went there so early? She left the hotel at nine-forty-five. If she didn't meet you at that joint, who did she meet?"

"I wish I knew," Alan said haggardly. "Perhaps she went early because she had nothing better to do. I have her letters; one confirming the time and place for our meeting. That only proves that we were, originally, to meet at eleven. Ordinarily we leave my mother's at ten-thirty on Friday and I had to allow time to take Viola home. . . ."

"But as it turned out, she didn't go with you to your mother's, did she?" Michael said.

"No, she didn't. And Mother made herself so unpleasant about a—family matter that Louis and I cleared out at ten o'clock. He had his car but I said I'd walk. I hadn't driven the short distance to Mother's. And I did walk, in a very roundabout way to the Verde Vista, killing time because Greta had the key to the apartment and I couldn't count on her being there until eleven.

"It was twenty past eleven when I got there and I knew at once that something was wrong. There was a crowd about the place and I soon gathered that there had been a killing. I didn't know that Greta was the victim but I didn't dare to try to keep my appointment with her. I turned and went home. Today, I did know that she'd been killed, but before I'd made up my mind to any course of action, Cathie brought over this letter. . . ."

8

The envelope was addressed in sprawling characters to Mr. Alan Furness at a Vallejo Street address. Inside was a sheet of bluish, lined paper, on which was written:

"Thursday A.M. Mr. Furness, I come across something the other day that makes me think you'd like to talk to me. I inclose something that will interest you. I'm willing to talk for a G. but I want it in twenties and you better bring it with you. And I can't give you much time. To be safe, you'd better get here before Saturday noon. I'm a few miles from Hayward on the highway. You'll see my mail box. Yours sincerely, Bella Voss."

"The snapshot I showed you was the enclosure," Alan said. "But the letter was sent to Mother's address. We lived with her until we found a place of our own and were listed in the old telephone book at that address. If Bella consulted a directory, it must have been an old one."

Michael looked thoughtfully at the pile of old newspapers and magazines in the bookcase. "Has your picture appeared in any newspaper recently?"

"Why—about three months ago. They must have been short of material for the Sunday papers. They had my picture and Viola's and something about my connection with the firm I'm working for. But. . . ."

"But women like Bella Voss like to read even old newspapers and the child in that snapshot

resembles you so markedly. . . . It would be a long
shot, but Bella must often have wondered who the
child's father was. Then she would have had two
sources of income, you and Greta."

"Well, at least she did write the letter and send
it to Mother's place," Alan said. "I still should
have had it last night. Mother says that Cathie
volunteered to give it to me, but she forgot, so she
brought it over to our house late this afternoon. I
can prove that."

"I'm sure you can. But Bella wasn't killed tonight. She's been dead a good many hours. Where
was this letter from the time it was delivered at
your mother's home, until your sister gave it to
you?"

"Cathie said that the letter had been on the
hall table where mail is left and that even if she
did promise to give it to me last night, someone
else should have seen it and said something about
it. And ordinarily I would have looked to see what
was on that table since people still write to me at
Mother's address. But last night I was—perturbed
and I was late and I didn't stop in the hall."

"So presumably the letter lay there from yesterday morning until this afternoon?" Michael said.
"But when you'd finally read it . . ."

"I walked in on a—crisis this afternoon," Alan
said grimly. "Mother had just recommended that

we hire an elderly maid who would be fond of children and Viola went into hysterics. I told Mother the truth; that there would be no more children. Then I told her and Cathie and Nate to go home. And took Viola to her father's home. He's a mild, ineffectual soul but very restful, and Viola's old nurse is his housekeeper now.

"I stayed there until she was quite calm and was asleep," Alan went on, "and then I got my car and came here. No one answered the doorbell. The door was not locked. I came in and went through the place. I thought there was no one here. I came into the kitchen, decided to look into the out-buildings. When I realized someone else was lurking about this place I became panicky, with disastrous results to myself. . . ."

He touched the back of his head regretfully. "Of course you couldn't know who I was, but neither could I know that your—um—intentions were of the best. And I went through the house quickly but I saw no one at all. No trace of a child—Where is he? What's happened to him?"

When Michael did not answer at once, Sam said, "Everything points to Bella's being ready to take a powder as soon as Greta had gotten here. At least, that's what I'd think. I don't know. . . ."

"Oh, she must have meant to clear out," Michael said. "She told Mr. Furness to get here before noon of today and Greta said that she had an engagement out of the city tonight. So Bella must have wanted you to get here before Greta did, Mr. Furness. And since Bella was leaving this place, Greta must have planned a new setup for the boy."

"Why not, with him going on six?" said Sam. "Or maybe Voss was just leaving here anyway, going into some new racket. In any case. . . ."

"Where is the boy?" Alan broke in. "I saw nothing belonging to a child except a broken toy engine, but I didn't see the Voss woman, though you say. . . ."

"Oh, she's plenty dead, Mac. Hidden under the bed where you wouldn't see her unless you looked. Head bashed in. I guess someone didn't want her found right away. I'll bet she told folks around here that she was going away and so they won't be expecting to see her around. . . ."

"Eventually, we can check on that," Michael said. "But just now—I'll be frank with you, Mr. Furness—none of us is in an enviable position. We've all withheld information from the police. We should go to them at once. . . ."

"But do I dare?" Alan said. "If this is—if it is kidnapping . . ."

"I know. You meant to accept the boy and take him into your home. Obviously you believed your

wife would accept him, too. That would establish
his position so that you could provide for him
very adequately, legally. And you would have?"

"Yes. I know this would greatly have changed
Cathie's expectations. And Uncle Nathan's. I'll
make a new will and I don't feel that the promises
I made before I knew I had a son are binding now.
If I still have a son! If—"

"Yes," Michael said repressively. "And there is
more than money to be considered."

"The inevitable scandal? I'd planned that we'd
move to some other city. The story would follow
us, but people wouldn't take it too seriously away
from here where Viola was born. Fortunately neither of us cares for social position or so-called
society. . . ."

"But has your mother planned to spend her
declining years in San Francisco?"

"Y-yes. She wouldn't want to follow us into ex-
ile. She sets great store by legitimacy; she doesn't
care for children; she'd hate the scandal. But,"
Alan added quietly, "though ordinarily she can
bully me, she knows that when I really want something I can sweat it out to the bitter end."

"So? And you are well able to pay ransom if
someone has kidnapped Greta's son. You will pay,
of course? So though Greta's child, dead, would

probably mean money in the pocket for your
uncle and sister, it would also be simple to collect
ransom from you. And Louis Hilton couldn't collect from you in any other fashion."

"But how," Sam said practically, "did anyone
find out about the kid?"

"I wish I could tell you! That letter from the
Voss woman did lie in Mother's hall for more than
twenty-four hours. I suppose it could have been
opened and resealed. I tore the flap across when I
opened it. . . ."

"And you'd better keep this." Michael handed
the letter back to him. "But what about your letters to Greta and her answers?"

"I wrote to her at the office and mailed the letters myself, at once. But I made carbon copies."

"That was sensible of you."

"Yes, but I didn't dare leave anything like that
in the office. I kept the carbons at home. Viola
would never go through my desk. Greta's own letters are in it, too . . ."

"Do your relatives come and go as they wish in
your home?" Michael asked.

"They—drop in. And the desk is in the living-
room. Our mail is put on a hall table, too, so
sometimes Greta's letters have lain there until
I'd get home. I told Viola they were letters from

an uneducated chap I knew in the Army. Greta's scrawl might have been a man's. But it's too fantastic to think—to suppose that—anyone opened my letters. . . ."

"But the child is gone," Michael said. "If he's been kidnapped, kidnappers are apt to take drastic action if the police are called in. I suggest that we go home and wait to see if you receive any communication regarding the boy."

"It's the only thing we can do that won't endanger him," Alan agreed. "But you haven't told me why you came here tonight."

"Greta called me on the telephone just before she was killed. She asked me to remember the name, Bella Voss. I made inquiries, found out who, and what, the woman was, and where she was living."

"Oh. Well, I don't like to think of her just lying here. . . ."

"Does it matter, now that she's dead?" Michael said indifferently. "And before too long we'll arrange to have her found. Sam and I will put things in order here. . . ."

"In order?" Alan repeated.

"Remove a few fingerprints for one thing, Mr. Furness: Hadn't you thought of that? I fancy whoever killed Bella Voss did clean up, so there's no point in leaving just ours for the police to find."

He turned to Sam who was looking through the suitcase he had found in the bedroom closet. "Anything helpful there?"

"Sort of. Only about five dollars in silver in her purse, which is funny because here's a coach ticket to Chicago—thirty-day limit. She'd need more money than that before she got to Chi. But she was going away and I'll bet a few people around here knew it and will just suppose she's already left. That may be a lucky break for us. . . ."

The suitcase also held a stock of plain underwear, a cheap toilet set, several inexpensive dresses and a sweater. There were even a few pocket books and a camera that Sam said was a Premo 2-A—old, but good for snapshots. "Look, Mr. Dundas, how's about me trying to take a few shots in the bedroom in case someone got bright ideas and managed to rearrange things here before the body's officially discovered? It's kind of a grisly job but I don't mind."

"Have you the equipment to take pictures indoors at night?" Michael said, surprised.

"Sure. I travel prepared." Sam slapped his protruding pockets. "Camera here. Not expensive, but I get results. And a small flashbulb attachment in the other pocket."

"Go ahead. I'd better repack this suitcase if we want it to look as if the contents hadn't been disturbed since Bella packed it. You'd better get going, Mr. Furness. Here's your gun. But," Michael added, "I'll expect to hear from you tomorrow—Sunday."

9

When they had passed the toll gate to the Bay Bridge, Sam Weller said mildly, "I'm not bitching, pal; I'm with you all the way. And I'm no calamity howler, but though we did find out a lot, it might've been better if we'd found Bella Voss alive instead of dead. . . ."

"Might have been?" Michael let out a sound that was half-groan and half-sigh. "Bella could have told us almost everything we want to know. I don't like the way things are going. I feel as if I were trying to play against a stacked deck. Being able to find out so quickly where Bella lived, was a lucky break that encouraged me. But we find her dead and to save ourselves further embarrassment, have to conceal evidence. We're worse off than we were this afternoon. But what is it that you're determined not to complain about?"

"Oh, wouldn't it have taken the pressure off if you'd hustled Furness to the cops? Of course, if you believe him—and you've almost got to—there's the kid to consider though it seems to me he should've had some kind of ransom note by now if the boy's been kidnapped."

"Whoever killed Bella doesn't necessarily know that such a letter is being expected. And while it is possible that someone read Bella's letter to Alan, before he did, it's also possible that someone learned of her existence without reading her letter."

"Someone? Who? How?"

"Whoever killed Greta. Don't forget the box she carried to the Verde Vista with her. It's missing, and one will get you ten, that she carried more than one prized possession in it. Such as Bella's letters to her regarding her son, and the snapshots that she sent her regularly. I think it's reasonable enough to guess that Greta, meaning to talk to Alan about their son, would take those with her. And I'm concerned for the boy's safety. I don't think anyone would kill him unless they thought it necessary. . . ."

"Yeah, kill the kid only if that would keep you from getting caught," Sam said. "Then if you still got caught and it was proved you'd killed him, you wouldn't be any worse off."

"Precisely. And then, looking at it from a purely personal standpoint, I can't prove that I didn't visit Bella in the early hours of the morning after I took you to your hotel."

"Won't they be able to tell when the dame was killed?"

"Not to the minute and hour. No one's going to be able to say when she may have eaten her last meal, for one thing. And besides, I want to avoid public investigation and publicity. Alan told us his story because he hoped that we'd give him a break. But if we'd thrown him into the laps of the police, do you think he would have told them the same story?"

"I suppose not," Sam said slowly. "It would be his word against ours and we'd all have a lot of plain and fancy explaining to do."

"And I wish to avoid that. I'd like to hand over airtight evidence to Hoyt. For one thing, it would save trouble and for another, I'd like to rub his nose in it. And if we turned Alan over to the police, Viola wouldn't talk to me."

"That's so. But do you believe Alan's story?"

"Much that he told us had the ring of truth though I don't doubt that he told a few lies," Michael said. "He didn't ask one question he might have asked. . . ."

"He didn't gnaw on me for falling down on the job. Of course. . . . What's the matter, doc?"

"A worm crawled down my spine. I'm ignoring something that could be important. . . . Well, I want to talk to Louis Hilton. I doubt that he has much family feeling. But even he wouldn't speak freely if Alan were being detained by the police. There it is again. And I'm interested in Catherine Furness."

"Yeah. Alan kept starting to say things about her—her plans and so on, but never finished. What do you have in mind for me?" Sam asked.

"I'd like you to rise early and keep an eye on Mrs. Hester Furness's household—Hester herself, Nathan Ridley and Catherine."

"Oh, my aching back! You know what it's like to try to loiter around some house in a residential district. And if I had to follow someone who used a car. . . ."

"I know someone who will provide you with a car—with false license plates. His name is Squiffy Bain and he'll be very glad to do me a favor," Michael said with a sardonic smile. "I'll call him before eight A.M. Go out to the Excelsior Garage. . . ." He mentioned an address in the Mission.

"Look, chum, you seem to have plenty of moola and a position in this city, so how come you know all these characters that do you favors?"

"I'm one of Horatio Alger's boys—rags-to-riches. I knew Squiffy in my early days here. He feels I know a little too much about him. He has nothing to fear from me but I don't tell him so. I learned my sociology the hard way," Michael said reflectively. "That's why I was a trifle severe with Mr. Furness."

"Oh? Well, can you arrange to have the Voss dame's body discovered?"

"An anonymous telephone call will take care of that. Little man, it's going to be a busy Sunday."

Having finished talking to Squiffy Bain, Michael lay back in bed, reflecting that it would not be wise to try to see Louis Hilton before ten o'clock on a Sunday morning. Therefore he had better sleep for another hour and a half. But sleep flitted coyly just before him. He admitted finally that he still had a cold, crawly sensation down his back and settled himself to track down its origin.

He had said, of Alan Furness, "He didn't ask one question he might have asked." And Sam Weller, not quite comprehending, had remarked, "He didn't gnaw on me for falling down on the job . . ." Sam had fallen down on his job because "a little twerp" had gotten into a cab just behind Greta's, before Sam could. So it had taken Sam longer than it should have to reach the Verde Vista and as a result. . . .

"*Sacra Maria!*" said Mr. Dundas fervently and snatched up the telephone. He dialed the number of the Brighton Hotel, asked for Mr. Weller and when Sam said sleepily, "Hello?" demanded, "What did that little twerp who managed to get into the taxi just behind Greta's look like?"

"Why—he was chicken-chested and pimply; pasty-faced with a lot of Adam's apple and no chin. . . . Hey! Something wrong?"

"Egbert to the life," Michael said briefly.

"Jeez! And he was sore at Greta as well as you, because she laughed when you pinned his ears back. . . . And he had an eye for the main chance, so he hung around the St. Francis. . . ."

"I don't require a blueprint," Michael snapped. "And I could be wrong but. . . . Take this down." He gave Sam the address of Egbert's rooming house. "I'd better not go there, but since the place is on Pine, it's not too far from your hotel. Find out if he's home and let me know."

He got up and had finished what, with him, passed for breakfast, when the telephone rang. Viola said, "Mr. Dundas? I'm calling from my father's home. Will you take down this address? . . . Yes, that's right. Daddy will play golf at eleven and Alan will go to church with his mother. I know you can't have told the police about me and I promised to talk to you. . . ."

"Will as soon after eleven as I can make it, suit you? Very well," Michael said, "and thank you for calling me."

Before he was completely dressed the telephone rang again. Still a little early for Sam to be reporting, he thought, glancing at the clock as he crossed the room. Possibly Costello. . . . It was Alan Furness. Michael suspected that his voice sounded lifeless because it required some effort for him to keep it low and even.

"The maid—she sleeps out—found a letter under the door when she arrived this morning. Cheap envelope, no address, the usual words or letters cut from newspapers and pasted on a plain sheet of paper. It says, '*The boy is safe and will be as long as you don't go to the police or tell them too much that you know about Greta Mallon. Keep quiet and you'll hear from us again.*'"

"Brief, comprehensive and typical," Michael commented.

"It says 'us.' Do you think. . . ."

"It may be merely an editorial 'we.' But two people could easily be working together on this."

"Y-yes. I'd—thought of that. But what can I do!"

"Do as you're told, for today at least. So far as I know, you've no way of getting in touch with whoever concocted that note. You'll simply have to play it safe for a reasonable length of time."

"Yes, but. . . . Could I meet you later in the day?" Alan asked. "Viola wants me to placate

Mother by going to church with her and lunching with her, as usual. But later on. . . ."

"I'll call you this afternoon or evening at your own home," Michael said. "Or you can call me here, on the chance that I'll be in."

He sat down on the bed with the telephone in his hand and willed it to ring again. In another five minutes, it did.

"Egbert's not home," Sam told him. "But he was alive and kicking an hour ago. The landlady saw him go out to breakfast. She thought he'd be going over to Marin county; says he likes to spend Sundays out-of-doors."

"Egbert a nature lover? Well, perhaps he thinks that fresh air will increase his chest expansion."

"The landlady told me to try the greasy spoon where he usually eats, when I said I'd like to catch him before he got out of the city. He ate there, all right, and had sandwiches put up to take out. I haven't traced him farther than that."

"Well, if he got to the Verde Vista last night in time to see Greta's murderer arrive or leave, either Egbert's already approached him for hush money—or Egbert hasn't," Michael said brilliantly. "If I hadn't been abysmally stupid, we'd be watching him now."

"He don't seem to have any pals," Sam broke in. "I've got a way with landladies. This one was surprised that Egbert had any friend that was anxious to see him. But I can hang around this neighborhood if you think it'll pay off in the end."

"No, if he bought sandwiches and went off, instead of back to his room, the chances are that he doesn't mean to return there for some time. He may think, and he'd be right, that he's safer until after the pay-off, if his whereabouts aren't known. There's nothing we can do just now about Egbert, I'm afraid.

"The Furnesses will be going to church and then home to lunch," Michael added. "You needn't follow them to church, but you can see what happens afterward. You might try to call me here after three o'clock. Squiffy Bain has a car for you at his garage. Meanwhile, I'll go over to see Louis Hilton."

PART FOUR

1

"You are the victim of circumstances, aren't you?" Louis said, his long mouth twisting into a mocking smile. "Because, in some ways, Greta was a circumstance beyond one's control. You'd better console yourself with another coffee royal. . . ."

Michael had a high enough opinion of Mr. Hilton's intelligence to believe that he had outlined the case against himself in some detail, though he had not mentioned his own activities following his discovery of Greta's body. He had expected that Louis would appear to find his predicament slightly diverting. Louis did, but as he poured coffee and added a generous dollop of brandy, his smile faded.

He put the cup back on the table in front of Michael and said seriously, "You haven't told me all this just because you feel the need to confide in someone. You know that you can prove, eventually, that you didn't have an affair with Greta back in 1940—and who did."

"Yes. First, Viola fainted for no apparent reason, just after Greta had sailed out of Gisele's. Then you and Nathan turned up at Greta's little brawl and he made a point of explaining how you two came to know her. . . ."

"I'm fond of the old boy but he's about as subtle as a herd of hippos."

"Then the elevator operator at the Verde Vista said that Nathan knew the Yellands. After that, I learned that you two were related to the Furnesses. Then, Greta mislaid a cocktail napkin that was a valuable clue. And I ran into a private operative that a man who could have been Alan Furness had hired to follow Greta up here from Los Angeles. . . ."

"The poor, damn fool," Louis said pityingly. "But if this gumshoe was following Greta, why can't he tell us who killed her?"

"Circumstances beyond his control."

"Oh. But why did Lanny want Greta followed? Did he. . . . Look, you'd better talk to him. . . ."

"He was forced to talk to me. He had Greta tailed because he thought she might visit their son before she went on to Reno. He was trying to find out where the child was. You don't seem surprised to learn that there is one, Mr. Hilton.

Alan thought no one knew but Greta. He swears
he didn't, until lately."

"That babe in arms! But I don't see how he
could have known, because he went East so soon
after Nate and I told Greta—for him—that it'd
been nice while it lasted, but that it was all over.
I didn't know, when I talked to her then, that
she was going to have a baby. I doubt if she did,
either, because that was certainly the time for her
to have spoken of it."

"Apparently she never did speak or ask for help."

"I concluded that she had honest-to-God guts
and a lot more pride than you'd expect," Louis
said. "But you want to know if I knew, or suspected, she'd had a baby? Yes, I did. I get around.
I always have. And one day, about August of that
fateful year, I found myself in the neighborhood
where Greta lived."

"Were you considering renewing your acquaintance with her?"

Louis grinned. "Well, even in those days, there
was something about Greta. We could have had
fun, too. But I saw her going into the corner grocery and one look was enough to make me decide
not even to say hello."

"And you didn't report your findings to Alan?"

"Good God, no! He might have married her. I'd
have asked first—how do I know it's my child? I

know; I'm a wise guy and I didn't do her justice. However . . ." Louis reddened slightly—"I sent her an anonymous fifty bucks just in case, since I happened to be in funds just then. When we met again, in exactly the way Nate said we did, I kept my yap shut. More power to her, I thought. And she was affable to me but she never talked over old times."

"The thing is," Michael said, "that if, back in 1940 you considered trying to get to know Greta better, Nathan was probably more susceptible than you. . . ."

"I know. But if he did see her again in this city, I don't know it," Louis said quickly. "He'd have called it 'guarding dear Alan's interests.' Lanny's a good guy but people have always looked after him."

"The fact that you call him 'Lanny' made me suspect that."

"And I called him a babe in arms because he thinks only Nate and I knew about his little interlude with Greta. He thinks that because his mother never said anything, she didn't know anything. But that's the sort of thing Hester would never mention because as long as she doesn't acknowledge an unpleasant fact, she thinks it doesn't exist. But Lanny certainly knows that she has the Indian-sign on poor old Nate."

"So that Nathan might easily have been tricked or bullied into telling her about Greta and Alan?"

"Yes. And if Nate knew and told her that Greta was going to have a baby, Hester would have said, 'There are charitable organizations to care for sluts like that.' What did Lanny intend to do if he found his child or persuaded Greta to tell him where it was?"

"He says he intended to persuade her to give it up to him; to acknowledge it as his own and provide for it as generously as possible," Michael said. "Do you think that he is telling the truth and that his wife would have accepted the child, too?"

"You said it's a boy?" Michael nodded. "Then I think he's telling the truth. He wanted a son so much that I was sorry as hell when their baby died. Uncle Zach and Lanny are—were—slightly hipped on this business of perpetuating the family name."

"I have a son," Michael said, "but he was born before the war. I honestly don't know, after what I saw in Italy, France, Germany and even England, whether now I'd have the infernal gall to bring another child into the world. But I've known men whose wartime experience made them think quite differently."

"My reaction would be yours. Though I didn't get overseas, I saw too many youngsters killed in

training because they—or I, as their instructor—
weren't good enough. It seemed a terrific waste.
Lanny saw just enough of real war that he came
back feeling that millions of fighting men are
going to be another lost generation; that a new
generation's the only hope for humanity and that
a man who doesn't have children hasn't much
reason for existence."

"And besides," Michael said unkindly, "he realizes that he is 'a superior type' who should have
offspring." Louis shrugged and did not deny it.
"Also, Hester Furness is his mother and he resembles her enough to be a man of property. I think,
though he doesn't realize it, that he considers
Greta's son his property. But will Viola co-operate?"

"I think so. Alan is nuts about her; don't ever
think he isn't. But unconsciously, he feels she
owes him something because she didn't produce
a healthy heir. And she thinks so, too, poor kid.
When they married, she was a charming little snob
and something of a prig, and no wonder. She'd
been convent-educated and sheltered from unde-
sirable contacts. But following Lanny about from
one camp to another, she learned how the rest of
the world lives. That, and losing one child prema-
turely and then this other one, made people out of
Viola. Of course you can't be certain, ever, what a
woman will or won't do. . . ."

"But you can be certain that Hester Furness would oppose Alan's plan?" Michael asked.

"God, yes! Dear Hester would blow her top and she's a dirty fighter. She'd consider Lanny a soft-hearted fool even if he made just moderate and discreet provision for his son. But if he's really made up his mind, she can save her breath. There's no shaking Lanny on the rare occasions when he really makes up his mind to something."

"Catherine knows that, too? And did she know of Alan's little interlude with Greta?"

Louis reddened again. "I told her. I've always been sorry for Cathie and so would you be if you. . . ."

"I had an opportunity yesterday to observe Mrs. Furness's manner toward her daughter. It shouldn't happen to a dog."

"Check! Of course Cathie is a fool; she never learns. She'd always been devoted to Lanny and admired him because he was a 'big man on the campus' and all that sort of manure. She remained 'mamma's home girl' while Lanny made the ideal marriage. I got fed up with her saying dear Alan deserved all his happiness, he was such a little knight in shining armor. I thought it would do her good to know that her idol was even as you and I."

"Did it?"

"I think so. She took a more normal, healthily critical attitude toward him after that."

"And her father's will was a strain on fraternal feeling, wasn't it?" Michael said.

Louis frowned. "You know about that? Yes, and I don't blame Cathie. I suppose you know, too, that Lanny promised, after the baby died, to make a more nearly equal division of the estate this fall?"

"Yes. Why doesn't he think Catherine can be trusted to handle any great amount of money? What sort of plans or impractical schemes does she have?"

"If I knew, I wouldn't tell you. I don't know how much of Cathie's farewell conversation on my doorstep you heard Friday night. But since I don't owe Hester one goddam thing, I'll tell you what that was all about.

"Nate and I were late to dinner. He said we'd been hobnobbing with screen royalty—Greta Mallon. Hester merely sniffed. But later on, after Lanny and I left, earlier than we are usually allowed to, Hester was expressing her displeasure with everyone to Cathie, and she referred to Greta as 'that Malinowsky person.'"

"Oh?" Michael said. "Had Cathie known that Greta Mallon was once Gertie Malinowsky?"

"I didn't peddle gossip about Gertie after she became Greta Mallon. But I'd told Cathie the name of Alan's little diversion and she remembers things. She said nothing to Hester. Cathie isn't supposed to know about Lanny's wild oats. Cathie is sent from the room when Hester and her pals discuss any subjects that involve the basic facts of life."

Michael grimaced. "And Lincoln freed the slaves. So Catherine concluded that her mother knew all along about Alan and Gertie Malinowsky?"

"Yes. That upset her. She realized that no matter how long Hester had known about Alan and Greta, she must have taken it in stride. I had to convince Cathie that Greta hadn't dropped into town just to make trouble for Lanny or anyone; that to rake up the past would be the last thing she'd want to do."

"And so far as you know, Catherine has no notion that Greta and Alan had a son?"

"I'm sure she doesn't know," Louis said. "But, of course, if Lanny goes through with his quixotic plan, it will make a difference to Cathie, financially. And to Nate. And now I'll ask the sixty-four dollar question. . . ."

"I wondered when you would."

"If I thought you'd answer it, I'd have asked it before. Where is Greta's boy? Alan's boy, now. I think that if you knew, you would have told me. Or Lanny would have and called a family council.

The possibilities of this setup hit you in the eye
at once and . . ."

Louis stopped as heavy feet ascended the steps
outside the cottage; someone pounded on the door
and then, without waiting, Nathan Ridley burst
in, very much the country gentleman in sloppy
tweeds but otherwise considerably agitated.

"My dear boy, we must put our heads together
for Alan's sake though I could hardly credit my
ears, it's so fantastic. . . . But we must consider
Hester, too, and Cathie, though in a different . . ."

"Yes," Louis said warningly, stepping away from
the door and gesturing toward Michael, "but, you
see, we are not alone, dear boy."

2

"I'll leave you alone," Michael said, rising. "I've
been here too long as it is. But I take it, Mr. Ridley, that Mr. Furness showed you a communication that he received this morning?"

"Yes. The poor fellow's off his head with worry
and naturally. . . ."

"Well, since he doesn't know who put that note
together but is anxious to co-operate, perhaps
he will get action more quickly if he confides in
everyone and anyone who could possibly have sent
him that note."

"Mr. Dundas, I resent that and I fail to see. . . ."

"I'll remove myself from your resentment if you'll answer one question. When you were at Mrs. Hester's on Friday night, could any, or all of you, have made a telephone call some time between nine-twenty-five and nine-forty without having to announce your intention to the others present?"

"Easily," Louis said. "There are phones in the library and the upstairs hall, both private enough. Lanny used the one in the library to call Viola, around nine-thirty. And the rest of us were in and out. Both Nate and I had to go upstairs and Cathie was bustling about, doing the little errands Hester always finds for her to do. Is that all? We'll be seeing you—I'm very much afraid."

Michael had parked his car just off Mason, below the steps that went down past Louis's cottage. There was another car parked close to his now; an elderly, but unremarkable sedan, with remarkably dirty license plates.

Michael got into his own car, grinned and said, "Do you happen to have a match, Mac?"

"Sure, pal . . . The others are off to church," Sam told him. "Alan evidently got to his Ma's before I got this heap from your friend and parked where I could see the front door. At least, he was there to go off with two dames I guessed were Mom and Cathie. In two shakes more, this middle-aged guy comes out and high-tails it over here. He walked, but he sure did ankle along. I thought I'd better tail him. When we got here I recognized your car and thought I'd wait to ask if you want me to stay with Ridley—that's who he is?—now."

"N-no," Michael decided. "I think these two will watch their step and I'm more interested in Catherine and her mother. Of course, there are two of them and only one of you. But go back and watch the Furness house. I'll come by it myself when I've seen Viola, in case you're still just sitting there."

"Oh, my aching back! I should have brought a book—or a bottle," Sam grumbled. "Okay, but I'll probably have a nice, long sit."

Mr. Weller did have a nice, long sit and before it was over, was beginning to be apprehensive regarding his cigarette supply. Hester Furness's home was an unpretentious brick dwelling with a driveway to one side that led to a red brick garage. Sam, having no notion what one paid for property in this district, thought rather disparagingly that the house was a nice enough dump but nothing you'd ever look at twice.

And finally, since he had nothing to do but stare at the house, he realized that, though its more showy neighbors still looked war-worn, somehow Mrs. Furness had dealt with wartime shortages of material and labor and maintained her standards. . . .

He became very busy with non-existent wires below the dashboard as Mrs. Furness, Catherine and Alan came along the street from the direction of Fillmore. But none of them glanced his way. They went into the house and, just before one o'clock, a car drove up and Nathan Ridley got out.

From Michael's description of him, Sam knew that the car's driver must be Louis Hilton. Louis leaned over to close the door and said in his languid but clear and carrying voice, "No thanks. Hester's Sunday luncheons give me a bellyache. I don't mind their being cold so that the servants can go to church when they'd rather not, but. . . ."

Nathan shook his head and a warning forefinger but Louis continued calmly, "But the odor of sanctity in which said food is eaten makes me want to heave. If Lanny wants to milk my feeble brain, it's at his disposal—if Hester isn't present to confuse the issue. Personally, I think he'd better string along with Dundas."

Nathan said something that Sam could not hear and Louis broke in impatiently, "So he isn't one of the sacred family! But he's involved in this, though he'd rather not be. And I'd rather have him for me than ag'in me. I know more about him than you do. He's not only as smart as they come, but he could be very vindictive, and personally, I don't want any part of Mr. Dundas's animosity. You may tell Lanny that. I'll be home around three if anyone wants me. . . ."

Louis drove away and Sam, who was beginning to feel hollow below the belt, sat and thought of after-church meals; not a cold lunch, but the sort his mother had served—roast beef with browned potatoes during the winter, fried chicken and a freezer of ice cream in summertime. . . .

These recollections moistened a mouth that was dry from too many cigarettes. He swallowed and then put up a hand to shield his face when, at a few minutes past two o'clock, a roadster with Catherine Furness at its wheel suddenly backed from the garage.

"Allah be praised!" said Mr. Weller devoutly and stamped on the starter.

It was almost absurdly easy to follow Catherine. She was a skillful but prudent driver; she went steadily along, not too fast, not too slowly, observing all signals and stop signs. Sam felt that his lack of familiarity with San Francisco handicapped him. As Catherine swung from one street to another he could not always locate a street sign quickly enough to be able to say by exactly what route they had traveled, the San Francisco authorities having apparently no set rules for the erection of, or painting on, of such signs.

But he was aware that they were on Haight Street some time before Catherine swerved into the curb and parked before a large, dilapidated, gray building. To one side of a narrow staircase was a discouraged cleaning and tailoring shop; on the other, what had been meant for a small shop had been converted into an apartment by the simple expedient of putting Venetian blinds behind the small show window.

Catherine disappeared up the central outside staircase. Sam, following her cautiously, discovered a brass plate screwed into the riser of the fourth step—JACQUES' HEALTH CULTURE AND CONDITIONING CLUB.

Mr. Weller whistled noiselessly. "Dundas said she was one of these better-health-through-better-living dames. Could be," he thought and went on up the stairway until he found himself facing a door that bore a sign like the one on the step below.

Sam studied the sign thoughtfully. "I've got plenty of health, but no culture, so maybe conditioning is what I need," he muttered.

There was a doorbell, but automatically he nudged the door with his toe and placed an experimental hand on the doorknob. The door swung

open and he stepped into a small room furnished
with a spittoon, an ash stand, a rigid, formida-
ble chair, and a square desk with a dog-eared
appointment book spread open on it, besides several dozen photographs of muscular young men
posed in those postures and costumes best calculated to display their muscle.

Mr. Weller gazed wistfully at another door,
labelled PRIVATE which was a little ajar. He could
hear voices on the other side of it, and when no
one appeared to ask what he wanted here, he slowly edged closer to the door and, finally, risked a
quick look around it.

He saw a huge room with rowing machines and
various pulleys and exercising apparatus against
the walls, rings and horizontal bars at one end of
the hall, medicine and volley balls resting in cor-
ners. Catherine's back was to Sam; she was facing
a brawny young man who wore shabby slacks and a
singlet cut low enough to show a great many muscles and a mat of curly brown hair on his chest.

He said, in a deep, rather pleasing but entirely uncultured voice, "Look, babe, we've had this
out several times before and I thought the last
time was final. You agreed with me there was just
one thing to do. You said you wouldn't argue any
more. But now, just because things haven't turned
out like we planned, you come running to me. . . ."

"Oh, Jack! Please, Jack, please! You don't understand; no man could. . . ." Catherine burst into tears and drooped against the stalwart chest.

He upheld her manfully, patted her shoulders and said in a piercing whisper, "Are you sure no one followed you here, babe? Could happen, you know."

Sam stepped hastily back from the door though not so quickly that he did not hear Catherine's, "Of course not, Jackie. You're the one that's nervous now. Oh darling, things aren't going right. . . ."

Sam swore to himself because they lowered their voices so that he heard only the sound of them, until Catherine burst out, "But we can't wait too long! This is our chance. . . ."

Sam slid closer to the door though he did not put his ear to the keyhole. Jackie, whom he had personally christened 'Muscles,' was making soothing noises and he thought that Catherine was crying again.

He heard her say, "So frightened. . . ." before she went on, quite clearly, "Yes, I'd better be getting back, though Mother and Uncle Nathan always take naps on Sunday afternoons and they won't miss me . . ."

Sam turned, half a second too late. Something exploded inside his head and sent him spinning down into darkness.

3

The upstairs sitting room in her father's home was very shabby—and immeasurably more attractive than Viola's own correctly furnished living-room. The books had been read, the chairs were taken for granted, the bits of china, brass and pewter looked as if they had been acquired merely because someone had happened to like them, and there was an unabashed display of family photographs.

Viola took one of these from a bookcase before she sat down opposite Michael and said, "I told Alan that I would stay in bed; that he shouldn't come after me until he'd had lunch with his mother. Even though he said that he must talk to me— at some length. Obviously he doesn't know what you know about me, though I think he must suspect. . . . But he remarked, in passing, that he had occasion to talk to you last night."

"That's true, but I think you'd better let him tell you what the occasion was, Mrs. Furness."

"I want him to; not you. But I must ask, how much do you know? How much must I explain?"

"I know all about Alan's relations with Greta Mallon," Michael said. "It's only your connection with her that you must explain."

"I see. Well, even before I met Alan, I'd heard a little gossip. His friends thought it was too amusing of him to take what is loosely called a pick-and-shovel job and to try to live as the men he worked with did. Now and then someone would remark, 'Well, I understand Alan's found his little sociological experiment has added attractions he never expected. . . .' That sort of thing."

"Yes, those things do get around and if Alan had been older, he would have known that they do."

"Alan won't repeat gossip himself," Viola said defensively. Then she smiled deprecatingly. "And I was a tiresome little prig. I was always saying, 'Perhaps it is amusing, but is it kind?' So I wasn't told things. My mother still spoke of young men 'sowing their wild oats.' So did Mother Furness. I didn't think that Alan's wild oats would be very many or very wild and I was prepared to forgive him. I was determined to marry him as soon as we'd met.

"I also expected to be courted; to be wooed and won, not too hastily. And then take time to fill a hope chest with the proper linens, properly monogrammed. . . . Alan went East that April. I was to go in May. Meanwhile, his mother didn't lose touch with me. And she threw out some broad hints about 'men will be men, you know,' and 'while it's a pity, it has nothing to do with a man's wife and it's best for him to have his little fling

before marriage. . . .' Almost prehistoric, but I
accepted it as a matter of course.

"It was in late April," Viola went on, "that I
was waiting for Mother Furness one afternoon at
her own home. No one else was there. I heard a
slight argument at the front door. I went out into
the hall. Mother Furness's downstairs maid who
has been with her for twenty years, was trying to
keep a girl from coming in, saying that Mr. Alan
wasn't in the city and his parents were not in and
'wouldn't see the likes of you, anyway.'

"I guessed at once who the girl was. For the first
time in my life I dared to make an important decision by myself. I told old Millie that I would talk
to 'the young woman.' We went into the living-
room. I told her that I was Alan's fiancée, which
wasn't true, and asked what she wanted.

"I wasn't discerning enough to see what she
might be, if she'd had half the care lavished on
her that I'd had. And she—wasn't too clean,"
Viola said distastefully. "Her clothes were dread-
ful; her hair needed washing—I'm telling you this
so that you may understand my reaction to her.
And showing you this, too. . . ."

She gave him the photograph she had been holding: her wedding picture. In it she was slender,
but healthily so; her eyes were clear, self-confident and unafraid. There was a little hint of arrogance in the curve of her smile that was attractive

because it was so youthful and so obviously justi-
fied.

"That's how I was the day I told Greta exactly what any person of breeding and refinement
would think of her. I was courteous; I didn't raise
my voice . . ."

"But you dissected her in a nasty, nice way; made
her feel like a bug squirming on a pin," Michael
said. "And she never forgot it."

"But she took it without whimpering," Viola
said somberly. "In her place, I would have wept.
. . . But she told me only that she wanted to see
Alan or Alan's parents. She did say, 'I let him off
too easy.' And truly, Mr. Dundas, I was so ignorant and so certain that I must have what I wanted, the way I wanted it. . . . I really didn't know
she was pregnant. One couldn't tell, at a glance.
Still. . . ."

Viola pressed her thin hands to blue-veined
temples. "I may deliberately have deceived myself
in this. Perhaps I just thought what I wanted to
think. I assumed that she thought that Alan might
marry her, and I pointed out to her just how un-
utterably ridiculous that was. . . ."

"You're being a little severe with yourself,"
Michael said. "It would have been ridiculous. Or,
more important, extremely impractical, except as
a purely temporary measure."

"Yes, but— Well, I reached for my purse. I was going to offer her what money I had. She got up and left the house. That was the afternoon's work I did six years ago. I was quite pleased with myself. I suggested to old Millie that it would be as well not to mention the unfortunate episode to Mrs. Furness. She agreed. . . ."

"Do you think that she did keep it a secret?"

"I think she—tried. She adores Alan and Mother Furness's servants always try to avoid 'upsetting the madame.' But Mother Furness referred today to Greta as that 'Malinowsky person.' She has never read a movie magazine or newspaper column in her life, so she didn't learn, that way, that Greta was once Gertie Malinowsky."

"That fact wasn't too often mentioned by Greta's press agents, anyway," Michael said. "But you knew?"

"She told me her name. I recognized her the first time I saw a picture of Greta Mallon. Alan and I were married but didn't live quite happily ever after. I was a poor Army wife; I should not have tried camp-following. I began to find myself remembering Greta when I saw how much better other wives—women I would once have dismissed as common—managed than I did.

"So, you see, I was not mentally as unprepared for all this as you might expect," Viola said. "I

knew that something had happened to disturb Alan
seriously when he went south with Uncle Nate.
And Nate, who isn't discreet, mentioned their
having met Greta in some nightclub. Just boasting,
in a harmless way. Then Alan went south again in
a few weeks when I knew he didn't need to for any
reason connected with business.

"Just before that, I wanted to adopt a baby.
Alan wasn't enthusiastic but I thought he was
going to let me—until he'd made that first trip
to Los Angeles. Alan's a poor liar," his wife said.
"He insisted it would be less of a gamble to take
a child five or six years old instead of an infant."

"I don't know," Michael said reflectively, "why
we think we might deceive our wives with such
ridiculous rigmaroles. But we still will try."

Viola smiled briefly. "Then letters began coming for him from Los Angeles, addressed in this
third-grade handwriting. I did not decide that
Alan had found that he loved Greta, after all. I
finally asked myself, did she have a child by him?
And suddenly I knew—I just knew, that's all—
that she had! He flew south last week end. But
I don't read the newspapers. I didn't know Greta
was stopping over here for a few days on her way
to Reno.

"I'd thought of little else but her and Alan
and—everything, all last week. When on Friday

she passed me, leaving your shop, it was too much. I went home," Viola said rapidly, "found a newspaper and learned where she was staying. I called the St. Francis and was lucky enough to get her instead of a secretary. I asked if she remembered me, and if I could see her that afternoon."

"She agreed, but she deliberately chose an old hangout of hers as a meeting place, knowing it was the sort of joint you wouldn't like going into?" Michael said.

"I suppose that was it. She had something coming to her, didn't she? She was as much in command of the situation Friday as I had been six years before. She enjoyed herself. That doesn't matter. But I asked if she and Alan had had a child; told her that I knew he would want the child, and that I was willing to accept it and treat it as I would my own. I swore that I'd never remember that it was her child, but only that it was Alan's. . . ."

"And?" Michael said.

"She—laughed at me. She said I hadn't been so concerned for the child's welfare the last time we met. I can't blame her. She said she hadn't even had a doctor; only an old Italian midwife who would have wrecked her permanently if she hadn't come from good, husky peasant stock."

"And that was all, Mrs. Furness?"

"She insisted that I keep drinking and I couldn't handle the liquor and became a little incoherent. In the end, she laughed and said, 'I'll think it over.' And put me into a cab. I got home safely but hadn't pulled myself together when Mother Furness dropped in. She pronounced me disgustingly drunk and I had to tell Alan a fantastic story to account for that."

"So you didn't go to your mother-in-law's for dinner on Friday," Michael said. "Your husband called you at home around nine-thirty. But since a wife needn't testify against her husband, I suppose there's not much point in asking you when Alan got home?"

"But I don't know! Since he didn't take the car and walked home from his mother's, ordinarily I'd have expected him to get back about a quarter of eleven. But I know now that he left her earlier than usual because they disagreed. Only I pretended to be asleep when he came home and looked into my room, so he wouldn't know I'd been lying awake. And finally I got up in the dark and took a double dose of sleeping tablets."

She looked nervously toward the old French clock on the mantelpiece. "I know," Michael said. "It's approaching two and Alan will be arriving. He'll have a great deal to tell you and you'd better tell him what you've told me. I hope that the police need never know of your interview with Greta—but I make no rash promises."

4

Michael drove back to Fillmore, found a drugstore that was open, went into its telephone booth and was lucky enough to find Costello at home.

"On account of Hoyt's findin' excuses not to use me," Costello chuckled. "He had that dumb son-in-law of his tailing you last night. As if that jerk would have a chance with a guy that knows all the tricks. But Hoyt is plenty burned because Quinlan flopped so bad."

"Hoyt hasn't anyone on me this morning."

"Well, watch out tonight. I picked up what crumbs I could this morning, Michael. I wouldn't say Hoyt was getting anywhere very fast. Most of what he's dug up is negative. That rooming house where Greta first lived has burned down. . . ."

"Yes, I know that."

"And so far he hasn't found anyone still living around there that really knew her. They do remember Greta at the place where she had the housekeeping room later on. You said you never visited her there, but the dame that still runs the joint says you did. And you know you're easy to describe; you don't look like anyone else."

"But I never did. . . . Oh God!" Michael said disgustedly. "My memory isn't what it was. I did take her home from the shop one day when she had such a bad cold that she should have been in bed. Yes, and I went to a drugstore, bought whisky and aspirin, made her a whisky lemonade. . . . My boy scout training. Does the landlady remember that?"

"Yeah. Funny what dames like that remember though I guess you wasn't very polite to her. But it still ain't too bad—if you're getting somewheres. Are you?"

"Yes. I could give Hoyt a good deal to think about right now if I dared to go to him at once. No, of course you can't understand why I can't, and I can't tell you. But I may try to talk to Hoyt tonight. Tell me, have they decided what the murder weapon was?"

"The doc's my pal, you know. He insists there was two things used. The one that did the real damage was a heavy brass vase. You missed it; it was chucked under the couch. No fingerprints on it—wiped clean. But he says he don't know what made that bruise on her temple and a couple of the first wounds. He says those are odd; that whatever made them and the bruise—which may've stunned her to begin with—wasn't very large and that there's nothing in the apartment or that he can think of, offhand, that's the right shape."

"You people are strong on routine but short on imagination," Michael said. "It wasn't a blunt instrument; it was an object. . . . I suppose Hoyt is having the proper inquiries made in Hollywood?"

"Yeah, but it hasn't led anywheres. The guy she was going to divorce is in the clear. But this big executive Miss Jameson thought Greta might marry. . . ."

"Victor Borck?"

"That's the guy. He was in his hide-out in the mountains where there's no phone, so he didn't know about Greta until today. Then he flew up right away and he says him and Greta did intend to get married when she had her divorce. I talked to Jubal Chambers. He managed to interview Borck and he thinks Borck really is broken up about it. At least, he's taking a lot more interest in the way Hoyt is handling things than Hoyt likes. Then a couple of guys connected with Greta's studio came up. . . . Haven't you read the papers?"

"I'd rather my blood pressure remained normal."

"Oh, none of the papers has printed anything about you that you could . . ."

"They've printed nothing actionable, you mean," Michael said dryly.

"Not even that bad. They got plenty to write about so far."

"You wouldn't happen to know whether anyone called Greta's suite Friday night some time between nine-twenty-five and nine-forty, Costello?"

"No. I can try to find out. That must've been checked on but it's no cinch the phone operator would remember. They're awful rushed in a hotel like that, and God knows how many calls there was to Greta's suite altogether on Friday. And they haven't found out yet where she was between two and five that afternoon. . . ."

"I have. And I'm no longer interested in knowing what the Yellands were able to tell Hoyt so we'll skip that. I'll call you when things have shaped up a little more."

Michael dug a dime from his pocket and then stood looking irresolutely at the telephone. No, he decided finally, it's a little early to set the wheels turning out Hayward way. If Bella Voss's body is discovered this afternoon, the investigation would be well under way by tomorrow morning, and the murderer wouldn't like that. Oh Lord, things would be so much less complicated if it wasn't for this kidnapping angle. . . .

He considered trying to get in touch with Jubal Chambers and decided against that, too. He left the drugstore and drove past Hester Furness's home. Sam Weller's car was not parked anywhere near it, a circumstance which Mr. Dundas found pleasing. Someone, he reflected, had made a move.

Meanwhile, he realized that he had subsisted mainly on liquor and coffee for nearly two days. It was almost three o'clock; Sam might try to telephone him soon, but it was just as likely that Sam would not be able to get in touch with him for some time yet. Better eat while I can and want to, Michael thought, and headed for Fisherman's Wharf.

It was not until he got his billfold out and saw the eyes of the cashier at Fisherman's Grotto widen slightly, that he realized he still had the considerable amount of money with which he had hoped to buy information from Bella Voss. He was reluctant to continue carrying more than a thousand dollars on him. He did not care to risk losing it and also, while it was unlikely that he would be called on to explain why he had such a sum with him, unlikelier things had happened recently.

Since he had no safe at home, he'd better take it back to the shop and, he thought, as he got into his car again, if Sam's been trying to reach me, he'll have to keep on trying. . . .

Sam kept on trying and, after what seemed like several weeks or months, managed to raise his eyelids and keep them raised. He realized then that he hadn't been unconscious for very long and that he had been hit only with a ham-like hand. But that hand had been used expertly, at precisely the right place across his neck, under his ear.

He was lying on a couch in a small room off the big hall that he supposed would be called a gymnasium and Muscles was regarding him unapologetically and truculently.

"Okay, wise guy, what's your game? I don't like snoopers even before I find out they're private dicks," he said. "You were trespassing, anyway. . . ."

Mr. Weller discovered that, just now, necessity decidedly wasn't begetting invention. He said baldly, "I suppose Miss Furness took it on the lam as soon as you laid me out?"

"Miss Furness? Who's she?" Muscles said woodenly.

"Just a mirage, Mac; just a mirage." Sam wished fervently that Michael were here. Only Dundas knew how much he'd be willing to tell this guy to make him talk. Still, Sam was gratified to find that his mind was beginning to work again.

He said craftily, "Since you looked at my papers and know I'm a private op, you know I'm snooping because I'm paid to. And you ought to know who wouldn't approve of you being so well acquainted with this Catherine Furness you say you don't know. And who'd pay to have her followed and wants to know what your racket and your record and your real name are. . . ."

"My record's clean and my name's just Jack Edwards. 'Jacques' is better for business, that's all. People are more apt to remember it," Mr. Edwards said. "And I've never been anything worse than a wrestler and I'm not afraid of that old battle-ax."

"You ever meet her? Then wait till you have." Sam lighted a cigarette. "Look, doc, I got my living to make. I got to report to the old lady," Mr. Weller lied unblushingly. "She suspects her daughter's been seeing you on the sly. . . ."

"I wouldn't wonder," Jack Edwards said stolidly. "But that's okay by me. Catherine's of age and there's nothing her mother or brother can do."

"You mean—you two are serious?"

"We'll get married when—as soon as Catherine says the word. If that's all her mother wants to know, tell her so, with my regards."

"That won't please Mrs. Furness though she may be relieved to know you're on the up-and-up. She suspects the worst," Sam said plausibly. "Miss Furness may be past the age of consent but the old hellion would like to make trouble for you, bud. For instance, if she could prove you play around with your lady customers. . . ."

"The kind of lady customers I get, if a guy was on a desert island, even, he wouldn't make a pass at them," Mr. Edwards said gloomily. "And don't she know her own daughter better than that? Why, Catherine wouldn't ever even think of. . . ."

"Well, the gal was out late Friday night. Could you alibi yourself, Jack?"

"I don't know what Catherine would. . . ." Mr. Edwards frowned. His thinking, Sam decided, was as muscular as his development. "But I can prove that I was playing poker with a bunch of guys till midnight Friday."

"Yes, but the night was young then. What about after midnight?"

"I sleep here," Edwards said, indicating the couch on which Sam was sitting. "There wasn't anyone here with me Friday or last night either."

"You got a car?"

"I've got an old heap that'll run but. . . . Look, what're you driving at? What's me having a car got to do with whether me and Catherine ever slept together here, Friday night in particular? Maybe I better just not believe anything you say and if I decide I don't. . . ."

Sam had, for some time, been sitting on the edge of the couch. His legs were in working order again and he used them. He darted out of the room, across the gymnasium and down the stairway to the street. In high school he had been a better than average quarter-miler and Mr. Edwards did not come within striking distance of him.

He tumbled into his car, pressed his foot on the starter and drove off, muttering, "I'll be right home, Mom. But some day I'm going back and beat the living be-jesus out of that muscle-bound bastard. . . ."

It was past three o'clock. But, Sam thought, there's no use hurrying to report this to Michael over the telephone since Catherine's probably home by now and will stay there. I'd better talk to Michael in person and first, I might as well check on Egbert again. . . .

Egbert's landlady greeted Sam cordially but, "He hasn't come back at all, Mr.—uh—?" she said.

"Woodrow," Sam said. "Just call me Woody, lovely."

The landlady was forty-five and looked fifty but thought of herself as "over thirty." She smirked. "Oh—you! I'm surprised Mr. Knapp has a friend as nice as you are, Mr. Woodrow. People don't like him very much. . . ."

"Egbert," Sam said sadly, "is unfortunate."

"He must be," the landlady said sharply. "The police was here after you was, wanting to know where he was or might've went. I don't like that."

"I don't blame you. I've always made allowances for Eggie but if he's in bad with the police. . . .

Did you mention me? You didn't? That was sure nice of you. And I'll tell you what I'm going to do," Sam said winningly. "I'm coming back here in a few days to see if you've got a vacant room because if I stay in Frisco, I don't know anywhere I'd rather live than right here."

In the car again, he found a handkerchief and passed it over his forehead. "As soon have a female shark for a landlady," he muttered. "Goddam your soul, Egbert! If you'd stayed put, this case would be wound up by now because me and Dundas would've made you talk. . . ."

5

But no one would ever be able to make Egbert talk again. He lay face down in Michael's private office and he was extremely dead.

Mr. Dundas's reaction was not admirable. Had there been crockery available he probably would have smashed it against the nearest wall. He was shaken by that hot, hopeless and helpless frenzy that certain persons experience only when confronted with the undeniable perversity of inanimate objects. And as an object, Egbert was very inanimate. . . .

Still, in a very few minutes, Michael was going through the proper motions. He went through Egbert's pockets and found duplicate keys to the front door of the shop, as well as one that would unlock the door to this office.

"Perhaps," he told himself, "when I'm in my dotage I will finally have learned not to underestimate all those whom I heartily detest. . . ."

However, the two desk drawers where he kept some rather interesting records had not been opened. He let Egbert's body fall back onto the floor in what he thought was exactly the position it had been in when he had discovered it. Egbert had been shot neatly through the back, but the bleeding had been mainly internal and his lamentable sport jacket had absorbed very nearly all of it.

There was no gun in the office or anywhere on the lower floor. Having made sure of that, Michael delved into the wastepaper basket that was only a foot or two away from his desk and Egbert's body. He found a greasy, empty paper bag, put it back where he'd found it and then stood for an instant looking at it with a deep furrow between his straight, black eyebrows.

His office was at the back of the building and had an outside door that opened onto an alley used by trucks. There was a spring lock on the door. Egbert had had no key to it but, once in the building, he could have admitted anyone who wished to enter from the alley. Michael made

certain that the lock was in the proper position
and that it snapped shut behind him as he stepped
into the alley. Then he headed unobtrusively
toward his car which he had parked several blocks
away from the shop. . . .

"Christ Almighty!" said Sam Weller. "We just
don't live right. . . ."

"We?" Michael said. "I'd advise you to get back
to Los Angeles as soon as possible. . . ."

"You got rocks in your head?" Sam said rudely.
"Look, I parked the car four blocks away so it
wouldn't be connected with you and waited till
I saw you drive into this street your house is on,
and then sneaked up here. . . ."

"You catch on quick, and you handled Jack
Edwards admirably. If you want to stay in this
stinking racket, you should do well. You've done
nobly and I've done what I could but. . . ."

Michael got up, poured himself another drink
and ran his hand through his hair in what even
Sam realized was an uncharacteristic, because it
was so obviously an uncontrolled, gesture.

"I'm to blame," he said quickly. "I should not
lightly dis'regard vermin like Egbert. Of course
he would have duplicates made of his keys in case
I suddenly took away those I gave him. If nothing else had come up, he would have tried to gain

access to my private papers on the principle that the more you know, the more likely you are to be financially solvent at all times."

"I guess you do have to be discreet in a business like yours, Mac."

"You'll never know, bud," Michael said with a fleeting grin. "And I take my hat off to Egbert. I can't think of any better place to have a private chat with someone than Gisele's on a Sunday. A special patrolman makes the rounds every hour—after seven P.M. But until then. . . ."

"That neighborhood would be dead as ditch water on Sundays? Yes, and whoever killed Egbert would like that for a meeting place, too. Nice and private and no one could hear a shot fired in there. When do you think he was killed?"

"This morning. I'd guess the appointment wasn't for any set time, that Egbert went there early, to wait. And to improve the shining hour by seeing if he couldn't look through my private records. He didn't manage to open the two drawers he would have been most interested in. I don't think he could have. Those locks are rather special."

"Any signs he'd tried, with a hairpin, chisel or whatever?" Sam asked.

"None. What time did you get to his rooming house?"

"Just about nine. But he'd been gone from there long enough to have had breakfast and left the joint before I got there," Sam said. "So I suppose he could have gotten to Gisele's by nine—but not earlier."

"Yes. Viola called me here at about a quarter of nine; Alan at nine. . . ."

"And I called you back about nine-forty. I know this guy Hoyt wouldn't accept my evidence without question, but still there's only half an hour or so unaccounted for there."

"I could have done it in that time, using my car," Michael said impersonally. "Of course I did not take the car out, but people sleep late on Sundays and those who have a view of our garage never rise until noon. And I did tell Egbert that I'd break his goddam neck if he gave me any further trouble. I've no doubt he passed that threat on to the police. However, proving that I didn't kill him is a secondary problem just now. . . ."

"Is it? Look, pal, don't you realize you've gotten yourself into a prize jackpot? You're taking it very calmly and that's okay but just the same. . . ."

"But just the same, Mr. Weller, it does no good to wring your hands and scream to high Heaven that there ain't no justice and you're a most unfortunate man! You've knocked about a bit, which means that you've *been* knocked about, too. And when you have been, you learn that Heaven helps him who helps himself and the devil take the hindmost—or you don't survive!"

Michael had spoken with more feeling and vehemence than Sam would have supposed him capable of. Michael seemed to feel, himself, that he had stepped out of character and when he went on, he dropped his voice to a deliberate monotone.

"I know I've never in my life been in quite such a tight spot. And the trouble is that now I have so much to lose where, fifteen or even ten years ago, it wouldn't have mattered so much. Frankly, when I found Egbert's body in my office, I wanted to go out and get stinking drunk and wait for the axe to fall. But I've never in my life let anybody kick me around and I'm damned if I'll start now! Well. . . . What I dislike most is being saddled with Egbert's unwholesome cadaver. There it rests in my private office where, if I don't officially discover it myself tomorrow morning, Fanchon certainly will by ten o'clock."

"The kind of thing you've been trying to avoid all along?" Sam said tentatively.

"Yes. I couldn't, if I tried, conjure up a situation that would be more productive of ruinous

publicity than this one. It will give Hoyt an opportunity to tear Gisele's apart. . . ."

"Well, why don't we move Egbert? He won't
know the difference," Sam said casually.

"That can't be done until after dark," Michael
said, as casually. "And there's a snag. When we
hand the murderer over to Hoyt, said murderer may
very well remark that it's a little odd that Egbert,
having died in my office, didn't remain there."

"Hoyt wouldn't overlook that? Hell, give me a
guy with a sense of humor. Well, it's a GFU, all
right, but when you decide what's to be done, I'll
go along with you, doc. Meanwhile, it looks to
me like any of this gang had some spare time this
morning."

"You're good at timetables, aren't you?"

"Am I? Well, some guys remember phone numbers. But Alan had from the time he called you
until he went to church with Ma. Louis Hilton
lives alone. He was free till you called on him
after ten. Viola may have been on her own this
morning, too . . ."

"Yes. We'd have to check with her father and
the old servant who let me in," Michael said, "and
they'd lie if they thought it necessary."

"That was quite a yarn Viola told you. Do you
think it's true?"

Michael frowned. "You'd have been inclined to believe Viola if she, instead of myself, had told you her story. But we've only her word for it that she urged Greta to hand her child over to Alan. She might have begged Greta not to do that."

"That's what I was thinking. Well, as for Ma Furness, Cathie and Brother Nathan, I'll bet they have breakfast by eight even on Sundays."

"Yes, I fancy they would."

"And after that, till church time or till Alan got to his mother's place, which time will have to be checked on—I don't suppose the three of them sat around together holding hands," Sam said. "And when you think of Mrs. Furness, you always have to remember her brother's under her thumb and might be persuaded to do odd jobs for her that she couldn't manage herself."

"I'm remembering it. And that Catherine also has a possible handy man on tap—Jack Edwards. Apparently he could not have killed Greta, but he could have gone to Hayward and Bella Voss's place for Catherine. How intelligent do you think he is?"

"Hard to tell. He was smart enough to tell Cathie to keep on talking while he sneaked out a door from the gymnasium into the hall and took me from the rear. But he certainly isn't living high on what he makes from that crummy health institute. Even with just her measly three grand or so income, Catherine'd be a help to him. But maybe they had a lot more ambitious plans."

"Alan hinted that Catherine might have some plan or scheme in mind, of which he would not approve," Michael agreed.

"Well, before we get back to Catherine and what she said to her Jackie boy—which needs a lot of explaining—there's something I wanted to ask. Egbert bought some sandwiches and you found the bag you thought they were in—empty. . . ."

"Yes. That's one reason I think that Egbert didn't know at exactly what time his client would arrive. Six will get you ten that he expected to have to wait until after noon. . . ."

"And so he took his lunch with him? But you're pretty sure he wasn't killed later than—say, eleven?"

"Yes. Rigor was pretty well advanced though not complete. I found his body around four o'clock. A fair figure for complete rigor is six to nine hours."

"So he was killed before lunch—but the sandwiches seem to have been eaten?"

"I know. A post-mortem will tell whether Egbert did eat those sandwiches for a mid-morning snack. But I suspect that the murderer took those sandwiches away, leaving the greasy bag behind deliberately. Doesn't that little touch seem characteristic, Sam?"

"Maybe, since it bothers me. But I don't know or remember. . . ."

"Bella Voss's bed, neatly turned down and apparently unslept in, though she was in her nightgown, and I very much doubt that it was her habit to wait until. . . . Blast! I suppose that will be Alan Furness," Michael said and went to answer the telephone.

It was Jubal Chambers. "Look, Michael, that guy Borck expressed an interest in you. I think he might like to talk to you—"

"I'd been thinking I'd like to talk to him. But I didn't know if he'd see me."

"Oh, he will. He's a good egg," Jubal said. "Who knows, he might help you. And boy, if something isn't done to divert Hoyt, you're going to need help! I'll drop by to see you at the shop tomorrow—"

Michael told Sam what Jubal had said, adding, "Jubal's the best police reporter in the city though he resembles a dissolute cherub and would be insulted if you called him a journalist. But I'd trust him with anything but my liquor. If we're to see Borck tonight, I won't wait for Alan to call me." He turned back to the telephone. . . .

"I've talked to Viola," Alan's voice said, "and if I had known last night. . . ."

"If I'd told you that I knew that Viola had seen Greta, Friday afternoon, what difference would it have made?" Michael said impatiently. "Knowing that would not have improved your position."

"No," Alan said stiffly, "that would have made me even more anxious to co-operate with you, but. . . ."

"Do you know, I was under the impression that it was Mr. Weller and I who consented to a little co-operation; that the choice didn't lie with you."

"Oh, if you must quibble. . . . Nevertheless, I would not have allowed you a free hand with my wife."

"Therefore, I did not add to your problems by telling you that she'd already agreed to talk to me today," Michael said pleasantly. "She told you the whole story?"

"Yes, and I. . . . Well, I should have known that she would guess that I was under some mental strain these past few months. But I had no idea that she. . . ."

"Telephone conversations are not satisfactory," Michael broke in. "Are you at home? And can you ask your sister to be there, too, in half an hour?"

"Cathie? She said she'd drop by around six, and it's that now. But why. . . ."

"We must talk to her and it would be less difficult to do so at your home than at your mother's.
We'll be over in half an hour."

Michael broke the connection and then dialed
the Moffatt hotel and asked for Mr. Borck. Mr.
Borck answered his own telephone, in a deep,
pleasant voice with only a trace of accent.

"Yes, I had been wishing to talk to you, Mr.
Dundas. My poor Greta mentioned you and. . . ."

"And Inspector Hoyt has mentioned me, too—
unflatteringly?"

"The Inspector is a person of limited intelligence," Borck said casually. "I do not care to
confide in him. I have one very good reason for
wanting to meet you . . ."

"I think I know what it is," Michael said. "But is
there more than one reason why you want to see me?"

"There is—something I might tell to a person
that I believed would make use of it. The Inspector's mind is very inelastic. How soon can you be
here? Or, I will come to you . . ."

"No. And I'm afraid I can't promise to be at
your hotel much before eight o'clock."

"That will do very well. I will get some food in
the meantime. The room number is 709. You will
come up without inquiring at the desk. . . ."

Michael went out to the kitchen to find Sam
polishing off a plate of assorted cold cuts, a well-

aged slab of French bread and some decomposed cheese.

"Be right with you, pal. This reminds me. . . ." He indicated the cheese. . . . "what about Bella Voss? Not that it could matter to her."

"On our way to Alan Furness's, we'll stop at some pay telephone and I'll call the Oakland police. . . ."

"Oakland?"

"I've no idea how efficient the Hayward police force is, but I suspect the worst. I'll say that I suspect there's been foul play. . . ."

"Disguising your voice?" Sam said doubtfully.

"Do you think I can't?"

"Well, you've got a certain way of talking. . . ."

"Who hasn't? I can do a fair imitation of a South-of-Market tough, *amigo*. Of course they'll think, in Oakland, that I'm a crackpot but eventually someone will go out to Bella Voss's and look around. I'd rather they didn't do that too quickly. If you've finished that disgusting cheese—which I supposed only my wife was hardy enough to eat— let's be on our way. . . ."

Viola and Catherine were having Sunday evening tea but Alan, Sam noted at once, was drinking a very stiff whisky and soda. Catherine had the Spode teapot in her hand when they entered.

She saw Sam and splashed hot tea over the table in front of her before she managed to lower the pot. She stared at Mr. Weller and the harsh, healthy color faded from her cheeks. She turned on Alan:

"So you set someone to following me! You can't let me live my own life even if I am almost thirty! You've had everything and I've never had anything—not anything at all! You're as much of a tyrant as Mamma is, except that you're polite. Just because Papa was fool enough to leave all his money to you for a baby that didn't live. . . ."

Viola flinched, put her hands down on the arms of her chair and dug her pale fingers into the upholstery. Alan said, "Catherine! For God's sake. . . ."

"I don't care!" Catherine said childishly. "I don't care! I could have children though they wouldn't be Furnesses. I could. . . . Oh, I'm sorry for you and Viola, but you're sorry for yourselves and nobody else. And now you have all Papa's money to do what you like with and you think that means you can run my life, too. . . ."

She began to cry. The tears, since she did not produce a handkerchief or even raise a hand to wipe them away, made for an effect of nakedness.

"All right, I'm going to marry Jack Edwards and you and Mamma and everyone else will say he's unsuitable. But we love each other and we like the same things. He has a better war record than you have, big brother! He was wounded at Tarawa, so badly that he had to be discharged. He'd call you a 'typewriter commando. . . .'

"Yes, and I want the money you promised me!" Catherine said angrily. "I'll marry Jack regardless but I've a right to that much of Papa's money. We can get a place in Arizona for fifty thousand and make it into a popular health resort if we have capital enough. . . ."

"Cathie, you don't—don't seriously mean that you intend to. . . ." Viola began. Catherine looked at her and laughed unpleasantly.

"Why not? I can play golf and tennis and swim and ride better than most people. I like people when I'm allowed to; I'm efficient, a good house-keeper—or would be if I could take full charge of an establishment—and I never get tired. I'd love it and it's Jack's dream. But Alan would call it im-practical and not genteel, so he puts a detective to trailing me. . . ."

"So you stuck around while the boy friend went through my pockets, babe?" Sam asked.

"Yes, but. . . . He didn't mean to hit you so hard. He's so strong and he gets excited and after all, you were spying on us and. . . ."

"Catherine! I'd heard rumors that you were interested in some—some good-looking rough-neck that you'd met on a golf course. But I did

not," Alan said distinctly, "engage anyone to spy
on you. This is simply a trick that. . . ."

"Don't let fraternal feeling run away with your
common sense, Mr. Furness," Michael advised.
"Sam overheard some of your sister's conversation
with Mr. Edwards. The question is, to what extent
have you confided in your family?"

"I don't. . . ." Alan frowned, stopped and
then went on slowly, "I've told Viola everything.
After receiving that—that note, when I went to
my mother's this morning, I. . . ."

"What time was that?" Sam said.

"I don't. . . . It was about a quarter of eleven.
Mother and Cathie were not quite ready to start
for church but Uncle Nathan was downstairs. On
an impulse, I showed him that note and explained
what it meant. . . . That is, I told him that I knew
that Greta had a son, my son. . . ."

He could not keep his eyes from turning toward Viola but she was looking straight ahead.
Alan flushed painfully and continued, "And that
I'd been trying to persuade Greta to give the boy
up to—to us but that someone got to Greta and
the boy before I did. Does that. . . . Is that sufficiently clear?"

"Yes. I think I know what you didn't tell and
that was very wise of you," Michael said. "Your

uncle Nathan was, of course, confounded with amazement?"

"He swore he'd never suspected that Greta had had a child," Alan said briefly.

"Naturally. Then he passed the word on to Louis Hilton as quickly as possible. You expected that? And. . . ."

"I heard what Alan told Uncle Nate," Catherine said defiantly. "I listen at doors. Since I'm supposed to be still a *jeune fille,* it's the only way if I want to know what's going on. Then, after lunch, Alan went into a huddle with Mamma. I'd said I had a headache and was going to lie down. I didn't listen long that time. I slipped out the back way and got my car and went to talk to Jack. But I'd known about Alan and Gertie Malinowsky though not that she'd had a baby. . . ."

"If you heard so much, that would explain your remarks to Mr. Edwards—more or less," Michael said. "Though those remarks were a trifle ambiguous and. . . ."

He paused, abruptly, because Mrs. Furness had, even more abruptly, entered the room.

6

Hester Furness moved to the center of the room in somewhat the fashion of an old-time Shakespearean tragedy queen coming downstage to go into her big speech, while her brother, lagging behind her, was a very reluctant spear-bearer.

"I also listen at doors when I think it is necessary," she said in her crisp, high-pitched voice. "In this case it was most illuminating. I'd heard, Catherine, that you've been seen with some uncouth male specimen but I chose to ignore that. I supposed that even you, muddle-headed as you are, would realize that a man like that could be interested only in your money. I thought that such a lesson could be quite beneficial and that as long as you were reasonably discreet, I would not interfere. But it seems that I underestimated even your capacity for completely idiotic behavior."

For just an instant Catherine sagged a little, like, Sam Weller thought, one of these plump rubber figures that has developed a slow leak. Then she straightened her shoulders and said composedly, "It won't do any good to call names, Mamma. Jack and I understand each other and you have nothing whatever to say about what I do with my life and what money I have. . . ."

"Dear me, I had no idea that you'd reached such a degree of infatuation," Mrs. Furness said cuttingly. "Do you suppose I'll stand by and see my daughter make a laughingstock of herself and her family? If you've been indiscreet, the fellow will have to be paid off. I presume his services won't come too high."

Catherine half rose from her chair and then sank back, her face blotched with ugly patches of white. "Oh," she whispered, "if I could only—if just once I could really hurt you—could. . . ."

"Matricide, in some circumstances, is not such a very unnatural crime, do you think?" Michael drawled.

Hester Furness turned on him. "Oh yes—the dressmaker. Well, perhaps I should beg your pardon for allowing my natural solicitude for my daughter to cause me to forget that there are strangers present. But I should like to know, sir, what you and this person"—a contemptuous thumb disposed of Sam—"are doing here?"

"And I am glad to tell you," Michael said courteously. "But it would save your valuable time if I knew how much I must explain. You did know about your son's affair with Gertie Malinowsky?"

"Certainly. Naturally my dear friends acquainted me with any rumors they heard regarding Alan's little fling. I did not care to seem to attach undue importance to the matter by letting him know that I was aware of it. But Nathan has never been able to keep a secret from me."

"But Lanny, I didn't know the—the rest of it," Nathan bleated. "If I had—well, my dear boy, I am not inhumane and I know that you aren't and so I would certainly have. . . ."

"Made an unnecessary fuss about nothing," Mrs. Furness snapped. "And so would my husband since he was a softhearted fool. I suspected the girl had had a child. My old servant, Millie, had to admit that the girl turned up at my home one day, wanting to see Alan, Mr. Furness, or myself, and that Viola had talked to her. . . . I wouldn't have supposed that Viola would have been so sensible or capable of so much decision," she added with a faint accent of surprise.

"But the Malinowsky girl would have gotten short shrift from me. Gracious Heaven, why should one take her word for it that her brat was Alan's child? And if it was—well. . . ." She shrugged. "Once she'd embarked on a Hollywood career, she couldn't demand anything of us. She was in no position then to risk having her unsavory past made public. Is there anything else you think you must know, Mr. Dundas?"

"That's enough to go on. It's very simple. . . ."

You mean, Sam Weller thought, that you're going to try to make it sound simple.

"Oddly enough, Greta also felt a natural solicitude for her child, which she'd kept almost too well hidden—the child, that is. Just before she was killed she asked me to remember the name,

Bella Voss. I discovered that Bella was a woman who looked after stray children. Being, as Mr. Ridley so nicely puts it, not inhumane, I thought someone should contact the Voss woman and arrange for the child's future care. But when I got to her home she was—gone, and so was the child."

"I was with him. We'd joined forces by then," Sam said. "But I got into this because Mr. Furness hired me to tail Greta Mallon. He wanted to find out where this kid was though he didn't tell me so. . . ."

Mrs. Furness scrutinized him deliberately through an invisible lorgnette. Mr. Weller returned her look with interest and grinned impudently.

"No, ma'am, you can't buy me off. And if you don't believe that I don't have my price, let's say Mr. Dundas will top any figure you could name."

"Yes," Michael said, "I will. Well, Bella Voss had written to your son because she hoped to get money from him. He didn't get her letter as soon as she supposed he would. . . ."

"Oh," Catherine said, "was it *that* letter?"

"Yes. But Bella had already bought her train ticket to Chicago," Michael said speciously. "And Mr. Furness reached her place a little too late, but in time to run into Mr. Weller and myself. Then, this morning he had a letter warning him not to talk or act hastily if he ever wants to see his son. . . ."

"Oh, that absurd communication!" Hester Furness said. "Really, Alan, I thought that you were at least half my son, but apparently you resemble your father. You have the same sort of sentimental weakness that he called conscience. But at least he was reasonably shrewd. If you couldn't rest until you knew where this Malinowsky woman's son was, why put yourself in the power of a hired detective. . . ."

"I suppose, Mother, because I've been brought up to pay others to do difficult or disagreeable tasks for me," Alan said pleasantly.

"Don't be facetious. What's done is done. But so far as that ridiculous letter is concerned . . . Gracious Heaven, boy, you surely don't take it seriously? No one's going to harm that bastard brat. Someone knows a little too much and wants to get money from you. Louis Hilton is behind this. . . ."

"Oh, come now, Hester dear," Nathan said timorously. "I know you've never really liked Louis but he is a prince of a good fellow and. . . ."

"And Zachary didn't leave him as much money as he had hoped for; he has fifty thousand dollars which won't last long at the rate he's going. I have no illusions about Louis. . . ."

"But you have about Uncle Nate, haven't you, Mamma?" Catherine said sweetly. "And you could say the same things about him and money that you have about Louis, you know. . . ."

"Thank you, babe," said Mr. Hilton, shambling into the room. "And greetings and salutations, Hester. Is this a private dog-fight or can anyone get into it?"

Nathan managed somehow to smile, to shake his head warningly and say, "Tsk-tsk!" at one and the same time. Louis grinned and continued, "I wish I had thought up such a good get-rich-quick scheme. Lanny wouldn't miss fifty grand or so. But of course, Hester, you're made of stern stuff and you don't give a good goddam what happens to what you so charmingly refer to as a bastard brat, do you?"

Hester turned so that he had a view only of her very flat, straight back. "Alan," she said, "you've been extremely foolish. Of course Viola rather likes to think of herself as a long-suffering wife, taking your child by another woman into your home. . . ."

"Mother Furness," Viola said unexpectedly. "I want Alan to be happy, that's all. You wouldn't understand that."

Mrs. Furness ignored her. "But my dear boy, think of the consequences of such an action on your part! It would be a nine-day scandal. Come, let's be sensible and forget it and. . . ."

"*State zitt'!*" said Mr. Dundas abruptly. "*Punto en boca!*"

The sound was like that made by an angry cat. He's ready to fly into pieces, Sam reflected, and no wonder. If Egbert's body was lying in my private office, I don't think I'd have guts enough to pull a bluff the way he's been doing

"That is, would you mind shutting your trap, madame?" Michael said. "You are not only a very rude, elderly female with an oddly exaggerated idea of your own importance but you are also extremely tiresome. Which is not at all important. The important thing is that you are all together here and I can say this. . . .

"I've been influenced by what Mrs. Furness calls that absurd communication that Mr. Furness received this morning. I don't want any harm to come to Greta's son and I agree with Mr. Hilton that Mr. Furness can afford to pay ransom. I leave it to him to guarantee immunity to a kidnapper—who might be any one of you here. But you'd better make your demand for ransom quickly because by tomorrow night, I will have to tell the police what I know. And now I will leave you to the doubtful pleasures of a family council. Are you coming, Sam?"

7

Celebrity hunters, meeting the great Victor Borck, were always gratified to find him "so unassuming, so—so almost simple." Few of them reflected that, as simplicity entails a disregard of the non-essentials that are extremely important to most people, a man needs to be very self-confident and ruthlessly aware of what it is that he wants from life, to achieve simplicity.

Now Mr. Borck, having looked Michael over openly and for as long as he pleased, shook his massive, ugly head and said briefly, "No."

"No," Michael agreed. "While it is possible that Greta and I might have produced a fair-haired child, considering how very dark I am and she was, it's extremely unlikely."

"I did not think it was likely. She said nothing regarding you to make me think that it was. But you had known her before she came to Hollywood and I could not ignore that. I find myself over the horns of a dilemma. I do not want to make public anything that will smirch Greta's memory. But she had done her best for the child; she wanted to do better for him— more than anything else, she wanted that. . . ."

"But her wartime husband wouldn't help her?"

"How did you know that, Mr. Dundas?"

"Greta said that she and young Ainslee didn't see eye to eye about more than one thing, and that one of those things was something that was rather important to her, which was one reason why she was divorcing him."

"Of course Greta did not at all understand young Ainslee," Borck said. "The war delayed somewhat his becoming the stuffed shirt that he too soon will be. The poor child thought she'd only to urge him to allow her to adopt a child that she'd become interested in and that he would agree at once and ask no questions. She did not tell him the truth, however. She was shrewd and always proceeded carefully.

"With us, it was different. I understood Greta, not because she was a typical Hollywood product, but because she was not. She would never have been an actress; she was only a personality. She did not even like acting. She worked and slaved at it because she did value the rewards of being a star: things that many people take for granted—just the means of being always clean without taking too much effort and will power to keep yourself so; food and good clothes and a comfortable bed. . . . I'm the son of a Czech peasant. Greta's father was a Polish peasant. We knew."

"I think your marriage might have been a very successful one," Michael said.

"It would have been. Once we knew each other, we did not pretend. She was to give me children. She wished to. In return she would have had all that I could give her. I was prepared to adopt her son. There would have been talk," Borck said simply, "but I do not regard talk. Her son did not resemble her, so many people would have thought he might be my son."

"She showed you his pictures?"

"Yes, I saw all of them, from the time when he was a small baby to the last one, labeled 'Stephen, five years and three months old.' It was a pathetic little collection she had—the snapshots and letters from a woman who had charge of Stephen. . . ."

"And a baby shoe cast in bronze," Michael said, looking not at Victor Borck but at Sam.

"Yes, the boy's shoe that he had worn at three years. But how did you know? No one else seems to have guessed what might have been in that mysterious box that she kept always with her, took to her final rendezvous and which is missing now. . . ."

"It was only a guess," Michael said.

Mr. Weller grinned at him, came to attention and snapped off a salute. "You win, Mac." Then, "Jeez! Was that what stunned her?"

"I'm afraid so. The police surgeon couldn't think what might have made the bruise on her temple." Michael turned back to Borck. "But Greta didn't take you entirely into her confidence?"

"No. She was instinctively cautious and had carried on alone for so long. It was only last, month that she confided in me; showed me the boy's pictures. She didn't tell me who the father was or the name of the woman who looked after the child. Only that some new arrangement must be made. The boy was going on six. She meant to see him on her way to Reno. She was counting the hours until then. She knew that she could count on me for aid, and I made that known in the right quarters. I hinted that it would be as well if she was allowed to follow her own wishes, not those of her publicity department, on this trip of hers. But I did suggest the boy's father might have to be considered. And Greta said, yes, it seemed that he must be."

"And you let it go at that?" Michael said.

"Oh, I would give much now if I had not! But I thought that Greta was capable of seeing it through and she preferred that. We would not have married at once after her divorce; we meant to wait several months."

"I see. What else was it you had to tell me?"

"Someone had blackmailed Greta," Borck said. "Of course the woman who cared for the boy made her pay more and more as she was able to.

I told Greta that if necessary, I would handle the woman; would pay her off once and for all. But Greta believed she could arrange that, too. This other was, she said, a matter of chicken feed. The party concerned referred to the sums she gave him as temporary loans. Yes, it was a man. . . ."

Borck frowned. "I am trying to remember how she came to mention that. I think it was that she said she expected the woman who cared for the boy to make her pay through the nose, as they say, but had been surprised to be approached by this other person."

"Recently?" Michael asked.

"Within the last six months. And only once or twice and, as I have said, the sums involved were not large. That was all she told me but there was a look in her eye that boded no good for that gentleman, eventually."

"I have been wondering," Michael said with apparent irrelevance, "who suggested that she try to get taken on as a model at Gisele's in 1941. Because I doubt that at that stage of her education she'd have known that Gisele's existed."

"Ah yes, I see what you mean. Well, she never told me who suggested she might be a good model, Mr. Dundas. I am sorry I cannot help you and I had hoped that you might help me. . . ."

"You needn't concern yourself about Greta's son, Mr. Borck. There's nothing you can do to help."

"So? The father, then, is finally concerned for his son's welfare? Don't trouble to answer. That is as it should be. I will be here until tomorrow night," Borck said. "Or at least until the authorities here permit me to take Greta back to Hollywood. . . ."

"For a Hollywood state funeral?" Michael said sardonically. Borck grimaced. "I think Greta would have liked that," he said. "Meanwhile I will be here, at your service. . . ."

"Nice guy," Sam commented as they got into Michael's car again. "But he wasn't much help."

"Oh, wasn't he? He told us one thing that's very important. But I wonder—what reason could have been given that would have satisfied. . . ."

Sam waited but when Michael did not go on, he said unkindly, "Okay, Master-Mind. But there's still Eggie, you know."

"Yes, damn you. And Egbert. It's *time* that I need, Mr. Weller."

"Sure. Well, you delivered your ultimatum to the Furness gang to try to speed things up, didn't you?"

"Yes, but ransom can't be collected in broad daylight. And if a ransom note were concocted and delivered today, it's still Sunday. . . ."

"And you can't get a wad of folding-money to-gether on short notice on a Sunday? I thought of that. Look, doc, suppose that gang decides to stick together and double cross you? Alan could guarantee the kidnaper immunity; settle the thing out of court and then deny everything. . . ."

"He might try that if he thought he could swing it. But Hoyt's an experienced cop. He wouldn't ignore the evidence that I can give him, though he would take an unconscionable long time verifying it. Bella Voss's death is going to be investigated; Alan knows that. And we can see to it that his wife is grilled by the police, and he'd do a great deal to avoid that. I'm willing to leave the Furness tribe to stew in their own juices for a while. Egbert's the monkey wrench in the works just now."

"Well, what do we do about Egbert, then?"

"Give me time to think." Michael stopped his car in its own garage. "Couldn't you do with some sleep while the sector is quiet? It's only nine; we can't make a move for several hours. I'll show you to the guest room. . . ."

When Sam woke it was because a large gray cat had settled itself comfortably on his stomach. He had left the guest room door ajar and he could hear Michael talking over the telephone in his own bedroom across the hall.

"I know it is late, Miss Jameson. . . . Yes, and I know that you don't trust me. But Mr. Borck does and I can appeal to him if you. . . . Thank you. I only want to know if there is a camera in Greta's luggage. . . . Oh? You bought it for her? A gift for a friend? That's all I wanted to know. Good night. . . ."

"Hey, cat! Take your claws out of my belly," Sam said loudly. Which, as he intended, brought Michael to the guest room door. "Awake? I see you've met Mehitabel. He . . ."

"Mehitabel? He?"

"Yes. He adopted us some years ago and Valerie—my wife—named him without first determining his sex. Would you like a drink?"

"I never refused yet."

"Good. And I hope you're not fussy about what you drink. We're going to a nightclub—The Black Sunflower."

"The black—I never saw a black sunflower."

"Nor have I—growing. But you'll see any number of them tonight. However, if you manage to down enough of their liquor, you won't mind. You'll be seeing purple snakes and cerise elephants, too."

"What's wrong with their liquor?"

"I believe that they flavor it with fusel oil," Michael said judicially. "I can't think, offhand, of any bar that has a more unsavory reputation than The Black Sunflower. We'll take my car; I've already driven it from the garage. So bring your equipment with you and come along, if you don't mind. . . ."

Some six or seven minutes later, as Michael turned from Jones into Union, Sam observed mildly, "I think we're being followed, Mac."

"I hope so. I'm counting on that though I'll try to make it look difficult by going the long way round. And, oh Lord, let it be Hoyt himself who is tailing us tonight. . . ."

PART FIVE

1

The Black Sunflower was one bright patch on a block of small, nondescript factories, warehouses and dingy flats.

It was not far from the wide street that Michael had told Sam was Columbus Avenue and near enough to the waterfront to be enveloped in a fine aroma of fish, oil, and salt water.

Michael parked across the street from the club; said to Sam, "Keep your head down," and waited. In a few minutes a car went past them, rather slowly but without stopping. Michael nodded.

"Hoyt, I think, and alone which is not sensible of him, though if I'd shaken him off, he wouldn't want anyone to witness that. He'll be back and I hope he'll follow us into the club. . . ."

"If he does, what does he look like?" Sam asked, as they crossed the street.

"A little as if he should have 'sacred to the memory of' engraved on his forehead. Otherwise, as if he were just on the point of sinking his teeth into Eliza."

"Bloodhound, hunh? Well, if. . . . Jeez!" said Mr. Weller protestingly as they stepped from a small, murky lobby into the club proper.

As Michael had promised, there were black sunflowers growing where sunflowers had never grown before. They were painted on the ceiling, stenciled on the tablecloths, climbing up the walls. There were enormous baskets of paper sunflowers in every corner and a vase of them on every table.

All but one of the booths along one wall were occupied. There were a good many vacant tables in the center of the room though every stool at the bar was taken. A small girl, violently blonde, with a moist, pouting mouth, was clinging tenaciously to her perch at the end of the bar nearest Sam and Michael.

As they edged closer, the bartender was saying, "Look, sister, I told you to scram! All the way back to that tank town you come from. We don't want dames like you hanging around. . . ."

"I paid for my drink," the girl said sullenly.

The bartender, who looked like a prize fighter who had not retired from the ring quite soon enough, made a derisive noise. "And you've finished it. Either order another and pay up, or . . ."

"Give the lady whatever she wants," Michael said. And to Sam, "Grab that vacant booth, will you? I'll be with you in a minute. . . ."

Sam slid into the booth with a firm, "Don't bother, bud, this suits me fine," for the headwaiter. He watched Mr. Dundas, at first disapprovingly and then speculatively.

He muttered, "Hell, he wouldn't dare. Or— would he?"

The girl was listening to whatever Michael had to say, frowning as she gulped down her drink. Michael signaled to the bartender. He scowled but slapped another glass down in front of the girl. She smiled doubtfully; finally laughed. Michael's hand slid into his pocket; then Sam lost sight of him for several minutes as four sailors, already well under the influence, rolled into the place.

They took over a large, centrally located table and shouted for beer. On their heels came a leathery Marine sergeant with his lady of the evening. The lady was finding it difficult to steer a straight course. She collided with a table and sat down. The fact that there was a chair beneath her when she did so, was incidental.

The headwaiter looked unhappy. The lady's shoulders were only six inches removed from those of one of the sailors. He suggested that she and the sergeant would be more comfortable at another table. The lady said sleepily, "Like it here."

The Marine said, "You heard her, she likes it here. What do you do to get waited on in this dump?"

The headwaiter beckoned imperatively to an underling and retreated with a glance toward the bar clock which said eleven-forty-five. Michael, passing the two tables on his way to join Sam, regarded their occupants pensively over the highballs he was carrying.

"Well?" Sam said as Michael sat down opposite him. He sampled his drink, shuddered and pushed it aside.

"I've done what I can with the material at hand. Now it's up to. . . . Here he is!"

Inspector Hoyt had the offended look of a man confronted with a very bad smell and making no effort to ignore it. But he tramped unhurriedly past the bar; waved the headwaiter aside and chose a corner table from which he could survey the entire room.

"*Sangre de Cristo!*" Michael murmured. "What a beautiful background! That gargantuan basket of black sunflowers behind and to one side of him. . . ."

"Strictly 4.0," Sam said stolidly. He was emptying his pockets under cover of the table. "Leave it to me, pal. . . ."

"I will. But get the hell out of here, whatever happens. I'll try to meet you at the car, but don't wait more than five minutes for me there. That's an order. Go home and I'll manage to get back there. . . ."

He had been looking toward the bar and now he nodded, quickly and emphatically. Sam said, "Okay, Mac. Five minutes it is . . ."

The little blonde was sauntering slowly across the room as if she were headed toward the door at the rear labeled LADIES. But suddenly she swerved, darted up to Hoyt's table and cried reproachfully, "Why, Matty-watty! Have you forgotten little Tiny already?"

Matthew Hoyt's jaw dropped. Before he could speak, little Tiny was sitting on his lap. She wound her arms about his neck, pressed her cheek to his and cooed, "But I haven't forgotten *you,* daddy. . . ."

Sam pressed the button that set off the bulb in the small flashbulb attachment he held in his left hand. Someone laughed, a woman squealed—facts of which Sam was vaguely aware but which he ignored. He was unscrewing the used flash bulb, scorching his fingers, as he slid down the room, closer to Hoyt's table.

Hoyt had managed to get to his feet but the girl clung to him desperately. Before he could shake her off, Sam had a new bulb in his reflector. He squinted into his camera, the second bulb flashed and Mr. Weller turned and made for the door.

He was just in time to see Michael stop and speak briefly to the Marine sergeant. The sergeant came to his feet with his hand closed about a half-empty beer bottle. His aim was not of the best; besides, by the time the bottle left his hand, Michael had landed, with one catlike dive, under a table.

Regrettably, the beer bottle bounced off the head of the nearest sailor. His three companions rose as one, swinging their beer bottles. Someone shouted, "Fight, fight!" and the lights went out. Sam kept going but he heard, before he went out the door, a loud crash of breaking glass and an anguished voice bawling, "Call the cops!"

He reached Michael's car, put his foot on the starter and looked at his watch. He gnawed a fingernail; thought, "When I get time, I'm going to bust a gut, laughing. . . ." And watched a trickle of patrons escaping from The Black Sunflower.

He glared at his watch, sighed—and then threw the back door of the car open as Michael raced across the street, dragging the little blonde with him. He fairly slung her into the car, gasping, "No, we can't go back for your shoe . . ."

Mr. Weller did not have to be told to get going. The car was moving as Michael scrambled into it; they were half a block away by the time he had closed the door. He said, "Turn right at the corner and hit North Point, Sam. It's a through street as far as we'll want to go. . . ."

He produced the torn half of a bill and handed it to the girl. "Here you are, my child. Paste it to the half you have and it's as good as gold. And . . ." He took his billfold from an inside pocket. . . . "two twenties as a bonus for a good job and to pay for the shoe that you lost."

"Gee, thanks. You're a good joe. You said you'd see that I got away from that dump all right and you did."

"But did I need to?" Michael inquired. "Though it was dark, I rather thought that our friend Matthew was on the floor, trying to rid himself of a chair or table. What do you think, Angel-face?"

"I think Matty-watty got tripped up somehow. Funny, isn't it? Of course," said Angel-face with a seraphic smile, "it wouldn't have anything to do with a Marine I knew having taught me a few tricks he'd learned. Glad to do it for a pal. And I had to stick around to collect the other half of this century note, didn't I? Not that I didn't trust you, just because you didn't trust me too much. I'm always looking for suckers but I don't really like 'em."

"Yes, well, your performance was cheap at the price, Miss. . . ?"

"Just call me Tiny. Tomorrow I'll be on a bus, heading for the tank town that sonabitch'n barkeep mentioned. The war's definitely over, sugar. The pickings are slim and I can hardly wait to get hayseeds in my hair again. You counted on that, didn't you? I don't know what it's all about, though I know damn well that guy was a copper, and I don't like 'em. I'm no amateur but I don't, you might say, belong to the union. I operate on my own and I don't like to be shoved around."

"Who does? Where do you live, child? We'll take you home."

"Bush Street, near Fillmore. I'll show you the dump. This's Van Ness. Turn left, hon. . . . What'd you say to that gyrene, mister?"

"Just what I was wanting to know," Sam said.

Michael hesitated briefly. "Ladies present, but. . . ." He told them what he had said to the Marine sergeant. Sam whistled admiringly.

"I wouldn't have supposed a guy that talks the brand of English you do, could be that good in the vernacular. That was plenty to start a fight but. . . ."

"I knew that the headwaiter at The Black Sunflower always douses the lights as soon as a fight starts," Michael said. "I didn't know, of course, that I'd run into anyone as co-operative as Tiny. I could only hope for the best."

"But what was that God-awful crash I heard as I was going out the door—like a mirror breaking?"

"It was a mirror breaking, Samuel; the mirror behind the bar. I also managed to locate a beer bottle. I am not," Mr. Dundas said diffidently, "at all athletic, but when I throw something, even in the dark, it usually lands on the target. Nightclub owners don't like to have their mirrors broken. When that happens, they sometimes call the cops. . . ."

"Well, God help the innocent bystanders if you were really athletic," Sam said.

Tiny giggled, moved closer to Mr. Dundas and tucked her head into his shoulder. Mr. Weller grinned but made no comment. In due time he stopped the car before a narrow-faced, raddled dwelling on Bush street. Michael got out, escorted Tiny up a short flight of decrepit steps to the front door. She put her arms about his neck and kissed him.

Mr. Weller did not credit Mr. Dundas with even token resistance. He did finally pluck Tiny off, spun her about, bestowed a quick, practiced slap on that portion of her anatomy nearest him and pushed her toward the door. And returned to the car to confront Mr. Weller.

"Grin, you damn baboon," he said testily, wiping lipstick from his mouth. "Manners, Mr.

Weller, manners. She expected to be kissed and—
well, let's just let it lie and not kick it around.
And we'll save time if I drive."

2

Sam slid out of the driver's seat. "But what about
those shots I took? I'd like to get them in the
soup. I think I got something. . . ."

"If you didn't, it wasn't for want of trying. I
saw you getting as close to Hoyt as you could, letting him get a good look at you. How long does it
take to develop pictures? What do you need?"

"I can make out with a closet, a flashlight and a
bathtub or kitchen sink but I'll have to have hypo
and developer and paper. Don't tell me," Sam said,
grinning, "that you don't know a guy that can't
help us out on this angle?"

"Yes, I do know someone who has a darkroom of
sorts. He's an artist and photography is his hobby.
He never goes to bed before two A.M. and though
he may want to see the pictures, his interest will
be entirely technical. He doesn't know Hoyt and
he's not curious. He lives in the Monkey block.
I'll write an introduction to him now. . . ."

Michael took a card from his pocket, jotted
down an address in the seven hundred block on
Montgomery Street and below that, a few lines
introducing Sam.

"That's all you'll need and you'll have no difficulty in finding the place. Go down Pacific and. . . ."

"Okay, if that's an order but what are you going to be doing meanwhile, Mike?"

Sam wondered why Michael looked at him so fixedly, not knowing that only a few hardy souls have ever tried to call him "Mike" and that those few have not tried more than once. Still, after a moment, Mr. Dundas grinned fleetingly.

"'Late, late in the evening Kilmeny came home. And nobody knew where Kilmeny had been . . .' I hope. Let's say that I'm going to return Squiffy Bain's car to his garage."

"How you going to get home?" Sam said.

"Squiffy will ferry me home. You left the car four blocks from the house, you said? Then I'll leave you there and you can go on to the Monkey block. There's no longer much point in trying to hide the fact that we know each other. So. . . ."

Michael took a key ring from his pocket. "Take one of those two keys in the middle. They fit our front door. I'll join you at home later on. . . ."

It was early, early in the morning when "Kilmeny" came home, to find Sam, minus coat, shirt and shoes, gloating over the handiwork that he had arranged along the back of the chesterfield.

Michael studied the pictures for a moment; sat down and laughed until tears came to his eyes.

"Just luck," Sam said insincerely. "Notice how plain that basket of black sunflowers shows up? And the vase of 'em on the table and the ones printed on the cloth, too. That proves where he was and you say the club has a bad reputation so that helps. I like the second one best. Hoyt was really trying to throw the dame off when I snapped it, but the way she plastered herself up against him, it don't look that way."

"No," Michael agreed. "If it were true that the camera doesn't lie, one would say that they were embracing each other fervently. You made three of each, I see."

"Just in case. I made glossies since your friend had a print dryer. He was interested but not curious. Anyway, there they are and I hope you can make good use of them. . . ."

Sam turned away from his masterpieces and, contemplating Mr. Dundas, frowned. Slim, wiry guys like him are gluttons for punishment, but he's beginning to look a little worn, he thought. He said, somewhat apprehensively, "Did—did you make out all right?"

"Oh yes," Michael said, almost listlessly. But in an instant he sat erect and went on, "I fancy you think it took me long enough? But I had to wait until the special patrolman had made his hourly round and erase all traces of Egbert's brief sojourn in my office."

"Uh—where did you. . . ."

"In a nicely overgrown vacant lot that slopes away from the street. You may have noticed that the property owners of San Francisco seldom burn off or cut down weeds."

"I hadn't, but. . . . Well, I suppose the simplest way is the best in this case."

"I think so. If we're lucky, the body may not be discovered tomorrow. When it is, Hoyt will be forced to question me, since Egbert had been my employee. That's routine and Hoyt won't deviate from it," Michael said.

"Then you don't think he'll come to you right away? That is, unless he has to?"

"N-no. It's instinctive with Hoyt to play a waiting game. No doubt he suspects that I was responsible for his embarrassment at The Black Sunflower tonight, but it wouldn't do him any good to burst in on me, hurling wild accusations."

"He could see you in that booth after he sat down, but not me," Sam said thoughtfully. "I don't think he even saw me come out of the booth to take that first shot. I was well away from the booth when I snapped the second one, so though he saw me then, he may not be sure we're working together. Will you go to him?"

"If I must. And when I know what sort of trade I can offer."

"You mean it depends on whether Alan Furness gets a ransom note at all—and how soon he gets it and what it says?" Michael nodded. "Well, dammit, you told that gang you'd have to go to the cops Monday night. We don't know what Alan said to 'em after we left, but we've all got to sweat it out until someone makes a move."

"Yes," Michael agreed, getting to his feet. "And you'd better sleep while you can."

"I slept this evening, pal. What about you?"

"Oh, I'm going to bed, too. I suppose you sleep raw? There are some spare toothbrushes on the top shelf of the drug cabinet. Good night. . . ."

Only, Sam thought at nine o'clock the next morning, the guy didn't look like he'd had a particularly good night. Michael, entering the kitchen, regarded Mr. Weller and the admirable scrambled eggs he had to offer, with a jaundiced eye.

"Oh, to be five years younger. . . . No, Samuel, I do not care for eggs. You'd better eat them."

"Look, Mac; don't you ever eat?"

"Certainly I eat," Michael said peevishly. "But not when. . . . I don't care for breakfast. I'll have just coffee, if you don't mind?"

"I don't mind," Sam said pleasantly, attacking the eggs. "But some day someone's going to hang one on your jaw for the way you manage to say those four words. And I'll bet your wife's learned to keep her yap shut until breakfast is over, even if she don't look like the meek and mild kind."

"How do you. . . . I'd forgotten that our maid put a picture of Valerie in the guest room."

"And one of you, too, bud, in your very best major's uniform, and all loaded down with fruit salad," Sam said maliciously.

"Our admirable English maid, Patton—no relation to the late lamented general—is a pearl beyond price but if she had her way, even our living-room would look like a photographer's show window."

"I like your wife's looks," Sam persisted. "I can see why—why you want to make that plane to New York tomorrow night. If you've thought of anything to do to speed things up. . . ."

"I had wondered if it wouldn't be a good thing to . . . Well, the first morning caller has arrived. Let it in, whoever it is, will you?"

3

"This is it," Alan Furness said tensely.

He spread a large sheet of cheap white paper flat on the kitchen table. It was covered with words and letters cut from newspapers, pasted on somewhat crookedly.

ONE HUNDRED GRAND IN SMALL BILLS. BRING IT TO THE GEORGE STERLING PARK AT ELEVEN TO-NIGHT. HAVE DUNDAS AND WELLER COME WITH YOU. USE THE STEPS UP TO THE PARK FROM LARKIN AND GREENWICH. TAKE THE FIRST PATH OFF THE STEPS. FOLLOW IT PAST THE DRIED UP DRINKING FOUN-TAIN TO WHERE TWO BENCHES ARE. LEAVE MONEY IN TRASH CAN BY LEFT HAND BENCH LEAVE BY STEPS THERE DOWN TO LOMBARD. GO HOME. YOU WILL BE TOLD WHERE TO FIND BOY IN FEW HOURS IF NO POLICE OR AMATEUR DETEC-TIVES INTERFERE.

Sam, reading over Michael's shoulder, whistled. "Why drag us into. . . . Oh, we're the amateur de-tectives in question and we can't interfere if we're with Mr. Furness all the time. One of your rela-tions thought this up, guy. Who else would know about me? Where is this park?"

"It's not far from here, between Greenwich and Lombard. It is usually called Lombard Place. You can enter it either from Hyde or Larkin," Michael said. "I suppose that's why one of the two approaches is specified for Mr. Furness's use. And, as I remember the place, we're to take the longest route to that trash can. Perhaps we're to be under observation. Because it isn't a formal park, neatly laid out, and there's plenty of cover there."

"Oh, it's a very good spot for this—this transaction. But whoever did this . . ." Alan flicked the message with his knuckles, "must be mad. What good will this do—anyone?"

"What did you have to say to that pleasant little family gathering after we left you yesterday?" Michael asked.

"I—I did promise immunity to the kidnapper in so far as I can guarantee it. I said that I would gladly pay any reasonable amount to have my son safe; that I would not assist the authorities in their investigation if the matter was investigated. But the boy's of an age to observe and remember. . . ."

"He couldn't do any observing if he was snatched out of a sound sleep and kept doped," Sam remarked.

"N-no. I suppose they would—though that's a dangerous business with a child and . . ." Alan shook his head as if to clear it and went on, "But what I had in mind when I said that this—this scheme is insane, is that I don't see how anyone can profit by it. What good will this money do the one who collects it? Who would dare use that money once he—they have it?"

"That's a question I've been asking since you received the first communication regarding the child," Michael said. "And it's occurred to me that it would be difficult for anyone to manage this sort of thing alone."

Sam snapped his fingers. "Sure! What's that old chestnut about the laborer being worthy of his hire? If the brain behind this called in hired help, the help has to be paid off. And if you're damn fool enough to hire someone to do dirty work for you, he can practically call his tune and you've got to dance to it."

"I hadn't thought of that," Alan said slowly. "Or—well, I did realize that. Catherine is involved with this Jack Edwards and he probably knows some—knows certain types that she wouldn't normally come in contact with. And he himself has been more or less a free agent. He may be a very admirable person," Alan added hastily. "But I don't know, do I?"

"No," Michael said. "And as to Nathan and Louis, they do get around, don't they?"

"That's one way of putting it. They both know an amazing—variety of people. But mother. . . ."

"Your mother has Nathan on tap. And I think she'd take for granted she'd be a match for anyone she chose as—shall we say, a deputy? Her servants have been with her a long time, haven't they?"

"Y-yes. But they. . . ."

"Let it ride. But tell me, would your mother find it easy to raise any large amount of cash on short notice?"

"No," Alan said slowly. "Her income is adequate but she maintains a certain standard of living and helps Uncle Nathan out. Of course she could sell some of the investments from which her income is derived. . . ."

"She couldn't do that quickly without employing brokers. They'd know what she'd done and they might wonder—and talk. She thought that your father should have willed her a rather substantial sum in spite of having already provided for her by settlement? You needn't answer. At what time is breakfast served in her home on Sundays?"

"Why, at eight o'clock. But. . . ."

"And after that, what's the schedule for her and Catherine and Nathan?" Michael asked.

"Mother has old-fashioned ideas about Sunday—rather dismal ones. She goes to her room and reads an improving book. Mother," Alan admitted with a reluctant smile, "considers reading a duty, not a pleasure. Then she dresses for church. Cathie does her own room on Sundays to help the upstairs maid so that she can go to church, too. Nathan reads the newspapers and if Mother—uh—persuades him to go to church with her, takes considerable time dressing. But I don't see what that Sunday schedule has to do with. . . ."

"Never mind. How was this letter delivered?"

"In the same way that the first one was. It was put under the front door and our maid found it when she entered the house this morning. She brought it to me, but Viola and I were together and . . . Well, of course Viola would have had to know about it."

"Then you intend to carry out the instructions given in it?" Michael said.

"What else can I do? Though it rests with you, too. . . ."

"Oh, Sam and I will play along with you though I wish an earlier hour than eleven had been named."

"That's another thing. Even at eleven o'clock how can anyone risk being absent from—from wherever he should be, at the time the ransom must be collected?"

"Maybe that's where a hired hand will come in," Sam suggested. "And they've arranged it so that I and Michael won't be any danger to them.

Nobody's going to watch Jack Edwards. Louis Hilton lives alone. Of course your mother, sister and uncle might be expected to be together all evening."

"Mother always retires at ten-thirty," Alan said slowly. "Of course, if she should stay up later than usual. . . . Uncle Nate regularly dines at his club on Mondays with two old friends. And—I suppose I must tell you that Cathie walked out on us yesterday evening. She took her car and didn't return home last night. She said that she wouldn't but I didn't believe her. I suppose she talked to Edwards again. I only hope. . . ."

"That she didn't spend the night with him? Why? It would be good for what ails her," Michael said coolly. "You had your little fling, Mr. Furness. . . . Sam and I will meet you at your home at ten-thirty."

His tone was in itself a dismissal. "I'll manage, somehow, to stave off the police. And," he added more pleasantly, opening the door from the kitchen into the dining-room, "I'll keep my fingers crossed

He did not immediately return to the kitchen. In a few minutes Sam heard a radio voice droning away in the living-room. "Newscast, probably," he thought, got up and began to wash the dishes with a praiseworthy attention to detail that would have satisfied even the Dundas's admirable maid, Patton.

Michael, coming back into the kitchen fifteen minutes later, raised an eyebrow and said unkindly, "At least the Army did provide excellent domestic training for many men."

"Yap-yap-yapity-yap!" said Mr. Weller disapprovingly, fluttering his fingers against his thumb. "It was Ma that trained me on account of she had four boys with hearty appetites and said one of us should've been a girl to help her out. And look who's talking about K.P. I'll bet you're one of those guys that was stuffed into a uniform and turned loose without even being shown how to return a salute."

Michael grinned. "Yes. The first time I ventured out in full regalia, I not only felt as if I were going to a costume party in broad daylight, but all the way down Market Street I was praying that I wouldn't meet anyone who would salute me. I've been listening to the only available newscast. . . ."

"That's what I figured. Any luck?"

"No. There was no mention made either of Egbert or Bella Voss. There's another newscast coming up at eleven-thirty over an Oakland station which is our best bet. If there's no mention of Bella then, we'll have to go looking for the first editions of the afternoon papers."

"Oh, my aching back!" Sam said perfunctorily. "The idea being, doc, that you'd like me to go over to Hayward and find out what I can about Bella."

"Do you mind?"

"I'll make a stab at it. Between here and there I can dream up some kind of bull to explain why I'm interested in Bella. And it's going to be a long time till eleven tonight. When we went to Bella's place, I noticed a country grocery about a mile from her."

Michael nodded. "That should be your best bet. You'll have to take my car. . . ."

"Okay, but what do you specially want to know?"

"Anything that you can pick up," Michael said vaguely. "How many children did she have under her wing, when did she first announce that she was going to Chicago—that sort of thing. . . ."

He stopped as the doorbell rang; said, "I'd rather expected that we'd have more than one visitor this morning. Let's see who this is. . . ."

4

Mr. Ridley was not happy. He sat in a large chair, drummed his well-manicured fingers against the upholstery and made meaningless bass noises which sometimes resembled a deep cough though at other moments this persistent throat irritation resolved itself into a deep, "Har-rr-umph!"

Michael did nothing to put Mr. Ridley at his ease. He sat and regarded him fixedly until at last Nathan said, "It's very distressing." Then, seeming to feel that this was inadequate, he added with unexpected candor, "It's a hell of a mess, that's what it is!"

"Yes?" Michael said receptively. "Have you talked to Alan this morning?"

"I have. Everyone consults me," Nathan said fretfully. "I'm a professional uncle. . . . However, I'd called Lanny just before I came here, to tell him that Cathie managed to get a room at the Y.W.C.A. last night. Cathie's a good child. She couldn't quite bring herself not to let someone know where she is."

"But she's staying on at the Y.W.C.A.?"

"Uh—yes. She refuses to come home. Alan said, don't urge her. Let her stay there. And then he told me that he had received another—uh—communication. Well, I. . . ."

"What are your plans for this evening?" Michael asked.

"I always dine with friends at my club on Mondays. Why should I alter my schedule? I suppose that I might insist that Hester and I remain at home, carefully staying together until after eleven o'clock. But frankly, m'boy, my sister's in such a devil of a temper that I don't think I'm equal to the strain even if I felt I must provide myself with an alibi for tonight. And Hester is displeased with me, too, and I doubt that she would agree to stay up past her usual bedtime."

"Yes, she would be expected to keep to her usual schedule, too," Michael said thoughtfully. "But you didn't come here to tell me where Catherine is or to discuss your sister's very bad temper, Mr. Ridley. Just why did you come?"

"I—uh. . . . Never drink before luncheon, ordinarily, but under the circumstances. . . . If you've anything in the house, that is. . . ."

He gulped down the very indifferent Bourbon that Michael produced and went on, "One doesn't know where one's first loyalty is. But I suppose one's own sister and nephew. . . . Louis and I have always been very congenial. Perhaps because we're more or less the family black sheep. . . ."

"What did Louis do before the war?" Michael said.

"A little of everything and nothing for long. His father was a charming ne'er-do-well. That cottage is the only property Hilton managed to leave him. Zachary—my brother-in-law, y'know . . . helped the elder Hilton and, later on, Louis, from time to time. He often found jobs for him but Louis always tired of them quickly. He took up flying as a hobby and I understand that he's an excellent pilot. But he's always been reckless and easily bored. I know that before the war he associated with some rather—doubtful characters and may have done odd jobs for them, mainly for the thrill of it.

"I know," Nathan said quickly as Michael smiled involuntarily. "Not all of my own acquaintances are 'our very best people.' I know a good many bookies and gamblers. I'm one of their favorite suckers." He smiled ruefully. "But Louis knew men, who could be called—uh—racketeers and I don't know just how well he knew them or if he has—uh. . . ."

"Renewed old friendships recently?" Michael said. "What's troubling you, Mr. Ridley?"

"Well, you've been in Louis's cottage. . . ."

"Only in the living-room which runs across the entire front of the house. Otherwise, I don't know what the layout of the place is."

"There are more rooms than you would expect though they are small. Kitchen, bathroom and two bedrooms. I've often occupied the extra bedroom though the bed in it is the sort that brings on lumbago. Louis gave me a key to the place. He understands that there are times when I need a refuge from—well. . . ."

"From Hester and her unalterable schedule?" Michael said. "Go on."

"You know that I talked with Louis, Sunday morning. There was nothing wrong then. He drove me over to Hester's in time for luncheon; drove away and said that he'd be home around three if anyone wanted him. Then, as you also know, he turned up at Alan's in the evening while you were there."

Nathan rattled the shrunken ice cubes in his glass and drank the slightly tinted water that remained in it. Michael rose and rather pointedly put the whisky bottle on the table beside him.

Mr. Ridley poured himself a stiff, undiluted drink and continued, "After you two left, we remained in—uh—conclave for quite a while. Then Catherine suddenly walked out, and in a few minutes, Louis followed. I whispered to him that I'd be over to see him later on. He said, very quickly, 'Better stay home and soothe Hester.' I thought nothing of that, and after a rather exhausting session with Hester after Lanny had taken us home, I did go over to Louis's place.

"No one answered the doorbell so I used my key and went in. The first thing I noticed was the odor of a pipe, but Louis doesn't smoke a pipe," Nathan said unhappily. "I went to the back of the house, to the bedrooms. And I heard a key grate in the lock of the guest room. The door was certainly locked and I even thought I heard sounds on the other side of it. But one can't be certain about such things, can one?"

"You didn't see Louis?" Michael said.

"Oh, yes. He'd been down to a grocery on Jones that stays open until late on Sunday nights and he had two large bags of groceries. He seldom cooks or has any food about the place. I made no comment, we talked for a few minutes and I left."

"Maybe Hilton has a lady friend who smokes a pipe," Sam said facetiously.

Nathan gave him a pained look, shrugged and admitted, "If it hadn't been for that, I would have thought . . . But though Louis knows many indiscreet ladies, few of them would consider me a stranger and would trust to my discretion."

"It's very interesting," Michael said, "but you didn't ask questions last night and the time hasn't come yet when I can do so."

"There's probably some very simple explanation but. . . . Well, I talked to Alan this morning and he mentioned the possibility that some outsiders might be involved in this business; have been hired to do some of the—uh—dirty work. It's all very bewildering. . . ."

"Why didn't you tell Alan what you've just told us, Mr. Ridley?"

"I don't dare, m'boy. Lanny's beside himself with worry now. He might snatch at any slight straw and do something reckless, something that would upset the arrangements that have been made. And I feel that he'd better follow instructions. Besides, Alan and Louis are not very good friends. They just happen to be first cousins, that's all."

"I see. Well, do you intend to have a little chat with Louis this morning?" Michael said.

"I don't feel up to it. But I thought you should know, in case—well, just in case. Alan told me that you and Mr. Weller have been ordered to go with him to pay the ransom. Of course, if you wanted to—well, I do have the key to Louis's cottage and. . . ."

"You'd better keep it in your possession," Michael said virtuously. "Louis may give you an explanation later on today if he feels one is called for. He may even want to talk to Mr. Weller and me. We are. . . ." He looked at the clock on the mantelpiece, "rather popular this morning—"

Nathan flushed and rose at once. "I dare say you have a good deal on your mind this morning," he said rather maliciously. "I can't know just exactly what your problems are. I don't think, Mr. Dundas, that frankness is your long suit. However, thanks for listening so patiently to a tiresome old codger like me. Good-morning, gentlemen."

"I wonder if he's the well-meaning old fuddy-duddy he likes to call himself," Sam said, "or if this story was just an excuse to keep in touch and maybe throw dust in our eyes."

"Could be," Michael said and turned on the radio.

5

The announcer dealt with foreign affairs, national events and finally, toward the end of the short time he allowed himself for local happenings, remarked that the police were still investigating the death of Bella Voss. The body of the middle-aged woman whose antecedents were somewhat "mysterious," had been discovered late Sunday night. However, she had been killed some time previously, probably early Saturday morning. According to the police, the woman was known to have recently had a considerable amount of cash in her possession and this money was missing. Several itinerant workers and vagabonds had been questioned but. . . .

Michael turned off the radio. Sam whistled. "Remember when I looked through her purse and said it was funny there was only some silver in it? You ignored that. I suppose you thought that the guy who killed her had taken her money to throw the police off the track? There'd be no point in taking her ticket since the chances were that a few people knew she was going away. Well, maybe it worked, if the police really think it's just a case of robbery and murder."

"No doubt they'd like to believe that," Michael said. "But in spite of that, I'm sure they're trying to find out as much as they can about her past history. Evidently what we just heard was a follow-up. The story must already have been given out on an earlier broadcast. You'd better get an *Oakland Tribune* and a *Post-Enquirer* when you're across the Bay."

Sam nodded. "Then I'll know just how much the general public knows, which is all I'm supposed to know. You want me to start now? What're you going to be doing?"

"I'll go to the shop and try to work. Since you can't say when you'll be back in the city, you'd better meet me there."

"Okay. I'll get my coat and . . . Well, hear them bells go ting-a-ling-a-ling. If it's not the door, it's the phone," Sam said. And, getting into his coat and slicking back his hair in the guest room, listened to what Michael was saying at the telephone.

"Yes, Costello? Oh, they did? This morning. . . . I see. I know it's a bad break but I'm not surprised that someone. . . . I know! And I'll be available whenever Hoyt wants to talk to me. But we'd better not talk longer now, since you're risking something, calling me like this. . . ."

By now Sam had come out into the hall off which the bedrooms opened, not bothering to pretend that he was not listening. "They found Egbert?" he asked.

"Yes. I did know, when I chose that vacant lot as a dumping ground, that vacant lots are popular with dog owners and that dogs are inquisitive beasts. But I had to take the chance that a dog might be turned loose on that particular lot, discover Egbert and bark his silly head off."

"So that's how it happened? Well, those are the breaks, pal," Sam said philosophically. "You'd probably have had to see Hoyt some time today, anyway. If you like, I can stick around and go across the Bay later. No? Well, give me your car keys, Mac, and take it easy till I get back, will you?"

"'Nother bottle of beer?"

"Sure thing, Mr.—er—?"

"Just call me Pop. Everyone does," said the proprietor of the roadside grocery and fruit stand, throwing back the lid of a square box filled with bottles and large chunks of ice.

They were sitting behind the counter of the ramshackle fruit stand to one side and in front of the store because, Pop said, "We won't be bothered much here. It's late in the afternoons, mostly, that folks stop to take peaches and watermelons home."

He opened two bottles of beer, poured half a bottle down his throat and said, "Well, so you're a private detective and this friend of yours that was in the Army with you wanted you to locate Bella Voss?"

"That's it," Sam said patiently. He had already shown his credentials and told the story he'd fabricated on his way over. But Pop, he'd seen at once, couldn't be hurried. He belonged on a cracker barrel before a potbellied stove in a Norman Rockwell painting of a country grocery.

"My pal's wife died and left these kids and he's going nuts trying to find someone to look after 'em. He remembered his wife had this Aunt Bella that was good with kids. He only saw her once and the last his wife heard from Bella, she was living somewheres in the East Bay. He'd heard some family gossip that Aunt Bella could be a doubtful character but he thought it was worth a try. I'm just starting in this business and I thought it'd be good experience. . . ."

Pop nodded sagely. "And soon's you got up here, you read in the papers about Bella being killed? That was discouraging. But she's the woman you was looking for, all right, from the description your friend gave you of her. And she was good with children, all right."

"Was she? Long as I've come this far, I might as well take back what information I can to Bill. He might know something about her relations to tell the police, though I doubt it. His wife left Chicago when she was a kid and he's never met any of her folks there."

"Bella told me she was going back there but she didn't mention no relations," Pop said. "She come here over two years ago. She always traded here and I thought she was a real pleasant woman though she was close-mouthed. Whatever they say, she took good care of them kids."

"Oh, then you saw her nursery?" Sam said.

"No, can't say I was ever in her house except the kitchen. Seeing's she give big orders and my house's a couple miles past hers, durin' the war I'd stop and deliver on my way home. But there never was no complaints about her. While the war was on, she looked after a lot of kids during the day for girls I know that had jobs in war plants. They thought she was fine with babies and she certainly bought the best of ever'thing for 'em here."

"Oh, I thought maybe she boarded kids."

"She did, but I don't know just how many. She was investigated by some of these here organizations or boards or agencies. Don't know their exact names," Pop said scornfully. "Usually something to do with welfare and just busybodies if you ask me. But she satisfied them and they left her alone. . . ."

He got up to sell what looked to Sam like a decidedly under-ripe watermelon, to two passing motorists, who thumped it inexpertly and finally said weakly, "Well, if you're sure it's ripe enough. . . ."

"Where was we? Oh, a few at a time, after the war ended, Bella lost her day boarders as their mothers quit their jobs or was laid off. Till finally she had just these three boys. That was when she begun tellin' me she was leavin' here soon's she could wind things up. I see the kids now and then but not to get a close look at 'em. . . ."

"How was that?" Sam said.

"She had this old car and these kids were old enough she could bring 'em along and leave 'em in it while she was in here. Though as I recall it, I hardly seen her for about three months from May on. She didn't need so many groceries and I guess she shopped around for 'em. Then one day two or three weeks ago, she comes in here. . . ."

"Alone?" Sam asked.

Fortunately Pop was letting the last drops of beer trickle down his throat and did not realize with what eagerness Sam I had put the question.

He said, "No, she had this one boy with her— cute little towheaded shaver. That's when she says to me she's going back to Chicago. She wants to sell her car and radio and asks me to pass the word along."

"Oh, I see," Sam said. "She was going as soon as she got rid of the last of the kids she'd been looking after?"

"Yep. Said his mother was comin' for him soon's she could. Bella said she was ready to take a rest. I didn't have no trouble selling her car and radio, and then one day I seen a load of baby cribs and stuff going past, so I guess she sold all that, too. She rented the other furniture with the place."

Pop opened two more bottles of beer and handed one over to Sam. "So she had that money and I heard she'd closed out her account in the Hayward bank and bought her ticket at the Western Pacific for Chicago. So I guess poor Bella had too much money around and some bum heard about it. Too bad. 'Spite of what the cops was hinting about her, Bella was a nice kind of woman."

Mr. Weller nodded sympathetically and reflected, "I better not break away from this old guy too quick. . . . but I wonder if Michael's talked to Hoyt yet. Probably. . . ."

6

At a little after one o'clock, Inspector Matthew Hoyt stumped along the salon toward Michael's office, seeming to spurn the deep, gray-green carpet beneath his feet as an unnecessary and slightly indecent luxury. Though none of Mr. Dundas's employees is permitted to use any sort of perfume, and flowers are not tolerated in the salon, still the place has a definite, delicate, feminine odor, compounded of expensive scents and cosmetics, bath powder and sachet. The Inspector's nostrils dilated virtuously and he arrived in Michael's office with a "just as I thought" expression on his rugged countenance.

To find that the inner sanctum reeked only of tobacco smoke, that the floor was uncarpeted and needed re-finishing while any self-respecting secondhand dealer would sneer at the chairs and desk. The latter was piled high with correspondence, sketches and swatches of materials and Michael was very successfully giving the impression that he had a great deal of work to do and was trying to dispose of it as quickly as possible.

"Sit down, Inspector," he said politely. "I'd expected to see you again before this—though I'm sure that you've been very busy. Frankly, I wish that you hadn't chosen this morning to call on me. I'm taking a plane to New York tomorrow night, you know."

"Oh, are you?" Hoyt said. "That's what you think. . . ."

"That," said Mr. Dundas without emphasis, "is what I think. What's on your mind, Inspector? Did you get your sleep in last night? Because—I trust you will pardon my mentioning it—you look as if you'd had a hard night of it."

Hoyt eyed him warily, passing his tongue over his lips. He was, Michael reflected with reluctant admiration, groggy but game. He said, "That bookkeeper of yours, Egbert Knapp, was found in a vacant lot on Larkin Street this morning with a bullet hole in his back."

"So? I'm not surprised. . . ."

"Oh, aren't you now!"

"No. Egbert thought he might blackmail me and found that he couldn't. But he'd listened to Greta Mallon's conversation with me and she offended his sensitive ego by laughing at him when he was scurrying around to get his belongings from his locker. . . . Didn't he mention that?"

"No. I've only got your word for that." Hoyt hesitated, but he had a great reverence for facts and he was forced to admit, "We all knew he was pretty sore at both you and Miss Mallon. I have to ask myself how a guy like Knapp would get along on the witness stand. And I knew a smart lawyer could've tied him in knots, he was so boiling over with spite for you and her."

"Yes, a smart cop does have to think of those angles," Michael said flatteringly. "And you probably suspect, as I do, that Egbert decided to watch Greta, to pick up any crumbs that fell from her table. If he did that, he followed her to the Verde Vista and waited outside and he saw her murderer enter the building and leave it."

"That's one way of looking at it. But it may've been only you that he saw. And you threatened him. . . ."

"Yes," Michael said coolly. "I told him I'd break his neck if he annoyed me further. But you can't prove that now, can you? Greta heard our conversation but she, also, is dead. Where was Egbert killed? Surely not in a vacant lot?"

Hoyt sucked in his breath. A number of his back teeth were missing so the resulting sound was rather trying to sensitive nerves.

"Of course he wasn't killed in any vacant lot! He was killed somewhere else and his body was dumped there. We haven't got the gun that killed him but we know from the bullet it was a service revolver. Oh, I know! You're going to say there's a lot of those floating around now. All the same, that kind of gun was used on Knapp. He died between nine and ten yesterday morning, between an hour and an hour and a half after he'd eaten breakfast."

"Oh—breakfast?" Michael murmured. "What? I was only mumbling to myself, Inspector."

"Yeah?" Hoyt sat back in his chair and looked deliberately about the small office. "I see you've got a door into the alley. I don't suppose you ever gave a key to that to anyone, but you could let people in by that door. On a Sunday, with every place in this neighborhood closed up, this'd be a nice place to meet someone on the q.t."

"You think Egbert met whoever killed him in this office?" Michael managed to appear mortified with his own stupidity. "I hadn't thought of that. I confiscated his keys to the front door and this office when I discharged him. Did he have some spare keys on him?"

"No, he didn't! He. . . ."

Matthew Hoyt had had a trying Saturday night. He'd been slightly stunned when "little Tiny" had managed to trip him. He hadn't been able to get away from The Black Sunflower before two patrolmen had rushed in to quell what was beginning to be a small riot. They'd recognized him, he'd had to explain, and. . . .

He said recklessly, "I know damn well that guy Knapp was killed in this office! Ten to one, you killed him. And even if you didn't you moved his body and that's a criminal. . . ."

"Yes, do let's cut the cackle and come to the horses," Michael said crisply. "I admit nothing.

But I do think I know who killed Greta and Egbert. . . ."

Hoyt made a rude noise. "I don't expect you to believe me," Michael said. "But since I know that *I* did not kill Greta, I haven't been handicapped by preconceived notions. I've gotten around and. . . ."

"All right, tell me who killed them and prove it!" Hoyt snapped.

Michael shook his head. "No. I need time. That's what I want from you, Inspector. Don't bristle or look even more self-righteous than usual. Let me finish. I'm not a timid soul. I don't think there are many things in this world that I am really afraid of. But. . . ." Michael's tone was the leisurely one of polite conversation. . . . "I will go to some lengths to avoid being made to appear ridiculous."

Hoyt moistened his lips again. "I—I don't know what you're driving at."

"The hell you don't!" said Mr. Dundas in a sudden flash of uncontrolled temper. Then, very gently, "I do sympathize with you, Mr. Hoyt. Lately I've been the victim of circumstances. And so are you, pal; so are you! Here. . . ."

He yanked open a desk drawer, drew out and threw down on his desk two copies of Mr. Weller's candid camera shots of the Inspector and Tiny.

"I have the negatives for these. You see, I have a friend who's interested in this sort of thing. . . ."

VIRGINIA RATH

"You. . . . I . . . . It was a frame-up. . . ."

"Why, Inspector! We just happened to be in The Black Sunflower and you just happened to be tailing me." Michael lighted a cigarette, took two drags from it, crushed it out in a battered ash tray and said abruptly, "We won't play cat and mouse though it could be very amusing. I'll give it to you straight. I'll make use of these pictures—if you force me to.

"I don't think any newspapers would use them—now," he added thoughtfully. "But they might file them away for use the next time we have one of our periodical graft investigations. Of course, I know that you were at The Black Sunflower in the line of duty, that you were framed—and that everyone who knows you will believe that you were. . . ."

"Yes. Well, then," Hoyt said hoarsely, "what good would it do you to. . . ."

"They'll believe you, but they'll look at these pictures and oh, how they will laugh. Your very rectitude will backfire against you. You've preached the gospel according to St. Matthew too often to your less upright colleagues. Inspector Maxon, for one, would burst his buttons laughing at these pictures."

Hoyt winced, opened his mouth and closed it hastily.

"And there's the newspapermen," Michael went on. "My very good friend, Jubal Chambers, dean of the police reporters, has a very peculiar sense of humor and doesn't, I regret to say, like you very well. But then," he added cruelly, picking up the picture in which Hoyt seemed *not* to be trying to cast Tiny from him, "these photographs can't be dismissed with a passing glance. Such passion, such abandon. . . . Who would have thought you had it in you, at your age, Inspector?"

"What do you want?" Hoyt said thickly.

"Time. I want you to forget that I exist until—well, I will say one A.M. tomorrow morning. That's item one. Item two, is that after I have handed the murderer over to you—told you who he is, at least—you will, if necessary, act the part of a fairy godmother, though God knows you don't even remotely resemble one, and grant me one favor."

Hoyt swore. He was a godly man but he had rubbed elbows with ungodly characters for nearly forty years and his remarks were such that Michael listened to him with admiration. When Hoyt paused for breath, Michael said approvingly, "That covers the situation very adequately. But that's my proposition and you can take it or leave it. If you'll go along with me, I'll turn these negatives over to you as soon as the festivities are over."

"How do I know you will?"

"You'll have to take my word for that. If you'll give me your word that you won't interfere be- fore tomorrow morning, that's enough for me," Michael said slowly.

"Oh. Well. . . ." Hoyt was silent for a minute and then he said unwillingly, "All right. I don't know anything and I'll give you till one A.M. After that. . . ."

"After that, if I don't produce, it will be just too bad for me. I know. And it would be a good idea for you to stand by tonight. You'll be hearing from me—I hope," Michael said, let the Inspector out by the back door into the alley, sat down again and reached for the telephone.

7

"So I thought I'd got as much out of Pop as I could without him wondering why I asked so many questions and I let it go at that," Sam concluded. "I told him I wasn't wanting to get mixed up with the cops and he thought that was natural, on account of he listens to all these radio shows where the police and the private ops are always at each other's throats."

"You can talk your way out of almost any situ- ation, can't you?" Michael said.

Sam snorted. "'Approbation from Sir Hubert Stanley is praise indeed.' Oh, I was exposed to education," he said, as Michael looked at him with an elevated eyebrow. "I just sluffed it off and don't let it bother me. Well, is it any help—what I managed to find out?"

"It clears up some details that aren't too important, except to those who would be unhappy if every incidental fact wasn't firmly fixed in its proper place. And one thing that you learned, answers a question I've been asking myself. . . . It's after three," Michael said, "and you might as well check out of your hotel. They may be wondering why you didn't sleep there last night."

"And why pay for a room when I'm not using it?" Sam said thriftily. "Then what? You want me to join you at home or are you going to stay here until closing time?"

"I'm not achieving anything here." Michael scowled at the litter on his desk. "Yes, I'll go home. You still have your latchkey. . . ."

"And I'll walk to the hotel and then grab a taxi," Sam said. "You use your car. I parked it off the alley in back of this place. Seeing you. . . ."

It was after four o'clock before Michael managed to leave Gisele's, and then he did not drive home by the most direct route. He turned into

Van Ness, went on to Pacific, followed Pacific to Mason. Continuing along Mason to Vallejo, he could look up the steps from Mason to Taylor to Louis Hilton's small hillside cottage. He did look up, frowning indecisively and then, at the foot of the hill, he saw a parked car that he thought he recognized.

Abruptly, he stopped his own car, got out and climbed the steps to Louis's cottage. Catherine Furness was on the doorstep, unbecomingly flushed, batting her eyelashes very rapidly to shake off the tears that were gathering on them. She jabbed at the doorbell as if she'd already done so a great many times and had resolved that this would be the last.

Then, becoming aware that someone was watching her, she turned, stiffened and said to Mr. Dundas frostily, "Oh. What do you want?"

"Since I, too, am on Mr. Hilton's doorstep, it should be evident that I also wish to see him," Michael said mildly, going up the steps to the front door as he spoke. "But obviously he isn't in. . . ."

"He doesn't—no one answers the doorbell. . . . I mean, he isn't home," Catherine said. "I—I wanted to talk to him. Uncle Nathan called me after he'd talked to Alan and you, and I—well, I needed to talk to someone and so. . . ."

"Haven't you seen your fiancé today, Miss Furness?"

Catherine was plainly pleased by his offhand use of the term "fiancé." She said, "Jack is sweet and he wants to do everything he can to make things easier for me, but he doesn't know us—my family—and it's not fair to make him suffer for—our—our. . . ."

"Sins?" Michael said helpfully.

"That's a rather strong word though. . . . Jack can understand Mamma. She's a perfect type," Catherine said unexpectedly. "The tyrannical dowager duchess. But it's Alan who's caused all the trouble with his tendency to be quixotic and his overdeveloped paternal instinct. Though of course, it was Papa's will that made things worse. Alan likes to be benevolent, but he likes controlling the purse strings, too.

"I can't admire Louis or approve of some of his—his habits, but I'm not supposed to know about that," Catherine said primly. "And he does manage to look at things impersonally and keep calm and cool and so I wanted to talk to him. . . ."

"So did someone else," Michael said.

He pointed to the protruding corner of a card that had been thrust under the front door, stooped swiftly and came up with the card in his hand. It was Viola's and she had written on it, "I wanted to talk to you, Louis. Any time this morning will do if you find this soon enough. Alan doesn't expect to be able to lunch at home."

"Oh," Catherine said. Then, indignantly, "Put it back. It's none of your business. I mean, if Viola. . . . I do sympathize with her, even if she is just too good to be true sometimes, but. . . . Well, haven't you made trouble enough already?"

Mr. Dundas slid the card under the door again, very meekly and followed Catherine down the steps to her car. "Are you still at the Y.W.C.A.?" he inquired as she settled herself in the driver's seat.

"Yes. I don't care to go home to Mamma, and Alan doesn't care to have any of us around today. He told us so," Catherine said briefly and drove away.

Despite this detour, Michael got back to Russian Hill Place before Sam did. When Mr. Weller arrived he was carrying one battered suitcase, a dozen eggs, a pound of bacon, two thick steaks, a carton of potato salad, a loaf of French bread, a bakery pie and a small bag of white onions.

"I knew you'd never think to buy groceries and had a hunch you wouldn't want to go out to eat," he said. "And all I had at Hayward was one hamburger and four bottles of beer."

Michael chuckled; said, "Don't forget to put that on your expense account—as if I needed to remind you," and wandered off to the living-room. Sam opened the back door to allow Mehitabel to enter, tied a tea towel about his waist and went to work.

He did not hurry. It was six-thirty before he had dinner ready and past eight o'clock before he rinsed out the dish-cloth and surveyed a spotless kitchen. Well, he thought, that's not bad. I've killed enough time in here that there's only about two hours to go. . . .

Nevertheless, no two hours had ever passed more slowly, and that despite the fact that Mr. Weller knew all about sweating it out until H-hour arrived. Michael was not only disinclined to talk; he withered all attempts at conversation almost before they put their tender little shoots above ground.

To Sam's question, "Can you trust Hoyt to stick to the bargain you made?" he said, "I can trust Hoyt to keep hands off until one A.M. If I can't give him something definite in the way of evidence by then or tomorrow morning. . . . Well, I don't know what he will do. It depends on whether his fear of ridicule or his devotion to duty wins out."

Sam said, "Oh," and got up to mix drinks for both of them before he ventured another question.

"Why did you want to know if Greta had a camera
in her baggage?"

"Don't you know? Well, if you don't, ignorance
is bliss and there's no reason why both of us should
be unhappy."

"You're bucking for a fat lip, Mac," Sam said
half-heartedly. And then, being nearly unsquelch-
able, "You only ate about three bites at dinner and
you look dead for sleep. Why don't you hit the
sack for a while and I'll wake you. . . ."

"Don't be motherly," Michael said ungratefully.

Sam snorted indignantly into his drink but at
that moment Mehitabel, replete with the trim-
mings and scraps from the steak, his face well-
washed, stalked into the room and settled himself
across Michael's knees.

"Well!" Sam said. "He don't strike me as the
kind of cat that likes to be petted, so why do you
suppose he decided to stay in tonight? He couldn't
know there's something going on, could he?"

"Any man who claims that he understands
cats—or women . . . is a damned fool," Michael
said. "And you're right. Mehitabel is thoroughly
conscious of his masculine dignity and doesn't
care to be cuddled, except by my wife. For her,
he'll roll over on his back and wave his paws inel-
egantly in the air."

He stroked Mehitabel's head. The cat purred loudly and dug his claws into Michael's knee. Sam found himself watching the slim, strong brown hand moving rhythmically back and forth over the cat's gray fur. He sipped his drink cautiously, listening to Mehitabel's purring. . . . and did not realize that he had fallen asleep until he suddenly jerked awake, saw Mehitabel curled into a circle on the chesterfield and heard Michael's voice from the hall beyond the living-room.

Evidently he was at the telephone again. He said, "No, the setup is the same. . . . Yes, that's it and I'm counting on you. . . ." Another minute and he was in the living-room. "Awake? Good— it's time to go. . . ."

Sam was still not fully awake. His eyelids were hung with lead and the back of his neck ached. He said contentiously, "Just like that, hunh? It's time to go, he says. . . ."

Michael turned on him so quickly that he blinked and stepped back. Mr. Dundas opened his mouth, closed it and finally said pleasantly, "Mr. Weller, we're throwing double or nothing and I don't see how anyone could be such a fool as to nibble at the bait that's being offered and. . . . However, if you still think I'm taking this too lightly, let me assure you that if this trick doesn't work, I undoubtedly will breakfast in jail, and six will get you ten, that you'll be keeping me company there. Meanwhile—it *is* time to go."

8

"I've counted it myself and the bank wouldn't make a mistake," Alan Furness said. "But—do you think twenties would be called 'small bills?' There are five thousand of these, which makes a rather bulky package, and if I'd asked for fives or even tens, I'd need a larger envelope. . . ."

On the point of blurting out, "For Christ's sake, stop acting like a fidgety old lady!" Sam reflected, he's trying to concentrate on unimportant details to take his mind off the really important thing. Didn't I keep bitching about that boil on my neck before Cassino, as if that was what was going to kill me. . . .

He said, "I'll count the money for you, Mac, so you'll be sure you aren't short even one twenty. Oh, it's a pleasure. I'll probably never have my fingers on a hundred grand again. And I should think twenties are small bills nowadays from what I hear people say about how they evaporate, with the cost of living what it is. Hand over the cabbage, bud. . . ."

Sam counted the money—limp, dirty, well-worn bills. "One hundred Gs, all present and accounted for," he said. "Here you are. . . ."

Alan put the bank notes, very neatly, into a large manila envelope. "I don't know," he said, frowning, "if this is enough. Perhaps this should be wrapped for additional protection. . . ."

"You might as well do that," Viola said.

She was sitting in a large chair before the sickly fire that was fighting a losing battle for existence in a too ornamental grate. Now and then she shivered and stretched her pale hands toward the fire, but Sam felt uneasily that the movement had nothing to do with the temperature of the room.

She went on, "There is wrapping paper and string in the bottom drawer of your desk."

"Oh—oh, yes, my desk." Alan looked toward the walnut secretary in one corner of the room and then walked toward it, slowly. "Yes, of course. Thank you, dear. . . ."

He wrapped the manila envelope in thick brown paper, wound string about it, knotting it carefully. Again Sam was on the point of protest at this preoccupation with detail, but Michael got to his feet abruptly and said, "We might as well be going."

"Oh—oh, yes," Alan said. "I know I am supposed to deliver this myself but I don't like to leave you alone, Viola. You will be alone. . . ."

"You didn't want anyone to be here at this hour," Viola said tonelessly. "And I'm sure that it's—wise that no one should be. Please do go on, Alan, and don't think about me."

"Well . . ." Alan's shoulders sagged as he walked toward the hall. Sam followed him, but not so quickly that he did not hear Michael say, "You're sure that you'll be all right—alone, Mrs. Furness?"

"Yes. Yes, I'll be quite all right," Viola said. "And they're waiting for you. . . ."

Michael parked the car in front of a square, soot-stained yellowish stucco apartment house. Larkin was a level street at this point, but what Sam termed "another of those damn hills," lay between it and Hyde. The hill took up a full block and was overgrown with freesia, veronica and other shrubs; small-leaved, low-growing trees, compact spruce and evergreen, a few heavy headed eucalyptus.

"I don't think there are any lights in the part of the park to which we're going," Michael said. "So if you'll get both flashlights out of the dashboard compartment, Sam. . . ."

They crossed the street; started up a long flight of concrete steps. There was a street lamp at the foot of the steps; Sam could see a gaunt eucalyptus toward the top of the hill and smell the odd, pungent odor of its fallen leaves. They passed one landing; came to a second. Michael switched on his flashlight.

"'First path off the steps,'" he said and turned left into a wide, dirt path.

Sam swung his light about in a half circle and saw that there was a thick growth of shrubbery and trees on both sides of the path before Alan said nervously, "Don't do that! Someone might think we were trying to—well, not obeying instructions. . . ."

The path widened suddenly. Sam's light shone across an old park bench on which only a few scattered patches of green paint remained. Beyond that was a sort of cairn of grayish stone blocks with a drinking fountain on top. But the bowl was filled with dirt and no water came from the spout when Sam turned the handle.

"'Dried up drinking fountain,'" he quoted. "Why'd they specify this one, I wonder?"

"Probably because there are fountains from which one can drink, on the upper level of the park," Michael said. He gestured toward the dark slope on their right. "There are quite a few benches up there and a sandpile. I've taken our youngster there. And there is a mosaic bench and a plaque to George Sterling. . . ."

"Who was he?" Sam asked.

"A local poet.

     "'Oh Singer, fled afar!
     The erected darkness shall but isle the
       star
     That was your voice to men,
     Till morning come again
     And of the night that song alone re-
      main.'"

For, he told himself, no good reason, Sam shivered. He wondered if Michael knew what he could do with that voice of his or whether he was just "doin' what comes natch'rally." Alan Furness reacted more violently.

"Oh God, is this the time for a lecture on local history! We didn't come here to discuss the inscription on the Sterling memorial plaque. . . ."

"No, but we did get here a few minutes before eleven," Michael said. "Go on. It's only a few feet now. . . ."

The path narrowed briefly and then they had reached one corner of the park. Here there was a semicircle of hedges, broken by another flight of steps with a bench to either side of them.

Alan muttered, "Trash can by the left hand bench. I don't see. . . . Oh, thank you. . . ."

Sam had thrown the light from his torch over a battered trash can. Alan walked toward it slowly, almost stiffly. It took him a little time to remove the lid which either fitted the can very tightly or was slightly rusted. He drew the neat brown paper package from under his arm beneath his topcoat and dropped it into the can.

For an instant he stood still, looking down. Then he put the lid back over the can but, Sam thought, his hands were not too steady, for there was a loud clang of metal striking metal. Sam started and was irritated because he did. He could not see Michael's face, though their elbows touched. It seemed to him that the other man was as motionless as if he'd been cast in bronze. . . .

"Listening," Sam thought. Because for an instant none of them moved or spoke. But about them was the sound of the wind murmuring plausibly to trees and leaves. The fog had blotted out the stars. It drifted up the hill, materialized briefly in oddly proportioned, ghostlike shapes.

Sam said with uncalled for vehemence, "I'll remember, after this, that you need an overcoat in Frisco in August. Weren't we ordered to go down these steps here? Why the hell couldn't we have come up them and saved a walk in the dark."

They were halfway down the steps in question before Alan said, "I suppose because if we had come to the spot where the ransom was to be left by the most direct route, it would not have been so easy for the—person who wished to observe us, to do so. I don't know. . . . Do you think someone was watching us? I felt that someone was. . . ."

"So did I," Michael said, "but that was to be expected because someone could so easily have watched us. I don't know if we three were alone up there. What do you think, Sam?"

Sam shrugged. "I've laid for hours waiting for a Nazi sniper to make the first move and at that, once I moved too soon." He touched the scar on his forehead. "I don't know. Up there at that trash can, I did feel like there was someone off in the bushes near it. But we're all on edge, and the trees and leaves make funny noises at night . . ."

They had reached Michael's car by now and Alan turned on him suddenly. "If someone was waiting there. . . . You said you wouldn't call in the police. Did you? Was a policeman waiting there? If Weller thought he heard someone, whoever was to collect the money would be warned away, too. . . ."

"Get into the car and we will proceed, at a reasonable rate of speed, to your home, Mr. Furness," Michael said coldly.

He stamped on the starter and continued, "There are other things I'd rather do than play wet nurse to you. But I'm involved in this business whether I want to be or not and I gave you my word that I would not call in the police until the ransom was paid. . . ."

"I . . . I am sorry," Alan said placatingly. "I know you . . . Well, but what are we to do now?"

"What we were told to do. Go to your home and wait for a message that will tell you where Greta's son is. . . ."

At first Sam thought that Viola had not moved from her chair before the fire since they had left her alone. But she motioned toward a table against the wall and said, "I made coffee and sandwiches, and the makings for drinks are there, too.

Sam's appetite was indestructible. He ate two sandwiches and washed them down with coffee. Alan had three whiskies with very little soda in them; Michael drank three cups of black coffee.

When he put his cup down on the table and mixed himself a highball, Alan said hesitantly, "How long do you suppose it will be until. . . . It's past eleven-thirty now and. . . ."

"I don't know," Michael said discouragingly. "It depends entirely upon how soon the ransom was picked up, and how long it will take the collector to write a message and deliver it or to get to a telephone. . . ."

"Write a . . . Oh God, you don't think . . ."

"I don't know," Michael said again. "I've never gone in for kidnapping myself. I hope, for your sake, that a telephone is used, but even if one is. . . ."

The doorbell rang. First there was a series of quick, staccato notes; then a shrill, prolonged sound that drilled deep into one's ears. Viola sat erect.

"There's no one to answer that." She said, "I know you told everyone not to come here but. . . . Oh, what does it matter. I can't bear that noise!"

She rose swiftly and left the room. In a few minutes they heard a solicitous masculine voice and Nathan Ridley came into the room, rather pointedly supporting Viola on a fatherly arm.

He said to Alan, "My dear boy, I know that you said you didn't wish any of us to be with you during this—this ordeal. But Viola must have been left alone and I don't think that was quite the . . ."

Alan looked at the clock. "A quarter of twelve," he said slowly. "You don't usually leave your friends until midnight on Monday nights. Didn't you dine with them, after all?"

"Yes, m'boy; yes, of course I did. But surely you don't suppose I'd be able to settle down to an evening of bridge on this particular night?" Nathan said reproachfully. "I left them soon after dinner. I. . . as a matter of fact, I stopped at the YWCA since it's so near my club. . . ."

"And talked to Catherine?"

"Well, no, Lanny. The . . . the fact is, Cathie wasn't there. She hasn't given up her room but she was—out. And—uh . . . Have you talked to your mother recently?"

"I haven't talked to Mother since yesterday evening," Alan said briefly. "Why?"

"Well, I thought that perhaps Hester might come to the point where she'd be glad to have her old brother around. That's one reason I left the club early. But I'm very much afraid Hester is sulking. The door of her bedroom is locked and she wouldn't speak to me. You know Hester does sulk now and then. It did occur to me, of course, that she might have ignored your wishes and come over here to be with Viola. . . ."

"No. No, she didn't come—here. . . ."

Michael moved over to the fireplace, humming softly to himself. Sam was not easily annoyed but the refrain, whatever it was, quickly irritated him. He felt that he should know the song; he was even fairly certain that he'd heard it on so-called cowboy radio programs. Yet, though the air was familiar, no cowboy ballad that he knew fitted it.

Michael pursed his lips and whistled the refrain, clear and true. Alan Furness frowned. It was getting on his nerves, too, Sam decided. Alan moved impatiently, started to speak—and the doorbell rang again.

Nathan Ridley said apologetically, "That may be Louis. I asked him to come over because. . . .

That is, he said. . . . No, stay where you are, Viola. I'll get it. . . ."

But it seemed that the front door must have been left unlocked. For, very suddenly a man entered the living-room. It was not Louis Hilton. It was Jubal Chambers. He was cold sober and his usually florid face was a little pale.

He said, "I waited a while like you told me to, but you were right—and here it is!" He flung a flat package toward Michael, a package on which the string had been broken but which was still wrapped in brown paper.

Michael ripped the paper away, opened the manila envelope, drew out two twenty-dollar bills— and a neat stack of brown paper cut to the size of twenty-dollar bills. He said, "Your mother's son, aren't you, Mr. Furness? Why risk losing a hundred grand to ransom a child that's been dead more than three months?"

9

Michael went on, "I didn't think you would risk it. But it's too bad for you that you couldn't bring yourself to part with that hundred thousand dollars. Because the fact that you refused to do so, proves that you knew Greta's son was dead. Only Bella Voss knew that. That means you saw her before she died, and you killed her so that—"

"I killed her because she let my son die!" Alan said thickly. "If Greta had chosen someone else to look after him. . . . They were both stupid and ignorant. The Voss woman thought I'd pay her to keep silent. She thought she could collect from me before she had to tell Greta on Saturday that the boy was dead. She thought all I'd care about was to avoid scandal and keep Viola from knowing there'd been a child. Then she said she was sorry. Sorry!" He laughed. "Well, she was sorry. . . ."

Nathan was making unhappy bleating sounds and ineffectual gestures of protest. "Lanny, you don't know what you're saying! You. . . . you. . . ."

Alan ignored him. His pale eyes narrowed slowly. "You said you didn't think I'd risk it? You. . . . why, you wrote that ransom note yourself, you. . . ."

He flung himself at Michael, his hands outstretched, claw-like. Sam caught him competently from behind and held him. "Take it easy, bub. . . ."

Michael said coolly, "Certainly I concocted that note. I went without sleep to do it. And put it under your door myself just before your maid would arrive, so that you wouldn't be the one to find it—and destroy it. If imitation is the sincerest form of flattery, you should be flattered, Mr. Furness. You'd dreamed up one letter from an imaginary kidnapper and delivered it to yourself to gain time, trusting that I would respect the feelings of an anxious parent. . . ."

"You damned, cynical, jeering—devil!" Alan strained as Sam tightened his grip. "You don't understand—you don't know. . . ."

"I know that up to a point you told the truth about your dealings with Greta. But when you saw that your mother was going to be disagreeable enough Friday night to give you an excuse for leaving her early, you called Greta and asked her to go to the Verde Vista as soon as she could, instead of waiting until eleven as you'd originally planned. And I know that Greta refused to surrender the child to you. She'd found a man eager and willing to look after the boy; one who could offer more than you could. And I'm sure she laughed at you when she told you so."

"She. . . . did laugh. That—that Hollywood producer, that—that peasant with no background to adopt my son! I—oh, for God's sake, will you stop!"

For Michael was whistling again, softly and almost reflectively. "I've noticed you don't care for that refrain. Is it because you know the words to that song? 'You will do this, won't you, mother? Put my little shoes away'. . . . No, you don't like that, do you? Because Greta showed you your son's bronze shoe and you took it. . . ."

"She—she stood there and laughed at me!" Alan said hoarsely. "She said that perhaps if I asked her nicely, she'd give me the shoe for a souvenir. I didn't mean to. . . . But when I'd hit her twice, I—I couldn't stop. . . ."

"No, you couldn't stop then. So you went away and didn't know that Egbert Knapp had been watching Greta. He saw you enter and leave the Verde Vista by the service elevator and he remembered you. I don't know how he learned your name. . . ."

"He'd seen my picture in the newspapers. As Bella Voss had," Alan said almost indifferently. "I had to agree to meet him, before church on Sunday. But of course, I didn't let him blackmail me. I shouldn't have gone on to Bella Voss's after I—after Greta was dead. But when I'd read her letters that Greta carried in the box with that—that shoe. . . . Her address was on them and . . ."

"I don't know what I thought I could do about the boy. But Greta was dead and I guessed what sort the Voss woman was and I thought arrangements might be made. . . . I wasn't thinking clearly. I had to get out of this house. Viola was asleep so I took the car and . . . The next morning I didn't remember as much as I wanted to. I shouldn't have gone back to Hayward Saturday night, but I had the woman's letter to me, then, for an excuse, and I was afraid I'd left some clue there. . . ."

His voice trailed away. He stood staring at
nothing, his mouth a little open. Sam thought, "I
guess you'd call this shock. There's all kinds. He's
realizing he wasn't very smart, after all, and that
he's caught. . . ."

Nathan's well-shaved, smooth, pink jaw was
jerking nervously. He'd tried several times to make
himself heard and failed, until now. He said, "Lanny, I came here because I thought that I might
help—advise you, that is. After all, I studied law
in my youth and. . . . You have others to think of
and you've spoken recklessly when you should not
have said anything. . . ."

He broke off as the front door slammed shut
and someone said truculently, "I'm a member of
the family so just try to stop me, copper. . . ." and
Louis Hilton burst into the room.

He said scathingly to Nathan, "Don't you know
there are two cops out there in the hall? And I
suppose Alan's been spilling his guts. . . . I persuaded you to come over here because I thought
you'd manage to keep him from talking. But the
cops are looking very pleased. . . ."

He turned on Inspector Hoyt as he appeared in
the doorway with Quinlan, complete with notebook, just behind him, "I know this isn't England, worse luck, but even in America, isn't one
supposed to be given a warning of sorts? You've

stood there and listened to whatever Alan's had to say. . . ."

"Now, now!" Hoyt said imperturbably. "We didn't try to conceal ourselves. The gentleman could have seen us if he'd ever looked in our direction."

"So I didn't deceive you, either, Louis," Alan said slowly. "If you thought. . . ." He turned toward his wife. "Viola, did you. . . ."

Sam had, during the past few minutes, glanced toward Viola now and then. She'd kept holding her hands out to the fire that had dwindled to a few smoldering coals, but except for that, she hadn't moved and she'd looked as if she was listening courteously to a story that she'd heard before.

But now she rose and said, spacing her words carefully, "I was afraid. I have been married to you for quite a little while. I am very sorry for you, Alan, and of course, I will stand by you. But now I think I'd like to go upstairs for a while. . . ."

Louis moved toward her and Nathan heaved himself from his chair, but she shook her head and left the room alone.

It was one of Hoyt's peculiarities that he was usually jovial and rather paternal when making an arrest. He said cheerfully, "You'd better come along with us, Mr. Furness. If you'll come quietly we won't put the handcuffs on you. Will you?"

"Yes, of course," Alan said dully. "I. . . . Does one take his own toothbrush to—to where you're taking me, or. . . ."

"You can take what you'll need with you," Hoyt said genially. "Take him upstairs, Johnny, and get together what he wants. No razors, though, and no drugs of any kind. . . ."

Quinlan thrust his notebook into his pocket, ostentatiously patted the gun he carried in a shoulder holster and said soothingly, "Come on, Mr. Furness, we'll get whatever you want to make you comfortable."

They left the room. Jubal Chambers hastened to the buffet and mixed himself a very strong drink. Nathan was just behind him; he mixed himself an even stronger one, and sat down in the nearest chair looking like an elderly, pink baby making a manful effort not to weep.

Jubal passed a grimy handkerchief over his round, rosy face and said, "I'm too old and fat for this kind of thing. Crouched down in some prickly bushes watching you guys come along so I could swear that I saw Alan himself put a package in that trash can. . . . Then coming out and tearing it open to see if Michael had guessed right. Holding my breath for fear there'd be just a hundred grand in good U.S. currency there, after all. . . ."

"Do you think I was happy," Michael said tartly, "accompanying Mr. Furness back to this house, trying to act as if I believed that Greta's son had really been kidnapped?"

"I know. And I appreciate the scoop because I'm going to collect a bonus to end all bonuses. When I saw what the so-called ransom amounted to, I did as you'd told me and dashed around to talk Hoyt into coming here with me and . . . Leaping Lena! What. . . ."

Quinlan was bellowing, "Stop! Stop, or I'll shoot. . . . Watch out! Watch out, I say. . . ."

They heard the ear-shattering roar of a gun. Viola screamed. Then, for an instant, there was no sound at all. After that, one had to listen intently to hear a woman sobbing, quietly, monotonously. . . .

Hoyt charged out of the room with Jubal at his heels. Louis stood up, drew a deep breath and followed them. Nathan half rose, collapsed into his chair and muttered futilely to himself, "Oh God! Oh God! Oh. . . . No, not. . . ." Michael said nothing at all. He sat where he was without moving for several minutes and then he put his elbows on his knees and took his head between his hands. . . .

Jubal came back into the living-room. He mixed himself another drink; one that was, even for

Jubal, definitely outsize. Then he said, "I'm sorry for his wife. . . . That ape, Quinlan! He got what Furness wanted from the bathroom but then, when they came out, Viola was standing in the door of her own room. Furness said, 'Viola, let me explain!' And he went toward her which Quinlan thought was all right. But when Alan stretched out his hand to her she drew back and shivered all over.

"She said, 'I'll be sick if you touch me.' That seemed to make him go haywire. He turned and started for the stairs. Quinlan warned him he'd shoot. He says Alan was muttering, 'I've got to get away—I can make her understand. . . .' And then he turned back and threw himself at Quinlan and somehow Quinlan's gun went off. Well, it's the best thing. . . ."

"Very obliging of him. I'd hoped he'd panic and make a break for it," Michael said.

The words slurred together. Sam Weller got purposefully to his feet. He looked questioningly at Jubal and the newspaperman nodded vehemently.

"What's he been doing the last three days?"

"He's had about fourteen hours sleep and one square meal that I know of. You tell Hoyt that if he wants an explanation in full, he can wait till tomorrow afternoon for it. . . ."

"It's nice work if you can get it," Michael said in the halting accents that were in such contrast to his usual clear-cut enunciation. "'Justice is a machine that, when some one has once given it the starting push, rolls on of itself.' And, rolling on like Juggernaut, breaks a few hearts as it goes. . . ."

"That's right," Sam said, hooked an arm through Michael's and hoisted him to his feet. "Come on. I know combat fatigue when I see it. You're going home, Mike. Call me motherly—and see if I care!"

10

The gathering was entirely masculine: Inspector Hoyt, Jubal Chambers, Sam, Michael and Louis Hilton, "to," as he had remarked with a twisted grin, "represent the family."

Sam had gone foraging that morning. He had acquired eastern liverwurst, pickled herring, smoked salmon and oysters, ryebread and potato chips. Which were appreciated by everyone but Mr. Dundas, whose nostrils dilated whenever he came within smelling distance of the fish though he had only remarked thoughtfully, "Some time you and my wife must get together for an orgy, Mr. Weller."

Valerie Dundas had left the refrigerator well stocked with the non-alcoholic beverages to which she was addicted. Matthew Hoyt drank a quart of ginger-ale. That had a mellowing influence on him and when he was offered root beer, he became almost affable.

He said, "I sent a man to Hayward this morning and we cleared up some details about Bella Voss. That poor kid didn't die on account of neglect. She called a doctor; one from Oakland who didn't know her. But though he's overworked, he remembered it and told the police about it yesterday. The kid had this encephalitis thing. It fooled Bella and he was too far gone even to move to a hospital when this doctor got there.

"She told him the boy was her niece's child and showed him a fake birth certificate. Said the niece was dead and the father still in Germany. So the doc gave a death certificate. She picked out a cheap Oakland undertaker and had the boy cremated. This was in early May. People around there knew Bella had been boarding three boys but they didn't see her, or them, for a while after that.

"I suppose she meant to clear out as soon as Greta had come up to see her," Hoyt said grimly, "but she didn't want to lose her monthly pay check from Greta till she had to. Greta didn't fill out check stubs or keep cancelled checks, but we know now that every month there was a single, large-sized withdrawal from her account. That

must have been Bella's take and she went on collecting it for June, July and August.

"We don't know when she got rid of the first
of the two boarders she had left after Greta's boy
died. But the mother of the towhead she had with
her up to the last, went to the police, too. She's a
war widow who kept on working. She persuaded
Bella to keep her kid until about ten days ago.
Then she went and got him. I suppose that confused you—Bella having a boy with her right to
the last that could've been Greta's."

"It confused me," Sam said, "but apparently
not my pal here—who didn't confide in me."

"It needn't have confused you if you'd bothered
to think," Michael said unkindly. "In early May,
Bella was still caring for three small boys. Then,
for some time, the owner of that roadside grocery
didn't see her, or them. When he did, just before
she was killed, she had only one boy with her. But
that boy wasn't necessarily Greta's son. It was just
as likely that he was what he's been proved to be—
the second of her two remaining charges."

"Okay, maestro," Sam said impudently. "You
tell us how you knew Alan was IT."

"Wasn't it obvious from the beginning that this
business either had been very carefully planned or
that it had been quite unpremeditated? As time
went on, it was very evident that nothing had been

thought out unless someone was trying very hard
to prove himself a plain, damn fool. I'll explain
that later.

"As to Alan's story when we caught him at Bella's cottage. . . . Well," Michael said, "he did have
her letter which was some excuse for his being
there. And much of his story had the ring of truth.
He did tell the truth up to a point, so that we've
surprisingly few details to fill in. But of course
we knew, even when we were inclined to pity him,
that he could have met Greta at the Verde Vista
earlier than he had originally intended. We knew
that she was alone at the St. Francis between nine-
twenty-five and nine-fifty. When Miss Jameson
returned, Greta had gone. She could have received
a telephone call during that time."

"One of the switchboard girls at the hotel thinks
she remembers that Greta did," Hoyt said.

"Then, later, I learned that Alan had called
Viola around nine-thirty from his mother's home.
He could so easily have called Greta, too, at that
time. Then, when he was telling his story while
we were at Bella's place, there was a question he
should have asked Sam and didn't."

"I know," Sam said. "He'd hired me to follow
Greta. He didn't ask, right off, 'Where the hell
were you when she went into the Verde Vista?' I
apologized for having gotten there too late to see

her murderer. He let that pass though he should have jumped on me for that. But he knew I wasn't around there when he arrived and was afraid to mention it, one way or the other. Yes, and that proposition of him meeting Greta there, when I was supposed to be tailing her, proves he didn't go there intending to kill her."

"Exactly," Michael said. "I had an open mind regarding Mr. Furness, in a negative fashion. I don't care for the young lord of the manor, King Cophetua type. And Mr. Hilton, who had no illusions regarding his cousin, confirmed my diagnosis of his character."

"I talk too much," Louis said. "But I doubt that anything I said, even though I was lacking in family feeling and discretion, made any real difference."

"No. From the first I was irritated by Alan's references to 'his son.' To him, Greta was just a healthy brood mare. And, much as he loved Viola, he felt that because she hadn't provided him with an heir, she should repay him by agreeing to carry out any plans he might make. He did," Michael said slowly, "have an unhealthy desire for a son. But still he felt that he was quite a noble fellow to be willing to recognize and provide for his illegitimate son. I don't think he ever understood why

Greta didn't accept his proposition with gratitude and tears in her eyes."

"No, he didn't," Louis said bleakly. "The boy was half-Furness—Furness property. And a hell of a life the poor kid would have had with Lanny. Yes, and though he was always saying that Uncle Zach's will wasn't fair, he liked having control of so much money; he really believed that it was best for everyone that *he* should control it."

Michael nodded. "Catherine made a remark more or less to that effect. But Inspector Hoyt doesn't care for this sort of evidence. . . . During our first informal get-together, Alan showed Sam and me a snapshot that Bella had sent him with that letter that was meant to rouse his curiosity and pave the way for blackmail. He said that Greta had showed him a copy of the same picture *in July*. He said it was the *latest* one she had. But then he remarked that Bella was under orders to send Greta snapshots of the child *every three months*."

"Oh?" Louis said thoughtfully.

"He would have been six in November. I don't know on what day he was born but he would have been at least five years and eight months old in July. If Bella took snapshots of him every three months, Greta should have received one in—well, we'll say, February. She should have had another in May when he'd have been five-and-a-half."

"When we found Bella dead, I had no idea what had become of the child. I was even willing to believe that he had been spirited away. Not kidnapped for ransom, but removed from the scene by someone who would have preferred that Alan should never find him."

"Someone, mainly Hester, probably acting with Nathan's help?" Louis said.

"I wouldn't have put that past her," Michael said. "But I had very little to go on when we parted from Alan. . . ." He's not going to mention Viola's meeting Greta out in that joint in the Mission, Sam thought as Michael went on. "But Alan very promptly gave me something to think about. He produced a note from the 'kidnapper'. . . ."

"And you thought, even then, that it was a phony?" Jubal asked.

"I knew that Alan must be very anxious that I should not tell my story to the police. That communication he claimed he'd received was designed to keep me from going to the police. But to achieve that purpose it had to be a typical letter from a kidnapper: we have the child, don't go to the cops and you'll hear from us later. . . ."

"But you didn't believe the kid had been snatched just so someone could collect ransom?" Jubal said.

"No, I did not. When I had manufactured that ransom note—it takes hours to do that sort of work, by the way—Alan couldn't ignore it because the maid found it. But when he showed it to Sam and me he did venture to say that whoever wrote it must be 'mad.' Though he'd made the grand gesture of guaranteeing immunity to everyone in the family circle, as Alan said, no one would dare use the money after collecting it. And I hadn't promised anyone immunity once the child was safe. So I couldn't believe that someone close to Alan had planned ahead to kill Greta as the first step of a scheme to kidnap her son and force Alan to ransom him."

"Alan had the right idea but not the guts to stick to it," Sam said reflectively. "Then he seemed to swallow your suggestion that the actual kidnapping might have been done by a hired hand who had to be paid off. And I helped out by swallowing the idea myself. . . ."

"And poor, muddle-headed old Nate thought maybe I was hiding a gangster in my place," Louis put in. "For the record, I did have someone there Sunday night. This guy got away from his army hospital and came to me. His face still isn't all it should be. He came down in flames over the South Pacific. He doesn't like to see strangers. I let him stay with me Sunday night and yesterday I went to see his doctors and then coaxed him back to the hospital. That's why I wasn't home when Cathie and Viola wanted to see me."

"Why did Viola want to see you?" Michael asked.

"There's no reason why I shouldn't tell you now. Lanny was fool enough to keep that baby shoe and she came across it when she was putting bureau drawers in order yesterday. She couldn't account for it and she was frightened. She wanted me to advise her. When I wasn't home, she finally hid the thing in the garbage can."

"Where we found it during our usual routine search of the premises," Hoyt said smugly. "And he hadn't even gotten rid of his own gun that he killed Egbert Knapp with."

"Yes. Go on, Dundas," Louis said. "I'm interested in this business of the snapshots. You should have traced it through for us and picked up dropped stitches later on."

11

"But I was more than once distracted from that line of thought," Michael said. "The fake note from a non-existent kidnapper that Alan produced was a distraction, though later on it fell into the pattern. Also, I wanted to learn as much about you people as I could. Then, too late to save him, it occurred to me that 'the little squirt' who kept Sam from getting the taxi just behind Greta's when she started for the Verde Vista, might have been Egbert Knapp.

"When I described Egbert to Sam, he had no doubt that it was Egbert who'd stepped in ahead of him. So then we tried to locate Egbert—and failed," Michael said casually. "And Alan couldn't let well enough alone. He wanted to talk things over. . . ."

You liar, Sam thought affectionately. You're going to leave Catherine and Jack Edwards out of it, too.

He and Louis exchanged grins as Michael went on, "But then we had a stroke of luck. Victor Borck wanted to talk to me. Borck said, and I believed him, that he had promised Greta that she could adopt her own son after they were married; that he'd give both of them the protection of his name and influence and wealth. Then he told me something even more important. Which was, that in July, Greta showed him all of the snapshots she had of her son, including the '*last* one,' labeled 'Stephen, five years and three months old.'"

"Hmm? Oh," Hoyt said. "I take it Borck didn't know Bella was supposed to send Greta pictures of the kid every three months? But Furness had told you that. So in July, Greta should have had—

should have gotten it by June, at the latest—a snapshot labeled 'five years and six months old?'"

"Yes. Why hadn't she had such a picture? It was certain that she'd been paying Bella very generously to care for the child and for her silence. She was entitled to a few special services and, according to Borck, she cherished those pictures and carried them with her in the box she'd had made to hold the boy's shoe. So Greta certainly would have wanted to know why Bella hadn't sent the usual snapshots on schedule.

"That was when I asked, could the child be dead? If he was, Greta obviously didn't know it," Michael said. "One could guess, too, that Bella would go on bleeding Greta as long as she could. But she would have to give Greta some excuse for not sending her the usual snapshots when the boy was five and a half. And the most plausible excuse she could have given was that her camera had ceased to function.

"When I talked to Miss Jameson, she said that Greta had asked her to buy a camera which, Greta said, she wanted for 'a friend who needs one.' I don't know why Greta put that off so long. But she did say that she'd hoped to be able to go to Reno several months earlier. While, on the other hand, she and Borck weren't to marry for several months after she had her divorce, so she wouldn't have her son with her at once, and would still want snapshots of him while she waited.

"However, in the suitcase that Bella had packed, Sam found a camera that he said was a very good one. All of which was enough to make me seriously consider the possibility that Greta's son was not to be found, simply because he'd been dead for three months or so. . . ."

"But that didn't wash out the possibility that someone had intended to kidnap the boy," Louis objected. "And since only Bella knew that he was dead. . . . That's pretty well proven, isn't it?"

"Greta was planning to the last to see him on Saturday," Michael said. "If she didn't know he was dead, who else would but Bella? And, after Greta was killed, who could know anything about the child but the one who interviewed Bella before killing her, too?

"Of course there was a possibility that even though the boy was dead, someone still intended to make Alan ransom him. But I did not, for reasons already stated, believe in a carefully planned scheme to collect ransom. And if the boy were dead, that fact did at least eliminate the possibility that someone had simply abducted him to keep Alan from claiming him and taking him into his home.

"Our talk with Borck was the turning point," Michael went on. "Not only because of what he said about the snapshots, but because he told us he'd promised Greta that he would adopt her son. I doubt that she would have turned the boy over to Alan in any case, though I'm sure he thought she was only holding out for a high price. She had the whip hand and she'd enjoy cracking the whip. She told me Friday evening that she'd already had fun and meant to have more. And she said, 'Isn't it English to say that you're getting a bit of your own back? And I am and I will!'"

"Using the phrase not just figuratively, but very literally, to mean that she was going to get her own child back before very long?" Jubal suggested.

"I think so. Greta was a literal person. She'd kept the child and done her best for him when she had nothing. Why would she turn him over to Alan now, when she had Borck behind her? We'd always known that Alan could have seen her earlier than he first planned to. He admitted he'd made the arrangements for their meeting. A fact that, being amateurs and wanting to do things the hard way, we lost sight of. . . ."

Now he's being diplomatic, Sam thought as Hoyt made a sound of agreement and then smiled sourly.

"So I began to wonder," Michael said, "what Alan's reaction would have been if Greta had not only refused to turn their son over to him but had told him of her plans for the boy—and laughed at him. For one thing, why did Greta call me, unless she had suddenly asked herself if she could handle Alan alone, and became a little frightened? Still, that didn't keep her from laughing at him when they were face to face. . . . Well, then I saw how I could bring matters to a head so far as my doubts about Alan were concerned."

"Hoist by his own petard, wasn't he?" Jubal said appreciatively. "He was supposed to be waiting anxiously for a ransom note. When he got it, he had to follow instructions. He had to get the money, make sure you guys saw it, do up a nice little package. . . ."

"Having already done up one with only forty bucks, real money in it," Louis said. "When did he switch the packages?"

"On his way out of the house," Sam said. "He went out first, into the hall. Michael and I hung back. He talked to Viola and I listened, so Alan had a minute or two in the hall alone."

"We found the package he'd done up in front of you with the whole hundred grand in it, in the hall closet," Hoyt said. "So he must have had the fake package waiting for him there. I'll admit it worked, Mr. Dundas. It was a short cut, but it wasn't necessary. If you'd told us what you knew, we'd have gone to work and Furness wouldn't have escaped us . . . ."

"But I wouldn't have gotten off to New York to-night," Michael pointed out. "Besides, while I still thought the child might be living, I'd told Alan and the others that I wouldn't go to the police before Monday night. I didn't. But why do you suppose I stipulated, in that ransom note, that both Sam and I should go with Alan to the park?"

"Why, to have two witnesses and so that Alan would feel safe, because we both were with him and not wonder if one of us was up to something," Sam said.

"That, of course. But I wish to live a few years more, Mr. Weller, and I hope that you will, too. If Alan had killed two people without premeditation, he was the impulsive type of murderer. He might have had the impulse to erase Sam and me before we could go to the police. That ransom note was not only a trap; it kept Alan busy and gave him something to think about besides how much Sam and I knew—that no one else knew. When we were together we were fairly safe. And I made the instructions in that note involved, to keep Alan occupied and to increase the strain on his nerves."

"Well, there's something in what you say," Hoyt remarked grudgingly. "And I guess that about cleans things up?"

"Borck said some guy had been blackmailing Greta," Sam said. "I'm curious; it's a failing of mine. . . ."

"I think Nate borrowed money from her," Louis said. "I don't believe he knew that she and Alan had a child, but he probably thought it was possible. He may have gone back to see her again in '40 and even suggested that she try to get a job at Mr. Dundas's shop. But I don't think he really blackmailed her in Hollywood. He was probably temporarily embarrassed, threw out a hint or two, and Greta thought she'd better oblige with the needful. Still, he has his uses. If he wasn't holding Hester's hand just now, someone else would have to. Thanks for including me in on this session. I'll be going along now. . . ."

Jubal Chambers went with him and Sam promptly wandered off to the kitchen. Michael walked over to the mahogany secretary, took a manila envelope from it and handed it to Matthew Hoyt.

"This contains all the—uh—exhibits in question," he said.

Hoyt flushed a dull red and took the envelope. "It—it wasn't just this, you know. I . . . You gave me to understand this was a kidnapping case. . . ."

"What I actually said was, 'There's a child involved in this and a matter of ransom to be paid.' ¿*Verdad?* I had no choice. . . ."

"What about that favor I was to do you later on, besides giving you the time you wanted?"

"Fortunately the—contingency I had in mind did not arise," Michael said.

"Yeah, Alan Furness died before he could say very much about how and where he killed Egbert Knapp," Hoyt said shrewdly. "Well, we'll forget that. . . ." He added unexpectedly, "I finally told my wife about what happened at The Black Sunflower. I was worried. I've been married to that woman going on forty years. You know what she did? She laughed! She laughed fit to kill!"

For the only time since their first meeting, Mr. Hoyt and Mr. Dundas regarded each other with complete sympathy and understanding.

"They are so apt to laugh when you expect them to weep—and vice versa," Michael said sagely.

"And her a grandmother seven times over," Hoyt muttered resentfully. "Well—give my regards to Mrs. Dundas when you see her. . . ."

"Is this the beginning of a beautiful friendship?" Sam inquired, coming back into the living-room.

"Probably no more than the beginning of unarmed neutrality. Hoyt won't change and neither will I. This has been good for him. It's had a chastening effect on him—temporarily. By the same token, it's been good for me. It may make me a little less obnoxious in the future."

"I doubt that," said Mr. Weller candidly. "But, bud, you were lucky that Alan skipped lightly over his meeting with Egbert, though you did your part by steering him away from that in a hurry. Pity you couldn't share that nice little point about Bella's bed and Egbert's sandwiches with anyone."

"Oh, you thought that out?"

"Sure. Wasn't important except it showed the same kind of bungling technique. Bella had been to bed. The way she was dressed pointed to that, and anyway, by the time whoever killed Greta could get to her, it would've been midnight at least. But the bed was made up so's it would look like she'd been killed before she ever got to bed; killed earlier than she really was—too early for Alan to have done it.

"Then Egbert's sandwiches were taken away, but the paper bag they'd been in was left in your office so it'd look like he'd been alive late enough to eat his lunch. If he'd been alive at lunch time, Alan couldn't have killed him. Not very smart, considering what post-mortems can tell you. But typical of Alan's half-baked thinking. Well, you're all packed, ready to leave. . . ."

Michael nodded toward the secretary. "There's a check there that belongs to you."

Sam strolled over to the desk, looked down at the check and whistled. "You won't die rich, Mac."

"No? I'm supposed to be rather canny where money is concerned. But in this case. . . . Well, you don't want to go back to Los Angeles, do you, Sam? Here in San Francisco we appreciate your sort."

"Rugged individualists, you mean?" Sam grinned. "They must like that kind in Frisco or you wouldn't have lasted so long here."

"If you wish to be happy here, don't say 'Frisco!' But if you want to continue as a private operative—and you should be a very successful one—I can probably throw a good deal of business your way. Meanwhile, why don't you take a well-earned vacation here?"

"In this joint—house, you mean?"

"*Nuestra casa es suyo.* And that is not just a phrase used in common courtesy in this case. Literally, our house is yours, *amigo.* I won't be in New York for more than five days and when Valerie has heard what I have to tell, she'll want to meet you. . . ."

"Do you mean you're going to tell your wife the whole truth about this business?"

Michael regarded Sam pityingly. "If you ever acquire a wife, you'll learn that there are times when you'd better tell her the truth at once. Greta's death made every newspaper in the United States. If I didn't tell Valerie the truth that area would be heavily mined, and one day something would explode in my face. And though there are not many to whom I'd admit this, I'll even weep on her shoulder. . . ."

"Well, that's damn nice of you," Sam said with unwonted sarcasm. "Hell, considering what your wife looks like, I'd say it'd be not only a privilege but a pleasure to weep on her shoulder, pal."

"Since you mention it, it will be. Yes," said Mr. Dundas slowly, "it very definitely will be, pal!"

COACHWHIP PUBLICATIONS
CoachwhipBooks.com

VIRGINIA RATH

DEATH AT
DAYTON'S FOLLY

COACHWHIP PUBLICATIONS
CoachwhipBooks.com

VIRGINIA RATH

AN EXCELLENT
NIGHT FOR
MURDER

COACHWHIP PUBLICATIONS

CoachwhipBooks.com

THE DARK
CAVALIER

VIRGINIA RATH

COACHWHIP PUBLICATIONS

CoachwhipBooks.com

MURDER

with a theme song

VIRGINIA RATH

COACHWHIP PUBLICATIONS
CoachwhipBooks.com

POSTED
FOR
MURDER

VIRGINIA RATH

COACHWHIP PUBLICATIONS
CoachwhipBooks.com

EPITAPH FOR LYDIA

VIRGINIA RATH

COACHWHIP PUBLICATIONS

CoachwhipBooks.com

COACHWHIP PUBLICATIONS

CoachwhipBooks.com

LAVERNE RICE

WELL DRESSED
FOR MURDER

COACHWHIP PUBLICATIONS
CoachwhipBooks.com

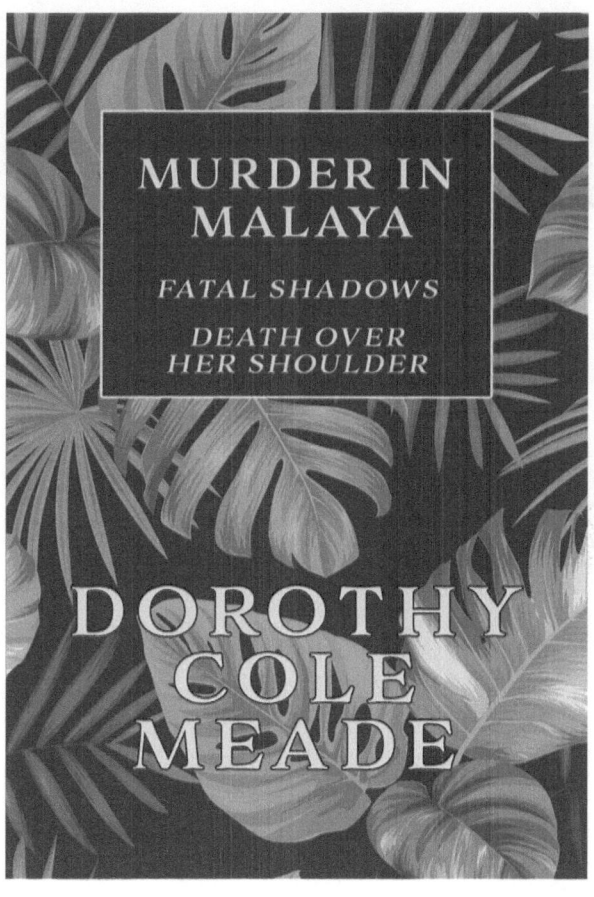

A HOUSE
A-HAUNT

CLASSIC STORIES OF HAUNTED HOUSES,
HORRIFIC ROOMS, AND OTHER GHASTLY ABODES

COACHWHIP PUBLICATIONS
COACHWHIPBOOKS.COM